The Ace of Westlake High

INTERNATIONAL BESTSELLING AUTHOR
NICOLE S. GOODIN

THE ACE OF WESTLAKE HIGH

BOOK TWO

ROYALS OF WESTLAKE

NICOLE S. GOODIN

The Ace of Westlake High
Published by Nicole S. Goodin

ISBN: 978-0-473-67885-2

First published July 2023
Cover design by Nicole Goodin
Images purchased from Shutterstock
Editing by Spell Bound

 Created with Vellum

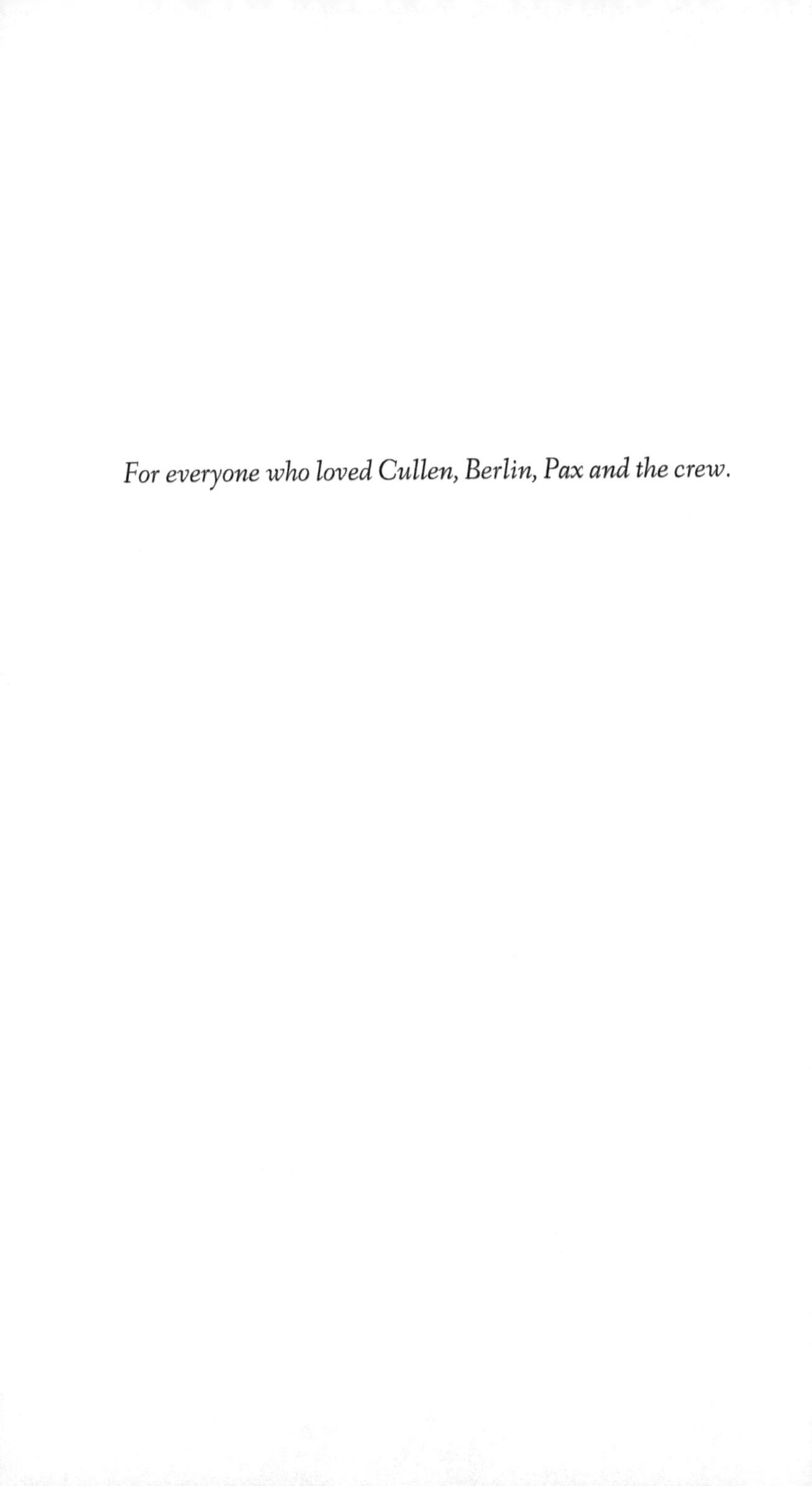

For everyone who loved Cullen, Berlin, Pax and the crew.

This book has been written using UK English and may contain euphemisms and slang words that form part of the New Zealand spoken word.

Please remember that the words are not misspelled. They are slang terms and form part of everyday, New Zealand vernacular.

I.e: I'm from New Zealand and sometimes we say weird things down here... please try and be cool about it.

PROLOGUE

Pax

The gasp sounds like a shout to my ears. I don't even know which one of us it came out of. Could have been me.

Siblings.

What. The. Actual. Fuck?

Son.

My hands are on my face, covering my ears. There's a ringing sound hammering my eardrums, it's so loud it hurts my brain.

I try to take a step backwards, but my knees start to buckle from underneath me.

I'm going to faint. I realise.

I'm going to flake out like some little bitch boy who can't handle a shock to his system.

"*Woah,*" I hear Cullen say as his arms steady me, but I

don't feel like I'm in the hallway with them anymore. I don't know where I am, I feel like I'm floating and sinking at the same time.

"*He's your son, Cole.*" It's echoing through my head on repeat. Over and over and over again.

Such a simple statement. On their own, such insignificant words, but when strung together like that, they're enough to ruin me.

Cole Davids is my *dad*.

Berlin is my *sister*.

I think I dry retch; I can't be sure before it all goes black.

ONE

Pax

Two weeks later

"Are you seriously fucking stoned again?"

I watch lazily as Cullen kicks my gym bag, still full of stinky workout clothes, across the room. I hear it thud into the wall on the other side of me, but I don't bother turning my head to see where it lands. I don't really give a fuck.

"*Well?*" he demands.

Well *shit*. I thought that was a rhetorical question, but apparently, he actually wants an answer. Like it's not fucking obvious.

Of course I'm stoned. My eyes are barely open, and

my room stinks like weed. Hardly need a trench coat and a magnifying glass to figure out that mystery.

I shrug. Words feel like too much effort.

He growls, crosses the room and gathering by the rude amount of light that slaps me across the face, I'd say he opened the curtains.

Son of a bitch. No offence to Mum.

I grimace when the air from the now open window greets me. Yuck. It's so... *fresh*.

"I know this is some fucked-up shit, but you're acting like it's the end of the world. So what, he's your dad? He's a good dude and he's *here*. You could have a relationship with him if you wanted to, for fuck's sake."

I give him a salute with minimal effort on my part.

"Fuck this shit." He grunts, before storming out again.

Grumpy prick.

"I can't deal with this shit. I don't know what the hell is wrong with him. You talk to him, because if I go in there again, I'm going to put his head through the wall." He's in the living room now, but I can hear him bitching. He's not trying to be quiet. He's talking to Berlin, no doubt.

We're the only three who know, we know what *they* know. I don't even know if that makes sense. It's like that *Friends* episode, and it's bullshit.

Mum, Ma. Cole... they've all kept this shit real secret squirrels. The private little threesome of lies. The trio of deception.

"Chill out. I'll talk to him."

I was right. It *is* Berlin.

Of course it is. She's here all the time... checking on me, covering for me with Ma and Mum, and she's probably the only thing stopping Cull from beating the crap out of me at this point too.

"He's high as a fucking kite again," Cullen sneers.

"I said chill out." I hear the jingling of keys. "Take my car, go and buy him a burger or something – he'll have the munchies soon and we need to sober him up before your mum gets home."

"You're too good to him," Cullen says.

She really is.

I hear Berlin sigh. "I know I am. Burger. Go."

There're footsteps in the hall.

I lie back against my pillow and shut my eyes. I'm tired. She's right though, I am getting kind of hungry, and a burger sounds pretty good. I'm tempted to yell out and ask for a shake, but I think I'd be pushing my luck.

I hear the front door open.

"Oh!" she yells after him, "and get him a chocolate –"

"Shake," Cullen cuts her off. "Yeah, I know."

I'm stoned as hell, but that makes me feel kind of warm inside. I lift my head and look down at my shorts, just in case that warmth I'm feeling is pee running down my leg.

Nope, I'm good.

I hear the sound of footsteps coming down the hall and shut my eyes again. I'm sure I'm about to get a lecture and I don't need to see the disappointment in her eyes; hearing it in her tone will be enough.

"You look like shit, Paxikins."

"I feel like shit, Ice," I murmur.

"You deserve to feel like shit."

Harsh but fair.

At least I'm not drunk at four o'clock on a Tuesday – not this week anyway. It could be worse.

"You know Cull is going to murder Tonksy if he keeps hooking you up with weed, and between you and me, I don't think it's going to take much convincing for Bry to help him do it – he's still dark on Tonks taking out Soph."

"Bry's a little bitch."

"And what are you then, huh?" she quips back.

I shrug.

I hear her sigh again. There it is. That's the disappointment. I'm fucking glad I can't see those big dark eyes right now.

Big dark eyes that she got from her father. Dark eyes that *I* got from her father too it would seem.

Her father.

My father.

Our father.

That still feels wrong.

I feel the bed dip and her crawl up next to me. I open my eyes, and she's lying next to me, her head on the pillow next to mine.

Breaks my fucking heart to see that look on her face. She looks so worried. It makes me feel like a piece of shit. It won't be enough to fix me, but I still feel bad for worrying her.

"I'm fine, really."

It's a lie and we both know it. I don't even know why I bother. She knows me too well for that.

"You're not fine, Pax."

No, I'm not fine. My whole life is a lie.

"I don't know what you want me to tell you."

"Maybe you could start with telling me why you're stoned out of your fucking tree twenty-four seven?"

I scrub my hands over my face.

"It makes me feel numb, Ice," I tell her honestly.

There's a long stretch of silence. So long that I think she's nodded off, and I almost do the same.

"Is the idea of being my brother really that bad?"

Fuck.

Now I've done it. Berlin doesn't cry much, and I've just heard her voice crack. Not only does that make me a total piece of shit, but it's going to make me enemy number one when Cullen walks back through that door and sees I've upset the centre of his universe.

I don't have the energy for this. I clearly don't even have enough to keep my own shit together, let alone take a run at hers.

I know I'm being a prick. That's the worst bit of it. I know this is hard for her and that I'm only making it worse – but I can't stop.

I know she's struggling too. She's probably the only person around here who can actually come close to understanding part of how I feel, and I'm pushing her away.

"I'm going to talk to my dad. I'm going to tell him we know."

"No," I snap.

"And why the fuck not?" she snaps back. "I can't deal with much more of this, Pax. You're a mess, I'm barely holding it together. My dad is walking around in a daze, and your ma looks like she's about thirty seconds away from having a full-blown menty-b. It's time we all came clean."

"No," I say firmly.

"Why?" she whispers.

"I want to see how long it takes. I want to know how much longer Ma plans to keep this from me." I barely even recognise my own voice.

It's filled with hurt and venom.

That's what this is really about. It's not about Cole or Berlin – not as much as it's about my mother. The woman who raised me. The woman who lied to me for eighteen years.

I feel her hand on my shoulder, but I don't look. If I open my eyes, the tears might escape.

"I love you, Pax. But I don't know what to do with you anymore. You need to talk to your ma, to my dad, to Cull... To *me*. I don't want to wake up in the morning and worry about what state I'm going to find you in. I don't know how to help you anymore."

Truthfully, I don't know how to help me either.

I don't have anything to say that's going to make either of us feel any better, so I don't say anything.

She doesn't speak again. The girl knows me well, I'll give her that. She knows she's not going to get anywhere with me today.

I must doze off at some point because I wake up to the front door slamming and an empty space next to me.

"I got the useless fucker his food," Cullen says, out in the hall.

My ears prick up.

"Good. Sober him up before Ma gets home. I flushed the last of his weed," I hear Berlin reply.

Motherfucker. Guess she wasn't napping with me.

"And kick Tonksy's ass if you have to because if *you* don't make him stop giving Pax that shit, *I* will."

I might be blazed as hell, but I'm still with it enough to hope that for Tonksy's sake, Cullen is the one to have that conversation. Ice is scary when she's mad.

TWO

Berlin

"Should he even be here?" Carissa frowns as we all watch
Pax do another beer funnel.

The dude has downed like twenty beers in the past
two hours and Cullen is looking more and more willing to
commit murder by the second.

I'd almost be willing to be his accomplice at this point.

"Probably not. He definitely shouldn't be drunk, he's
already on some pretty thin ice with coach. If anyone
finds out he's out here getting smashed, he'll be benched
for sure," I reply.

"I'm going to go out on a limb here and say he doesn't
care." Sophia grimaces as Pax stumbles forward, cheering,
and trips over a chair in front of him.

He goes flying forward, landing headfirst into the
ground.

We all collectively wince.

"I bet that tickled."

"Someone needs to stop him," Carissa says. She looks like she's about to cry. Poor bitch, she's softer than I am. Most people probably are, to be fair.

I think for a minute there, before all the shit hit the fan, she might have had herself a wee bit of a crush on Pax. I can't say for sure, but I'd be willing to bet all the money I've got on the fact that his behaviour over the past few weeks will have squashed that pipe dream long before it began.

I don't blame her.

I love the guy, and even I wouldn't recommend him to a friend at the moment. Hell, I wouldn't even recommend him to someone I hated.

He's a mess. A steaming-hot mess.

He gets up off the ground, groaning and holding his head, which has blood pouring out of it.

"Ah *fuck*," I mutter. "Alright, enough is enough. He can fight me if he wants, but he's leaving. *Now*. Before he bleeds out all over the carpet."

I stalk off in the direction of my newly acquired brother – something I haven't had thirty fucking seconds to really stop and think about, because I've been too busy trying to stop this dumb prick from going totally off the rails.

Cullen – who up until this moment has been standing in the corner, barely restrained, but doing what he's told – moves the second I do.

Carissa, Soph and I reach Pax at the same time as Bryson and Cullen.

"Time to go," Bry says, reaching for his arm.

Pax tries to shrug him off, but the fact that he's completely and utterly shit-faced, combined with the fact that he's now bleeding profusely from his left eyebrow, make it difficult for him to really pull it off.

"Don't be a prick," Cullen growls. "You're making a scene and there's fucking blood everywhere."

I can't imagine that Smithy's parents are going to be too happy about the state of their fawn-coloured carpet, but I've got enough on my plate without worrying about that.

People are starting to stare. Pretty sure one or two are filming this trainwreck of a situation.

Pax slurs something incomprehensible.

Bry and Cullen grab him from either side, but he starts thrashing around like a fish out of water. Drops of blood are flying everywhere. It's some rank-ass bullshit.

"Pax!" I yell.

He freezes and looks at me through his blood-covered eyes.

"You're done," I tell him. I'm so fucking wild, I'm literally shaking.

I can't do this anymore. I can't watch him go deeper into self-destruct mode, but something tells me this is only the beginning.

Everything is falling apart.

Dad has been a mess, but thankfully he's too wrapped up in his own head to notice that I'm not right either.

We're co-existing in the same space, each of us doing a shitty job of pretending nothing is wrong, while we both try and navigate how to handle the same secret from opposite sides.

It's super cool.

Pax blinks once. He looks like he's crying blood out of one eye. It's disgusting.

"We're leaving now. All of us. And don't you *dare* make this hard."

He might be smashed, but I can tell he knows that I mean business. I might be the only chance we have to get him to listen.

He nods once, just a little bob of his head, but that's all I need.

"Can you walk?"

A small shake of his head.

I look between Cull and Bry and give them a look.

They take hold of Pax's arms again, and this time he lets them. The six of us make a path through the party, beelining for the door. I don't know if it's the blood or the look on Cullen's face that gets everyone to move, but not one person gets in our way.

"Delete that or I'll shove that phone so far up your ass it'll come out your mouth," Cullen sneers at some guy filming Pax.

The guy's eyes bulge and he hastily starts tapping on the screen of his phone.

I give him a death glare as I follow after the boys.

"Jed, we need your van!" Bry calls out as we reach the door.

"What is it with you guys?" Jed whines as we exit the house and step out into the cold, winter's night. "Last time it was the spew queen over there, and now you want me to get blood all over my seats?"

He's bitching and moaning, but he's still walking towards his van, keys in hand.

He's a good mate and a Cullen worshipper. We all know he's going to give us a ride home whether he wants to or not.

"We'll put him on the floor. Just unlock the door already, he's fucking heavy." Cullen grunts as him and Bry struggle under the dead weight of Pax, who, if I'm not mistaken, has passed out. "I'll help you clean it tomorrow."

This is an absolute shit show.

Pax is drunk, injured, probably concussed, and now he's passed out.

Perfect.

We either need to take him to the hospital or take him home to Cullen's mum and hope like hell she's chill enough to stitch him up without going nuclear.

They get him in the van, and onto the floor, as promised.

"All aboard," I tell the girls with a roll of my eyes.

Sophia climbs in, carefully selecting the farthest seat away from Bryson.

I sigh and shake my head. I still can't believe those two haven't sorted their shit out.

Carissa jumps in, and I take the seat next to Cullen, with Pax at our feet.

"This is some fucked-up shit, new girl."

I look up at him, searching for his eyes. Those blue eyes are about the only thing I feel sure about anymore.

I rest my head on his shoulder, and he strokes the side of my hand. This probably feels a bit like déjà vu for him.

Cullen and the girls have been my rocks. They're solid. Everything else has turned to mush.

Even my dad...

I know none of this is really his fault. He had no idea he had another child out there – I know if he did, he would have *never* let it play out like this, but I can't help but feel resentment over the fact he's still keeping it from me, *and* from Pax.

I can understand that he might need some time to process the fact that he has a whole-ass adult male for a son, but it's been weeks, and as far as our parents are aware, we're still in the dark.

It's a ticking time bomb, and if Pax carries on down this path, it's going to blow sooner rather than later.

"What are we going to do with him?" I ask Cullen.

"Take him back to mine. Mum is home and Ma went away for the weekend with some friends. Mum will know what to do."

"What are you going to tell her?" I whisper.

He lifts a shoulder. "I'll pretend he got rejected by a girl or something. Got shit-faced to make himself feel better and fell down."

"It's half true at least."

"Seems to be a lot of half-truths floating around at the moment," he mutters.

He kisses my forehead and then leans forward to ask Jed to drop Bryson and the girls off, and then head to his place to unload the patient.

I don't think Hannah is going to be overly thrilled

with the mess about to turn up on her doorstep, but she'll sort it out. She's a good woman and she loves these boys.

We drop off Bryson, then Soph and Carissa, and before I know it, we're pulling up to Cullen and Pax's front door.

Jed helps get him out of the van, while I get the front door open and rush to find some towels to lay down on the couch.

There's a bunch of grunting and groaning as they lug the big dummy through the front door, and we've nearly got him on the couch when the hallway light flickers on, and Hannah appears in the doorway, rubbing her eyes.

"Boys, it's three in the morning, what the hell is going –" Her eyes lock on Pax and widen in shock as she takes in the state of him. "What the hell happened?"

"DO you think I should go home?" I whisper.

I've been hiding out in Cullen's room for the past hour or so, I'm not even sure if Hannah knows I'm still here. I probably should have escaped when Jed did, but I couldn't leave Cullen without knowing he was okay.

He's so busy trying to pick up all the pieces – keep both me and Pax on the rails, keep good grades, help out around the house, and still find time for training and rugby. He's maxed out.

"Fuck no," he replies as he strips off his jeans and t-shirt and flops down onto the bed next to me.

"I don't want to piss off your mum."

He grabs me around the waist and pulls me towards

him, my back against his front. He nuzzles into my neck, his breathing already sounding heavy.

"She's already pissed. We're the least of her worries."

I heard her ranting for the past twenty minutes, so it's hardly a shock to me that she's not happy.

Pax must still be passed out, because when she got done stitching him up, she started on Cullen – demanding to know what the hell was going on and why Pax was acting like this all of a sudden.

There was a moment there, in the middle of the argument where they both just stopped talking, and I think each of them were probably trying to decide if they should just come clean.

I wish they had, but neither one did.

And so, the secret of the century lives on. Just fucking great.

"Are you okay?" he murmurs.

I honestly don't know what the truthful answer to that question is.

Right now, I'm great. I've got him next to me, and Pax is safe, if not a little battered, but we're all here, under one roof. Alive to see another day.

"I think so."

"That's not very convincing."

"I dunno what you want me to tell you, golden boy. Our brother is a dipshit."

"Ew." He chuckles. "Don't say *our* brother, makes it sound like I'm fucking my sister."

"Yeah, weird kink." I laugh. "You should probably see somebody about that."

"You're disgusting."

"You're the one –"

He claps his big, warm hand over my mouth. "Don't even say it."

The bed shakes with our quiet laughter.

"Go to sleep, you little fruit loop."

I sigh and snuggle back into him, my eyelids growing heavy. I know he won't sleep well, but I will. I haven't got an ounce of energy left in me.

"We'll deal with Pax in the morning," he says.

I nod, unconvinced.

Yeah. Because that's been going *so* well for us so far.

THREE

Pax

"Come on... just let me take you out. Dinner, a milkshake, whatever."

She shifts her weight from foot to foot and fiddles with her red hair. I'm not fucking stupid, I know she's going to reject me, but I'm desperate. I just need to feel something other than the ever-present rage cycling through me.

"Pax... I don't know..."

"Carissa, babe, I'm back now, no more bullshit."

The look she gives me makes it pretty damn clear she disagrees with that statement, but she's polite enough to keep her opinion to herself, at least.

This is the third time I've asked her out in the past two weeks. Even I can feel how pathetic and desperate I sound.

"Don't take this the wrong way, okay? But it's never going to happen. You need to talk to someone, Pax." Her eyes soften, and I immediately look at the ground. "I don't know what's up with you lately, but you're clearly struggling with something."

One more dose of sympathy and I might explode.

"You're in no space to date, and honestly, I'm not interested in getting aboard the hot mess express. No offense."

Well fuck. So much for keeping her thoughts to herself.

"None taken," I mutter.

She reaches out to touch my arm, but I take a step back. She doesn't need to do this. I get it. She's not interested. I can't blame her for that, I wouldn't be interested either. I don't need her to feel bad about it.

I'm a mess. I've got stitches in my eyebrow, and coach has benched me for this weekend's game because of it. Mum is pissed beyond belief and Ma... I can't even look Ma in the eye.

"It's fine, Car, have a good day," I mutter as I turn and stalk away.

"Pax!" she calls after me, but I don't turn around. "I'm sorry!"

I've had enough humiliation for one day. Utter fucking disgrace that I am.

I need something to take the edge off, and I know just the man for the job. I glance at my watch and head for the spot I know I'll be most likely to find Tonksy.

Tonks isn't a bad guy – the fact that he's a small-time drug dealer aside. His older cousin is the real drug dealer, he just uses Tonksy to get a bit of weed and molly into Westlake. It's not like a thirty-year-old man is going to able to blend in, slinking around behind the art block with a pocket full of pills and grass.

I find him where I thought I would, but the look he gives me makes me think Cullen must have got to him first.

He points at me. "Nope, got nothing for you, bro."

I frown at him, still approaching. "*What?* Why?"

"You're cut off. Your brother is going to skin me alive if I sell any more shit to you. He threatened to tell coach if I don't cut it out and he gave me bruised ribs for my trouble."

"What the fuck? So, you're not selling anymore?"

"No, I'm just not selling to *you* anymore."

"That's bullshit. My money is as good as theirs."

"It's not worth a black eye or getting my ass expelled, bro, you're done."

Motherfucker.

"Why don't I go and snitch on you then? I've got nothing to lose." I cross my arms across my chest, full defensive mode.

"Because then I'll suggest a fucking drug test, and you'll go down with me. I might sell, but you're the one using."

Shit.

He looks pissed. I bet I look the same.

He's got me backed into a corner here, or more specifically, Cullen does. Berlin too. Meddling little do-gooders.

Fuck.

He's not going to back down. Not when Cull has put

his foot down. The golden boy has the pull power around here and he fucking knows it.

"Fuck ya, then," I say, and turn on my heel.

Maybe he won't sell to me directly, but I'll find a way. There's got to be a junior around here who will buy for me. I might have to threaten to knock a few sets of teeth in, but I can make it happen.

I round the corner of the building and come face to face with the man himself. Local Sheriff Cullen Carrington, doing his bit to clean up the streets. What a god damn hero. Someone better alert the media – get him a medal of honour or some shit.

"What the fuck, bro?" I demand.

He eyes me up and down. "He didn't sell to you, did he?"

"Of course he didn't – because you told him not to."

"Good."

"*Good?*" I yell. "It's just a bit of weed. It's not hurting anyone."

"Keep your voice down," he snaps. "And it's hurting *you*. You're like a fucking vegetable all the god damn time. I'm sick of it. I'm not going to sit around and watch you numb yourself up to avoid dealing with this. It's time to feel, Pax. Whether you like it or not."

My chest feels tight, like it's hard to breathe.

The reality behind those words suck.

He leaves me standing there, trying to catch my breath.

I don't want to feel. I don't want to deal with this. Not now, maybe not ever. Feeling hurts.

"We've got practice after school. I don't give a fuck if you're benched. Be there," he yells back to me.

I groan. That's the last thing I feel like doing. The only thing that sounds worse than playing rugby right now, is not playing. I don't want to sit on the side line like a schmuck with a ripped-up head.

Fuck.

This whole day is going to shit at a rapid rate of knots, and the one thing I could rely on to make it all feel less... *pointy*, has gone out the fucking window.

I give myself a mental uppercut and push off the wall that I was leaning on.

It was probably the only thing holding me up.

I've got one more class to get through, then I'll endure practice, and the day will be over. Two more things. I can handle two more things.

Even better, I decide, as I skulk off to class, I can scope out the team for potential drug mules. Some of those little pricks owe me, and I fully intend to cash in on some debt.

———

"MITCH, DROP BACK!" Cullen barks out another order.

The guy is way more fucking annoying to listen to when I'm not on the field with them. That's something I wouldn't have known if I hadn't been forced to turn up here.

At least I learnt one thing today, because I sure as shit didn't learn a single thing in any of my classes.

Mitch is covering my position on the wing for this weekend's game. He's making a piss poor job of it, but the kid's young and inexperienced, so he's not going to produce miracles.

"Out wide!" Bryson yells.

Coach is yelling about something, and Cole is making notes.

Cole. *Dad.*

I can't even bring myself to talk to him.

I quickly look away, back to the boys.

They're all running plays and throwing balls around. I heard talk of a team run after this, and there's no reason I can't participate in that, which gives me every reason to bail as soon as possible.

Jack jogs off the field and over to his water bottle. I still haven't found a kid to get me my weed, and this one suddenly looks like the perfect candidate.

"Jacko!" I call out to him and wave him over.

He grabs his water bottle and jogs over to me.

He starts making small talk about the cut on my brow and how it sucks I can't play this weekend. The kid's rambling, and it's starting to hurt my head.

"I need a favour." I cut him off.

"Okay, yeah, what's up?"

"I need you to get something for me."

He looks around the ground near us, confused.

"Okay..."

I glance over at coach and Cole, to make sure they're not paying attention.

This is fucking awkward, but I like sleeping at night,

and not feeling like I'm about to explode every thirty fucking seconds, so it's worth taking the risk.

"I need you to get some shit off Tonksy for me."

"What do you mean by *some shit*?" he asks, his tone wary.

Tonks's side hustle isn't exactly the best kept secret, so I'm willing to bet that even training wheels here knows exactly what I mean.

"Just some weed. Nothing serious."

His eyes bulge. "Fuck no, I'm not doing that."

"Why not?"

"My mum is a police officer, man, and my dad was a drug addict. I'm not an idiot. You've lost the plot if you think I'm going to buy your weed for you."

Fuck's sake. I would pick the one kid whose got a cop for a mother and a crack head for a daddy. This day just keeps getting better and better.

"It's for pain, I –"

"Don't even try." He cuts me off. "And I wouldn't waste your time trying anyone else, Cull has talked to all of us already."

What the fuck?

"What the hell did he say?"

He gives me a look of disapproval, and it makes me feel about an inch tall. Being looked down on by a kid sucks, but that's where I'm fucking at apparently. Rock bottom, I'll see you soon.

"I've gotta get back out there." He shakes his head at me. "I like you, man, but you're kind of a mess right now."

He drops his bottle and runs back out to meet up with the others.

I watch him go, and as he runs past Cull, we lock eyes. He knows full well what I just tried to pull.

He looks at me like I'm the biggest loser on the face of the planet. Coach and Cole are totally unaware of what just went down, but Mr. Captain sure as hell isn't. He well and truly got my number on that exchange.

Fuck this.

I don't even bother making some bullshit excuse for why I'm ditching, I just turn and leave.

Cullen will make the excuses on my behalf anyway. Anything to save face with his precious game.

I hear someone yell my name, but I pretend I don't, instead I swing my backpack onto my shoulder and gap it as quickly as I can without breaking into a run.

Fuck this shit.

I can't sit around here, sober as the day I was born, hanging out with a team that think I'm a full-blown druggy, and a dude who's my father but doesn't know that I know he's my father.

You couldn't write this shit.

I don't know where the hell I'm going to go, but I know one thing; I need a drink.

I'm going to have to walk home now that I've bailed on practice, and therefore, my ride home with Bry, but I don't give a fuck. I'll go right past a bottle store on my way, so maybe it was meant to be.

I've got a hoody in my bag, and maybe if I chuck that on over my school uniform, the prick who runs the place might let me buy a box of beers.

He's a real asshole usually, refusing to sell to anyone

in a school uniform, even if they're eighteen and have ID on them.

Bunch of bullshit.

I don't even know if it's legal, but that's his rule.

This day can't get much worse though, so I may as well give it a shot.

I fuck around for a while, dawdling along, taking my sweet-ass time to get there. It's not like I've got anywhere to be anyway.

I chuck on my hoodie when I see the bottle store in the distance, and decide I'll leave my backpack in some bushes out front. Nothing screams 'high school student' like coming in looking like fuckin' *Dora the Explorer*.

I stash my bag in the bushes near the door and stroll in.

Asshole owner gives me the once over but doesn't say anything when I walk past him. Not that he's got anything to complain about, I'm old enough to buy booze – not like half the students who have got away with using their older sibling's ID over the years.

I grab a box of beers out of the fridge and carry them up to the counter.

I don't say anything – just slide my ID across and wait for him to scan the box.

He doesn't even glance at my ID, just gives me a filthy look.

"No school uniforms." He points at the big sign on his door.

I tug at the hoodie I'm wearing.

He points at my shorts and the bit of collar I have poking out from the neck of my hoodie.

I groan. "Come on, man, it's like five o'clock, what do you care?"

"No school uniforms," he repeats.

"So, if I go home and change and come back here in five minutes, you'll sell to me? How the hell does that make any sense?"

"Those are the rules."

I don't know what it is about this exchange, but I feel the last shred of my patience snap. It's like there's a thin wire above my head and I can see it break in half.

This is just another cunt telling me I can or can't do something, know something, *be* something, based on nothing but bullshit.

I grab my ID and swipe the beers off the counter, sending them flying to the ground.

"This is a fucking joke!" I roar as the entire box of glass bottles hits the ground, smashing into a million pieces.

The noise echoes off the walls around me.

Part of me wants to smash something else, the rest of me wants to punch myself in the face for being such an agro piece of shit.

A cold surge rocks through me as the owner starts screaming and shouting. He reaches for something under the counter and my brain tells me to run. *Now.*

I flee the store, only pausing briefly to grab my bag from where I stashed it.

I can hear yelling behind me as I blindly run out into the street, only narrowly missing getting hit by a car.

"What the fuck?!" I hear the driver yell at me as I carry on running.

Jesus Christ.

I sprint in the direction of home, my heart pounding.

I don't know why the fuck I did that. *Who the hell even am I?*

A car comes flying past me and slams on the brakes just up ahead.

Shit.

I'm about to turn around and take off in another direction when I recognise the car as Bry's.

"Get the fuck in!" Cullen yells out the window.

I throw open the back door and dive into the back seat. "Go, go, go!" I yell.

I lie across the back seat, breathing heavily, relief flooding through me as Bry speeds off down the street.

It's short-lived though as reality creeps in.

I just fucked up, *bad.* And not only did I fuck up bad, but now my two closest mates are involved. I've dragged them into my shit, yet again.

I'm about to get ripped a new one. I can feel it building in the air.

There's nothing but eerie silence until the car comes to an abrupt stop and Cullen turns to glare at me.

"You wanna tell me what the fuck just happened?"

FOUR

Berlin

"What's going on with you lately?" Sophia frowns at me. "And don't you dare tell me it's nothing because I know you and you're not right. Something is going on and I'm not leaving here until you tell me what it is."

I just blink at her a couple of times. I don't know where to start. I'm so freaking tired. I feel like I haven't slept for a week.

"B, I swear to God, if you don't start talking soon, I'm going to –"

"Pax is my brother," I interrupt her.

She just stares at me. I can practically see her brain short circuiting as she tries to process the information.

I get up and shut her bedroom door, just in case Aunt A happens to walk by.

I go back and sit on her bed. She's still standing there, glitching.

I know what she's doing – trying to figure out the how, the what, the when. I see the moment it all clicks into place.

"Oh my god. Uncle Cole is the mystery man who knocked up Pax's mum in high school?"

"Apparently so."

"What. The. Fuck."

"I know," I say as I flop backwards so I'm lying on her bed.

She gasps, and I fly back up to a seated position. "You kissed your brother!"

Like I need reminding. I've thought about that at least five hundred million times, and it makes me feel ridiculously unwell.

You can almost smell the incest in the air.

"Ewwwww," she groans.

"Well, it's not like I knew! I'm not trying to be all *Game of Thrones* or anything, for fuck's sake."

She starts pacing. "I know. You're right, sorry. Tell me everything. Start at the beginning and don't leave anything out."

"I was over at Cullen's the other week and –"

"Oh my god I have so many questions already," she blurts out.

I cover my face with my hands and fall back onto her bed again.

I have so many questions too. This whole thing is killing me. Talking, but not really saying anything to my dad is killing me. Pax is killing me. *I'm* killing me.

"Oh my god. He's my cousin."

He sure fucking is.

"Sorry, keep going," she encourages.

So, I do. I tell her everything about what Cullen, Pax and I overheard. I tell her about Pax losing his gherkin ever since. I tell her about how the boys' mums and my dad haven't said a single fucking word to any of us.

By the end of it, I have tears in my eyes. Not because I'm hurt or scared, but because it feels so good to finally get it all out.

"Oh, B." She's lying down next to me now, and I'm not sure when she took it, but my hand is in hers.

I give it a squeeze.

I'm so fucking grateful for this little dork. I *never* would have thought on my first day at Westlake High, that she'd not only be tolerable, but turn out to be one of my best friends.

Maybe my old man didn't make such a dumb decision coming here after all. It sounds like he made some pretty dumb decisions over eighteen years ago though.

It's like the man had never heard of a condom, for crying out loud.

I can't help but wonder if I've got other siblings out there, or if after he knocked my mum up, he took a long hard look at himself and invested in a big box of rubbers.

Fingers crossed for the latter. I don't think I could handle any more of my DNA running around. The one half-sibling I've got has been causing me to lose enough sleep.

"What are you going to do? Do you think you should

tell your dad that you guys know? He might be able to help with Pax."

"Pax made me promise I wouldn't say anything yet. He's pissed off with his ma. I know what he's doing – he wants to see how long it takes her to tell him, and then he's going to punish her for it being too long. It's only going to make it all worse."

"She's already kept this secret for *eighteen years*, I doubt a few weeks is make or break in her mind. This is pretty shitty of her, huh."

I couldn't agree more. I've been trying really hard not to judge Julia too harshly, but it's hard when she took so much from so many people. I don't know why she did what she did. I hope one day I get the chance to ask her.

"He's not exactly thinking logically right now. He's seeing red, Soph. I'm genuinely really worried about him."

"He wouldn't do anything stupid, would he?"

I'm not so sure about that. He's already doing dumb shit left, right and centre.

My phone starts ringing, and I grab it quickly. I'm so on edge lately, even a message makes me nervous.

"It's Cullen," I tell her before answering.

"Hello?"

"Hey, baby."

He sounds tired. And not the kind of tired where you slept like shit or you had a long day, but the kind of dog tired that you feel right down to your bones.

"How was practice?" I ask him.

"It was all good, but ah... it's fucking Pax. I don't know what to do anymore."

Shivers race up and down my spine.

"What happened?"

Sophia meets my gaze, her eyes widening as she too realises something is wrong.

I can hear him pacing around, it's what he does when he's on edge – he can't sit still for more than about three seconds.

"He bailed on practice, and Jacko told me that Pax tried to get him to buy weed for him."

"What the fuck is he thinking?" I hiss.

"Oh, it gets worse," he mutters.

"Worse than trying to get a kid to buy you drugs?"

Sophia's eyes go so wide I'm slightly concerned they're going to bug out of her head.

I don't know what she's looking so shocked about; she's the goody two shoes who's practically dating the local drug dealer, but that's a situation to unpack another day. This one's maxed out.

"I don't know what to tell you, new girl, the prick is on a roll."

I run my hand through my hair. "What'd he do?"

"Fucked if I know. Me and Bry were driving home from practice, and he was sprinting down the street away from those shops a few blocks from home. Some dude was chasing him with a crowbar. We pulled over and he jumped in, and we took the fuck off."

"I'm sorry, *what*? I think I just blacked out. He was running away from someone who was chasing him out of a store with a crowbar?"

"He wasn't just running, he was *fleeing*. I don't know if he robbed the fucking place or what."

"Well ask him!" I demand.

"I tried, the bastard won't say shit. He's locked it down tight, and I tell you what, he's doing a pretty fucking good job of being non-verbal."

I hear someone talking in the background.

"What the fuck?" Cullen mutters.

I'm not sure I should even dare ask at this point.

"Bry said he just checked out the social media pages for some of the stores. The bottle store posted a grainy-as-fuck pic of Pax, and it says they're trying to identify a disgruntled customer who damaged property."

I groan. "*Seriously?* He couldn't get weed so he went to buy piss?"

"Must have. I swear to God, he's either going to kill himself soon, or I'm going to finish the job myself."

I ignore his death threat. "And you have no idea what went on in there?"

"Nope. He didn't have any booze on him though, I know that much."

"Jesus Christ, Cull... what are we going to do?"

"That's why I'm ringing you, B. You're the smart one. What are we going to do with your brother?"

"Uh uh, he's been *your* brother longer, don't you dump that on me."

It's only then I click that Bryson is in the room with him when he just called Pax my brother.

"You told Bry?"

"Yeah."

"I told Soph too."

"Good. You need more people to have your back."

I rub at the crease that seems to have taken up permanent residence between my eyebrows.

If Pax makes me get premature wrinkles, I'm going to string him up by his balls. And then make him pay for Botox when I'm forty.

Soph must have overheard Cull telling me about the bottle store's social media post, because she holds her phone screen up for me to see. It's Pax alright. I don't think I'd have recognised him from that picture without reference, but it's him. There's no doubt in my mind.

It's only a matter of time before this blows up and someone recognises him, then dobs him in.

"I don't know what to do, Cull... other than talking to my dad, I'm out of ideas."

"We can't talk to Cole yet. Pax will never forgive us if we do that behind his back. I don't know what he'd do."

I don't want to think about something happening to Pax – something worse than a bottle store raid, or whatever the fuck went on today – but that's where we're at right now. He's lost the plot. This can't go on.

"I know," I agree quietly. "But will we forgive ourselves if we don't... and something happens to Pax?"

FIVE

Pax

Cullen's not talking to me. Berlin cries when she calls me, and Bryson just looks at me like he wants to hold a pillow over my face for a prolonged period of time.

Basically, I've fucked up every good thing I had going for me.

But on the bright side, I found half a bottle of rum stashed under my bed, so I deleted that on my walk to school.

It helped keep me warm, especially since I had to walk the long way around to avoid going past the bottle store.

I'm stupid but I'm not *that* stupid.

I walk in the school gates, half cut, two hours late, and it occurs to me that I'm spiralling. I'm on a bad path here, but I can't see any other trails I can take. There's no life-line waiting to save me.

There's just lies and betrayal and hurt.

I lose my footing on a loose bit of rock and almost fall over.

Fuck. Maybe I'm more than half cut.

Three quarters. Let's go with three quarters.

Whatever I am, it's sure as hell not going to fly at school, yet here I am, stumbling my way through school grounds, on my way to PE class.

What could go wrong?

Last class must have just got out, because everyone is everywhere, walking to classes and shit. Talking, gossiping, making plans all around me.

Doing whatever they want without their lives crumbling around them.

Must be nice.

I think I must have downed the last of that bottle a little too quickly because all of a sudden, I feel *quite* pissed.

I stumble again, and this time a few people notice.

"What are you looking at?" I snap.

No one lingers long. Preppy assholes.

I squint against the sun that's peeked out from between the clouds and try and think about where I'm meant to be going.

PE.

I'm going the wrong way.

I slap my cheek a little bit, trying to sober myself up.

I shouldn't go to class like this, some prick will snitch on me.

I wander off in the direction of the gym, and halfway there, I remember that I don't have my gym gear, but at this point, I'm too far in to care, and definitely too far in to go back.

The idea of walking back to the lockers makes me want to knock my head against a wall. I feel like I've been walking for hours.

Fuck it, I'll fake a tummy bug or some shit. I'm sure I look bad enough to get away with it, and at this rate I probably will be puking soon, so maybe it'll all work out for the best.

A group of year nines are coming towards me, the girls give me the stink eye and take a wide birth. Snobs.

I emerge from the swarm and nearly walk straight into Carissa.

"Shit, Pax, look out." She steadies herself.

"Carissa, baby."

"Don't call me that." She frowns as she takes me in, looking me up and down from head to toe. "Are you okay?"

"I'm good as," I tell her, and even *I* can hear the slur in my own voice.

Fuck, I need to get a grip.

"Seriously, Pax, you don't look so good." She takes a step towards me, and I take one backwards. Doesn't take a genius to figure out I stink of rum, and I don't need her ratting me out to Ice.

I smack into someone behind me as I move.

"Oi, what the hell?" I grunt as I turn around to see who it is.

"*You* walked into *me*," the guy says.

I don't even know who he is, but he looks young.

"So move," I tell him.

"Whatever, bro, I'm out." He shakes his head at me.

He tries to step around me, and I don't know what it is, I don't know what makes me do it. Maybe it's the fact that I'm drunk, or maybe I've just completely and utterly lost it, but I shove him.

"Dude, what the fuck?" he demands.

I shove him again.

"What the fuck is your problem?" one of his mate's yells at me as he tries to intervene.

"Pax, stop it!" I can hear Carissa yelling at me, but I don't stop. At this point I don't think I can stop.

I grab him by his jersey and pull him towards me, shaking him a little.

"Get the fuck out of here, man," someone tells me.

I don't even know which one said that. There's at least three guys in front of me, they're all yelling at me, they're all in my face.

"Get fucked," I sneer.

Someone hits me, and I swing back. My fist connects. Hard.

I hear it as clearly as I feel it on my knuckles. That unmistakable sound of a nose breaking.

"*Pax!*" That's Carissa again. "Stop!"

I think it's too late for that.

I'm on the ground now, with three guys wailing on me.

The fucked-up thing is that this is the most alive I've felt all week.

I'm blindly swinging and kicking my legs. I don't

know who I'm hitting or why, but there's blood every-where, and I've got a handful of someone's school uniform. It's a shit show.

"*Paxton!*"

Fuck. Now that's a voice I have to pay attention to.

I don't even know how I hear her over all the screaming and yelling and the sound of flesh being pounded. We're surrounded by people, and I'm practi-cally buried under three dudes, but I hear her and she's not happy.

"Get the *fuck* off him."

I don't know what it is about that girl, but people take notice. They listen to her. They bow down. We all do.

"He started that shit!" one of them tells her.

"I don't care, just get out of my way."

Berlin Davids has got superpowers, and I'm no more immune to them than the boys being dragged off me.

I hear what sounds a hell of a lot like coach, yelling at students to go to class. I close my eyes.

Maybe if I close my eyes for long enough, this will all go away.

"Get up." It's Berlin, and she sounds broken.

I stagger to my feet and wince as I feel the sharp pain in my ribs. I hope like fuck that they're not broken, but it doesn't feel good.

My shirt is ripped wide open and the shit that was in my backpack is now all over the fucking show. Empty bottle of rum included.

Fuck.

"What the actual fuck, Pax?" The words rip through me, and I make the stupid decision to look at her.

Her face. Her eyes.

I'm tearing her apart, piece by piece. I'm *breaking* her.

"Get to class! All of you. *Now!*" Coach bellows.

Everyone is scarpering, but I don't even bother. I know there's no way out of this one for me.

"Jesus Christ," I hear coach mutter as he gets a look at me, and no doubt the forbidden glass bottle at my feet.

Ice is just standing there in front of me, the look in her eyes cutting me deeper than any words ever could.

"Berlin, go to class please." Fuck. I know that voice too. Cole Davids has entered the chat.

Berlin takes one long, last look at me.

"You're breaking my heart," is all she says before she's ushered away by Carissa.

Shit.

PRINCIPAL EVANS IS a tough old bastard. I've wound up in this office more times over the years than I'd care to admit, but this is by far the most serious.

I could be looking at getting expelled here. I *should* be getting expelled. I'd for sure kick me out of here.

Coach took me to the staff room, poured me a giant cup of coffee and told me to chug it.

I'm feeling ten times more sober than I did when I walked in the school gates, but I'm not sure that's such a good thing right now. I might want to be sloshed to hear this next announcement.

My shirt is ripped to shreds under the jacket that

coach made me put on over top, and I can feel my right eye is swollen, I've probably got myself a decent shiner.

My ribs are the worst of it though. It hurts to breathe, and that's not likely to be a good sign.

"Just shut your mouth and we'll see what happens," Coach mutters as Principal Evans comes into his office, a sour fucking look on his face.

Can't really blame the old geezer, I'd be pretty wild if I had to deal with me too.

It's just me, Coach and the principal in here. I don't know where Cole went, but hopefully it's to a land far, far away.

I don't know what happened to the poor pricks I chose to unleash my rage on, or the nose I broke.

Now that I've sobered up enough to think clearly, I hope like hell that they either got away, or got none of the blame. I deserved that hiding, but they didn't.

Quite honestly, I probably deserve another one.

No doubt Cullen will have one waiting for me the minute I get home. Once Berlin talks to him, he's going to be full-on fuming.

"Mr. Benson, can you shed some light on the current situation?"

I fucking hate when teachers do that. It leaves you wide open to say too much, which I'm sure is very intentional strategy on his part.

Coach told me to shut my mouth, so I do exactly that. I shrug my shoulders.

He stares at me hard, then sighs heavily when he realises I'm not about to run my mouth and spill all the tea.

"Coach Green?" he prompts, turning his attention to Coach.

"By the time I got there it was him and a small group of year elevens, fighting on the ground."

I glance at Coach out the corner of my eye, waiting for him to tell the rest of it. Like the fact that I was drunk on school property – with the evidence to support that claim, like some kind of dipshit.

Next time I want to get wasted somewhere I shouldn't, I need to at least dispose of the evidence.

Next time. Good one, Pax. Keep those dreams high.

But Coach doesn't say anything else. He doesn't rat me out about the smell of my breath or the bottle. Come to think of it, he must have disposed of it himself.

"Who started the fight?" Principal Evans asks me.

"I did, Sir. I don't know what got into me."

"You know we take violence very seriously here. It's completely unacceptable."

I nod. "I'm sorry. I'm dealing with some personal things at the moment, and I just snapped. I'll apologise... do whatever I have to do to make it right."

"You can start by going home and staying there until next week. You look terrible."

It's already Wednesday afternoon, so that's not as bad as I was expecting, to be honest. Probably helps that big dog Evans seems totally oblivious to the fact that I was full of rum and disrespect.

I nod, doing my best to look solemn about it. I can't say that a couple of days at home is going to feel like too much of a punishment, but the wrath of my mother sure as hell will when she finds out about this suspension.

"And then when you return..." He pauses, thinking, and I refrain from groaning. I was kind of hoping that was it.

I can tell the moment he's thought of what he clearly considers to be the perfect punishment.

"You're going to report to Mr. Higgins' chemistry class every lunch time and after school. One of our students is doing advanced grade chemistry and needs assistance with some of the more mundane elements of the practical work. We were denied the extra funding for the scholarship program, so you're going to fill the gap."

"Yes, Sir."

I've got absolutely no intentions of ever actually doing that. But I nod my head in agreement anyway. The nerd will have to wash his own test tubes or whatever. I don't give a fuck, but the likelihood of me doing that is slim to none.

"I'll be getting in touch with your mother, and I expect written apologies to each of the boys you led astray. I'm not going to enforce this, but I would recommend you see the school counsellor. I don't know what you've got going on at home, but you need to find some other techniques to deal with your frustrations if you wish to continue to attend this school."

"Okay," I tell him.

"You'll report to me first thing Monday morning, with your apologies. Understood? I don't want you setting foot on school grounds until then."

"Understood. Thank you."

He nods at me once, and then with nothing more than a look, effectively dismisses me from his office.

I exchange a look with Coach, and he ushers me out into the hallway. I do my best not to show that my ribs are screaming at me in pain. The last thing I need is anyone getting wind of that injury and telling me I can't play next week either.

Coach looks stressed, and I don't blame him. He didn't technically lie for me in there, but he didn't tell the whole truth either.

"You got off easy, kid. I hope you realise that."

I nod. "Thanks, Coach, for not ah... snitching about what a dickhead I am."

He purses his lips, his forehead creasing.

"You just make sure you do those letters and turn up to that classroom every god damn day."

I scoff. "Screw that. I'm not going to spend every lunch time and after school in some boring-ass science lab."

I grab my backpack from where Coach told me to leave it, outside the principal's office door. When I glance back at him, he's looking at me like he's run out of fucks.

"Then I hate to do it, kid, but you're out. I'm not having a guy on my team who can't take responsibility for his actions."

"I'm already benched, Coach."

"I'm not talking about benching you, son, I'm kicking you off the team."

"*What?*" I gape. "Coach, c'mon, you can't kick me off the team. Please, I need this."

He shrugs at me. "Then you do your time. You've got no choices left. You do your punishment or you're out. It's up to you, Pax. The only person that can help you, is you."

With that, he leaves me standing there, desperately trying to think of a way to get out of this but coming up empty.

"Fuck," I mutter to myself.

Oh well. I guess that's that, then. I either turn up to be some geek's science bitch boy, or my time on the field is over.

Cool, cool, cool.

I swing my backpack onto my shoulder, wince in pain, and trudge down the hallway. Walking all the way home is about the least exciting thing I could think about doing right now, but my options are limited. As are my brain cells, if today is anything to go by. It's going to fucking hurt too, these ribs are getting worse by the minute.

I round the corner and almost jump into the air when I come face to face with Cole. It appears he's been waiting for me.

"Coach told me what happened in there."

"What do you want?" I snap, pushing past him.

He looks visibly shocked.

"I don't know what's got into you, Pax, but I'm disappointed in you."

This clown. *He's* disappointed. The fucking irony.

"You're *disappointed* in *me?*" I huff out a humourless laugh as he narrows his eyes.

Fuck this shit. I'm done.

It's gone on too long. I don't care anymore. My life is

already going off the rails. I may as well pump the gas and really send it over the edge.

He turns to walk away.

"What do I care if *you're* disappointed in *me*? It's not like you're my dad, right, *Sir*?" I spit the words with so much spite, I almost choke on them.

His step falters and he turns back, his jaw slack.

"What is that meant to mean?"

"I think you know the answer to that already."

We stand there, only a metre apart, staring at each other. Him in shock, me in anger.

Father and son.

I guess the cat's out of the bag and the shit is about to hit the fan.

SIX

Berlin

The minute I walk in the door, I can tell something is seriously wrong.

Dad is on the phone, and it sounds like shit is getting *heated*. It takes a fair bit to get the old man all riled up, but he is maaaaad right now.

"I don't care, Julia, I'm telling you. *He knows.*"

Uh oh. Here we go. It seems Dad has finally caught on.

There's silence for a bit – I gather Julia is speaking.

"Don't treat me like an idiot, this is my life too. He knows. I'm telling you."

I drop my keys loudly into the bowl in the entrance, to give Dad the heads up that I'm home – and have functioning ears.

"I've gotta go," I hear him say quickly.

I decided on my drive home that I was going to

confront him about this whole fuck up of a situation and get everything all out in the open, but when he rounds the corner into the entryway, he looks so bloody tired, I don't know if I can do it.

I don't blame my dad for any of this really, it's hardly his fault, but I do blame him for keeping this from me since he found out.

Sharing is our thing.

I might not tell him every little detail about everything I do, but the big shit... the important stuff... he knows it all. I thought that worked both ways.

"Hey, kiddo."

"What's going on, old man? You look like shit."

He chuckles. "You sure know how to make a guy feel the love. That Cullen is a lucky boy."

"He certainly is."

"Did you talk to Pax yet?" he asks me warily.

I shake my head, my eyes narrowing.

He's ignoring my calls. I was going to go around to their house with Cullen; he wanted me to come, but I decided against it. I told him to go for a run and clear his head and then to call me. We'll see how that pans out.

"Nope. He doesn't want to talk to me. Which is probably for the best because I honestly don't know what I'd say to him after that fight."

I've seen some shit over my high school years. It's not like I've never seen a brawl before. Hell, I've been in a fight or two myself back in my more dramatic days, but Pax is a lover, not a fighter. And he'd never behave like that on a normal day.

Clearly today was far from a normal day.

"Come and sit down," Dad says, ushering me into the living room and sitting down across from me. "I think we need to talk."

Well shit.

Looks like this talk is happening now after all.

I nod my head. "Yeah, I think you're right."

"I'm pretty sure this is all about to come out anyway, and Pax's mum is begging me not to say anything, but I can't keep it to myself anymore, and honestly, you have the right to know."

I give him a small, sad smile. "I already do, Dad."

He looks up at me from his hands that he's nervously wringing together.

"*What?*"

"I know, Dad, about Pax. I know he's your son."

I've only ever seen my dad cry a few times in my life, but his eyes are tearing up now. He looks so... *sorry.*

"Pax, he knows too, doesn't he?"

I nod my head.

"I *knew* it. He said something today, and I just knew."

I sigh deeply. I had a feeling Pax would break sooner rather than later.

"How long?" he questions, his voice cracking. "How long have you known about this?"

"Since the night Julia and Hannah told you," I reply quietly.

I see the force the air exits his lungs in a big whoosh. "It's been a couple of weeks, B. You knew all this time?"

"I was over at their house the night you went around there to talk. We overheard everything."

He goes quiet. Probably reliving the moment he

found out he was a father of two, with absolutely no warning.

"What were you doing over at their house when you were grounded?"

"*Really? That's* what you're going to take from this?"

He laughs, but there's fuck all humour in it.

"Oh, kiddo." He sighs. I can see the guilt written all over his face. "I'm so sorry, I wanted to tell you right away, but Julia wasn't ready. She begged me to give her more time to figure out how to tell Pax."

"She's had eighteen years to figure out how to tell him."

He nods his head, his eyes glassy. "And how to tell *me*."

"*Dad...*"

I've never seen him look so hurt.

He rakes his hands down his face. "I know I'm the parent here, and I'm meant to have it all figured out, but honestly, I've got absolutely no idea what the fuck I'm meant to do."

"I don't know either... we've been trying... and failing."

"He's my *son*. He's your brother and I want a relationship with him, but I'm stuck between a rock and a hard place here. He *hates* me. I saw it in his eyes today."

"He doesn't hate you," I whisper, getting to my feet and moving to sit next to him.

He wraps his arms around me and hugs me tight. I think he's needed this hug as much as I have.

"How could he hate you? You had *no* idea. Julia kept

this from you too. He's got every right to be mad at her, but not you."

He lets me go but keeps one arm around me.

"She kept it from *everyone*. I don't know how she went eighteen years without telling a single soul who her child's father was."

"What about Hannah?" I question.

He shakes his head. "Not even Hannah knew. Julia only told her the day before she told me. She'd kept it to herself *all* this time. I guess when I showed up back in town, she finally cracked."

"Why didn't she tell you at the time... I don't understand why she lied."

"Your guess is as good as mine at this point, kiddo. I've asked her a million questions and only got a couple of answers. I'm trying to be patient, but it's breaking me."

"Well, I doubt she's going to be able to keep it quiet any longer. If Pax is on the war path, then I can only assume she's his target. I should warn Cullen."

"Pax fighting, not showing up to class or practice... it's all because of this?"

I swallow the lump in my throat. "He's going off the rails, and I have no idea how to help him."

"Today at school, was he –"

"As lit as a fucking Christmas tree? *Yeah*. Sure was."

He looks at me, pained as I've ever seen him.

"Coach Green threatened to kick him off the team."

Shit.

I'm no fortune teller, but I predict that things are only about to get worse.

SEVEN

Pax

Ma's in the kitchen when I get home, and I took that long to get here, I've got no doubt that she'll have already spoken to the big school boss man, and I'll be in fifty shades of shit.

I'd also be willing to bet that Cole has called her, and sworn black and blue that I know he's my dad. He saw it in my eyes. He heard it in my tone. I know. He knows. We all fucking know.

What Ma does next is up to her.

I sit down at the table, not saying a word. She knows I'm here. She flinched when I walked in the door.

She's just slowly stirring the pot in front of her, and I can see the shake in her hand.

I almost feel sorry for her, but I won't. Not now. I refuse. She's made her bed, now she has to lie in it.

The silence stretches for what feels like fucking forever.

She finally puts down the spoon and turns to face me. She's been crying, that's pretty fucking obvious – she needs to invest in some waterproof mascara.

I'm not going to let it stop me from getting the information I need though. I love this woman, there's no denying that. She's my mum, and normally, even a hint of a tear on her face would be enough to send me on a mission to fix it, but that's not the case today. I'm not going to let her emotions stop me from getting what I need out of her.

She's just standing there, staring at me. She looks like she doesn't even know how to begin.

"Just say it, Ma. This has gone on long enough."

She nods her head in agreement. "You do know, don't you?"

"I want to hear you say it," I reply, straight-faced and emotionless.

"Paxton, please, just tell me what you know," she begs.

"Why, Ma? So you can lie to me again? So you can only tell the truths you have to? It's not happening. I. Want. To. Hear. You. Say. It."

The silence stretches between us. I feel like I'm about to explode, but I'll sit here all night if I have to. I'm not leaving until she's finally honest with me. Eighteen years is a long time to be lied to and it's going to end now.

She takes a deep breath, and I'm just about to rip into her – demand that she tell me, when she finally speaks, and more than that, she's finally honest.

"Cole is your father."

I nod my head slowly. This isn't new information to me, but it hits me again when the words are said to my face rather than overheard from down the hallway.

"Why now?"

That might be the biggest question I have. Why keep a secret for all these years, only to turn around and come clean now?

She shrugs. "Because he's back in town... because of Berlin... I could see you two were close, and I know that she's with Cullen, but teenagers are scary these days. I couldn't take the chance that the relationship between you and her might turn... *romantic*."

I wince as I think about the fact that she was at least partially right, I kissed my fucking sister. That shit is whack.

"So, if they'd never moved back here, or his other kid wasn't a girl, you wouldn't have ever told me? You would have taken this shit to the grave?"

I can see the pain in her eyes. I can basically see her heart cracking open. She knows she's fucked up. She knows I'm probably never going to forgive her for this. I just can't find it in me to care about her pain. I've got enough of my own.

"I don't know."

That's about the most honest answer she's given me so far.

"I don't know how you could do this to me, Ma. I really don't. it's wrong. I had a right to know."

"Maybe one day if you have a child of your own, you'll understand what it's like. I lived in fear that if I told him, he'd try and take you from me. I was a young, single mother, barely making ends meet and making some questionable decisions. By the time I figured out who the father was, where he was and how to contact him, he was overseas, and a superstar playboy who'd proven to the whole world that he could handle being a single father like it was the easiest job on earth. I knew it would only go two ways. One, he'd take you from me, or two, he'd give up everything to come back here for you, for us. I didn't know what to do with either of those options."

"That's a total fucking cop out, Ma. So what if he came back here? He couldn't just take me from you. It would have been his choice to come back here and be a part of my life, or to give that up and stay there. But at least we'd have known. You took that from me. You took that from *him*. I don't know how you sleep at night. I don't know how you've slept a wink for the last eighteen years." I don't think I even get a breath in during my whole rant, I'm just *so* angry.

"You know what, I know you're hurting. I know you hate that I deceived you, I hate it too, but I'm not going to sit here and apologise for doing what I thought was best for my child at the time."

Is she seriously defending her shitty behaviour right now?

"At the time, *maybe*, and that's a big maybe, but all the years that followed... what about those? How was that what was best for me?" I'm almost shouting, I'm so fucking frustrated.

"I found myself in a hole so deep I didn't know how to get out. I thought about telling you so many times, but then it'd be real. And then I knew I might lose you, like I feel like I am right now."

"You deserve to lose me," I hiss.

"I'm sorry I hurt you. I'm sorry I lied to you, and I know that you hate me right now. But you know what, Paxton James Benson? I am still your mother, and you might not agree with my choices, but I did the best I could with what I had, and I'll tell you what, when you were a baby, what I had was fuck all. We survived on hopes and dreams, and I think I did a pretty good job of raising you, all things considered."

Oh shit, she full named me.

"That's all good and well, Ma, and maybe I can even understand why you didn't tell Cole back when I was born, or even when I was a little kid, but when I got older? All those times I cried because I wanted a father to be around? What about then? What reason can you give for keeping it from me then? From *him*? He's had another kid all this time and you just didn't feel like telling him? What the hell, Ma? That's some fucked-up shit."

"I can't take it back now. Seeing you like this, I wish I could, but I can't."

Way to state the fucking obvious.

"You should talk to Cole. I'm sure he wants to have a relationship with his son, and I want that for you too. You should get to know your dad."

The fucking irony. "Oh, *now* you want me to have a relationship with my father? After you denied me the opportunity my whole life. That's rich."

"I'm so sorry, Pax. I don't know what else to say."

There's nothing to say. Nothing that comes out of her mouth is going to fix this.

"I want you to know that Hannah wasn't in on this. She had no idea he was your father. Please don't punish her for my actions. She loves you and wants to be there for you." She pleads with me.

I know the words are going to cut her, and honestly, maybe that's why I say them – to hurt her, the same way she hurt me.

"Good. At least I still have one mother I can trust."

A fresh wave of tears roll down her cheeks.

I'm done with this conversation. I'm exhausted, and my ribs are killing me. I turn and leave the kitchen as she just stands there, tears streaming down her face.

I stalk off to my room, slam the door like a toddler, and in a fit of rage, tear up the best drawing I've ever done – the one I did of Ma.

***

BERLIN: **I talked to my dad. He knows we know. He told me everything.**

Five minutes later, another message.

Berlin: Cullen just told me you confronted your ma… are you okay?

Berlin: Pax, can you just reply once so I know you're okay?

Another five minutes passes.

Berlin: Please. I'm worried about you.

Berlin: I'm going to send Cullen in

Ah fuck.

I start to tap out a reply to tell her I'm fine, and to stop blowing up my god damn phone, but I'm too slow. My door swings open and Cullen stands in the doorway, his arms folded across his chest and a scowl on his face.

"She's got you firmly on the whip," I drawl.

He sighs, walks into the room and shuts the door behind him.

"She's losing her mind, worrying about you. I know I've had a thing for crazy girls in the past, but I actually like this one sane. You reckon you could help a guy out and stop making things worse?"

He sits down on the end of my bed. There's something different in the air between us now. He's mad, and disappointed, but more than that, he's worried, and sad. I don't know how I'd be handling this situation if roles were reversed and he was spiralling downwards. I don't envy him. As hard as this is for me, I can see how this is hard for him too.

"I'm trying, man, but honestly, I'm barely keeping my own head above water right now. I can't take on anything else."

It's silent between us for a few beats.

"Ma's gone to stay at her sisters for the night. She wanted to give you some space."

I nod my head. I didn't expect her to do that, but I'm glad, nonetheless. I can barely look at her right now.

"Berlin said that she talked to Cole. He's pretty cut up. She's really worried about him. I know he wants to talk to you, when you're ready."

I can't even begin to comprehend what that conversation might sound like. I know it's not his fault, but I still feel all this pent-up resentment towards the man.

"I'm not ready," I reply honestly.

"That's what I told B."

I nod again. I'm feeling kind of choked up all of a sudden.

"You know we're all here for you, right? I know I've been kind of a prick, and I've been coming down on you pretty hard, but I'd do anything for you, bro. Berlin too. Hell, I'd be willing to bet that Cole would as well. Mum... Ma... We all love you, Pax."

I don't think Cull has seen me cry since we were kids and he pushed me down a set of stairs and broke my arm. In fact, I'm not even sure I have cried in the past ten years, but I'm crying now.

Not only am I crying, I'm full-on bawling.

I expect him to start swearing or walk out. What I don't expect is him to shuffle closer and give me a hug.

This guy. We might not be related by blood, but he's my family. He's the one person in my life I can rely on no matter what. He's been there with me through it all, and he'll keep being there through it all, no matter how much of a dipshit I turn into. No matter how many stupid situations I put myself in, or how sick of my shit he gets, I know he'll always be there.

Like right now, as he sits next to me in silence, just being here for me while I fall apart.

I finally find myself all cried out. I've got nothing left.

I slowly pull away, out of his embrace and scrub my hands over my face to wipe away the wetness on my skin.

"I ordered pizza. Want to come get your ass kicked on the PS4?"

That's the best offer I've had all week.

"Tell me you didn't get pineapple on the pizza."

He gets to his feet and strolls towards the door. "Pineapple on pizza is elite, don't come at me because you have a basic bitch palate."

I chuckle quietly. "It's a fucking fruit. Get a grip."

He's out in the hallway now, but I still hear him yell back to me. "I'm getting extra pineapple next time, just because of that comment."

Asshole.

I grab my phone and reply to Ice.

Me: Thank you.

I take a deep breath, wipe my face one more time, and follow Cullen out to the living room.

I'll worry about all my problems tomorrow. Tonight I'm just going to enjoy the time with my brother and pretend my life isn't falling apart at the seams.

EIGHT

Pax

I'd honestly rather shit in my hands and clap than turn up to this chemistry lab and spit-shine safety goggles or whatever the fuck it is that I'm going to be doing for this dork genius, but unfortunately for me, that wasn't one of the options the principal gave me.

Apparently, I'm meant to show up, get signed off by Mr. Higgins, and then he's going to introduce me to dorks-r-us and give me a run down on the deal.

I hope the dude at least has some kind of a personality. It's going to be a painful however many weeks if he's some snivelling nerd who only talks in facts, or some shit.

I have to keep telling myself that I *need* rugby. I need one good thing in my life, and without doing this, I'm never going to make that team again.

It's a necessary evil.

I have to admit, without the weed, I can actually think a little clearer. See a little more sense. I'd never admit it, but maybe Cullen and Ice had a point. I was three quarters of the way to stonerville.

I walk through the science building, screwing my nose up, there's just something about this block that smells weird. It never feels quite right in here to me. It's kind of creepy. I can't say I'd be overly devastated if someone got a bit fast and loose with a Bunsen burner and burnt the place to the ground, but that's just me.

Physics is about the only subject that even remotely interests me from all of the sciences, and even then, I use the term 'interests' fairly loosely. It's participation at best.

I walk into Higgins' classroom and find it empty.

I decide to just quietly take a seat rather than go and snoop around out back. If I can kill even a minute of this torture without human interaction, then I'll be a happy man.

I manage to watch the second hand on the clock go around five times before I hear voices coming from the room out back.

I can't say I've ever spent much time in the advanced labs some of the classrooms have, but I'm willing to bet the super nerd I'm here to assist, basically has a bed set up back there.

"Record your findings and we'll go over them at the end of the week," I hear Mr. Higgins say before he appears in the doorway and notices me.

"Ah. You must be Paxton."

"Pax," I correct him.

"Pax," he repeats. "Well come on back." He waves me over.

I sigh, pick up my bag and cross the room to where he's waiting for me.

"I don't know what Mr. Evans told you about Lily's work, but she's..."

I stop listening after the word 'Lily'.

Hold up, nerd alert is a chick?

Well fuck me, this was bad enough when I thought I was dealing with a dude, but some nerdy little science girl is *definitely* worse. There's no way some white-coat-wearing female is going to want a dumb jock helping her out.

Fuck my life.

Higgins is looking at me like he's expecting some kind of response, but since I wasn't listening to shit all of what he said, I have no idea what the appropriate response *is*.

"Sounds really... *interesting*," I offer.

"It is. She's doing some amazing work, but unfortunately the extra grant money hasn't come through as we hoped it would, so that's where you come in." He carries on as I reach him.

He turns and I follow him into the advanced lab.

It's all pretty shiny and new in here, seems like *some* kind of funding must have made its way into this room. Doesn't smell like the hallways do. It's not all that bad.

I wish the boys locker room looked this clean.

"Pax, this is Lily."

She turns around, and the first thought through my mind is that she's pretty. Not like, trip over yourself trying to get another look, pretty, but she's a cute girl.

Dark blonde hair, round face and green eyes. She doesn't look like a super smart science prodigy, not that I know what I'd expect one to look like. She just looks... normal.

"Lily, this is Pax., He's here to help you with whatever you need."

"Hi," she says, looking me up and down.

"Hey," I reply.

She looks as unenthused about me being here as I am.

At least we'll have one thing in common.

"Mr. Benson here is at your beck and call. Principal Evans has given no indication as to how long this will continue, but for now, let's say lunchtime Monday, Wednesday and Fridays, and after school Tuesday and Thursdays for as long as Lily needs."

Could be worse. The big man made me think I was going to be here every day, twice a day. At this point I need to take the small wins where I can get them.

"Sounds good to me," Lily tells him. "Thanks, Mr. Higgins."

He turns to me. "I'll be in and out at times, but it'll mostly just be the two of you. Lily knows what she's doing, so just follow her instructions."

"Yes, Sir."

He looks between us, nods his head and leaves the room, leaving us all alone.

I wander over to the bench she's working at and turn a sheet of paper with handwritten notes all over it, towards me.

I'm trying to read it when her hand reaches out and she takes it away from in front of me.

I look at her, but she doesn't say anything, just raises her eyebrow. She's got a good 'what the fuck do you think you're doing' look.

"Don't worry, Einstein, I didn't understand a word of it."

"That's hardly surprising," she mutters under her breath.

That should probably piss me off, but she's not wrong, and instead of getting mad, I feel the corners of my mouth turning up.

At least it seems like she has a bit of personality. A backbone. I was expecting her to be the human version of an encyclopaedia, so that's a nice bonus.

"So, what are we doing here, brains? Need me to light something on fire?"

She's fucking around with something that looks a lot like an explosion waiting to happen.

She's got three glass vials in front of her with different coloured liquids in them, and a couple of smaller test tubes with what appears to be water in them, off to the side.

"I very much need you to *not* light anything on fire if that's at all possible. Do you think you can manage that?"

"I'm not willing to say yes... but I'm also not prepared to say no."

She gives me an unimpressed look.

"Why are you here?"

I frown at her; I'd have thought she'd be in the know. "Boss man gave me the orders."

She turns back to her experiment... if that's what you

call whatever the hell it is that she's doing. I watch as she puts on a pair of gloves and some safety goggles.

I take a step back. I don't need acid or some shit exploding in my face, and she doesn't appear to be too concerned about me having any safety gear.

"No, I know that you were told you *had* to be here, I'm asking *why* you have to be here. What'd you do?"

I shrug and run a hand through my hair. "Ummmm... a piece of work that I like to refer to as *a series of stupid decisions?*"

She doesn't speak, but somehow, I get the distinct impression she's waiting for me to lay them all out to her, so I do.

"Fighting, ditching school, playing up on the rugby field..." I list them off, sounding stupider by the second.

She mouths a word that looks suspiciously like the word 'WOW'. Now I may not be an advanced chem kind of smart, but I'm also not an idiot, and I'm pretty sure she's *not* saying that because she's impressed.

"Not my finest moments." I admit. "Very out of character.'"

"Well, that's something at least."

I'm transfixed on what she's doing. I have no idea what any of it means, or what she's trying to achieve, but she's tipping liquids around and making notes as though it all makes perfect sense to her.

"What are you doing?" I finally ask her.

"Observing chemical reactions."

I nod, as though that helps me understand, when in reality, it means absolutely jack shit to me.

"So, what am I going to be doing?"

"Right now, nothing. But I need some assistance with some of the practical elements of my study. Taking notes, sorting out equipment, cleaning, that kind of thing."

"Cool. Sounds like a hoot."

She pulls her gaze from the 'chemical reaction' she's 'observing' and shoots me a filthy looking side eye.

Damn. This girl means business.

I leave her to... whatever she's doing.

I stroll around the lab, looking at everything. Everything on the walls may as well be another language for all the sense I can make of it, but it looks cool.

I stop in front of a big poster of the periodic table. At least I recognise that.

I carry on, checking out everything else.

"You're like a small child who has to touch everything he sees."

I didn't even know she was watching me, but I glance down and, sure enough, I'm handsing something I can't even identify.

I put it down and link my fingers behind my back as I finish my lap of the room, peeking at her out the corner of my eye, every few seconds.

She's diligently doing her work and ignoring me at the same time.

Multitasking at its finest.

I come to a stop next to her and rest my hip against the bench she's working from. The table rocks a little and she pauses, sighs heavily, and then goes back to what she's doing.

I can't help the grin that spreads across my face. This Lily chick might be some fun after all.

"You know, I'd have expected a nerd like you to wear glasses."

"Great, so not only are *you* a walking cliché, but you expect everyone else to be too? *Lucky me*," she snaps.

Exactly the kind of reaction I was hoping for. I guess we're both out here observing reactions.

I've got a goofy grin on my face; I can feel it. "So, no glasses then?"

She scowls, puts down her equipment and crosses her arms across her chest.

She looks like she doesn't want to answer and that only intrigues me more.

"Come on, Lily, humour me."

She sighs heavily. "I'm wearing contacts, okay?"

My grin widens. "I *knew* it."

"Get out of my lab," she tells me.

I chuckle. It's a sound I haven't heard in a while.

"Oh, come on, Lily-boo, don't be like that."

Her eyes widen at the use of the nickname, and she points to the doorway I entered with Mr. Higgins.

That only makes me laugh again.

I shrug my shoulders. "Whatever you say, brains. I'll be right out there if you need me."

I hear her mutter something incomprehensible under her breath. It entertains me even more.

"YOU'VE BEEN A GHOST LATELY, BRO."

I can't be sure, but Bryson looks a little bit sad. Maybe he loves me after all.

"Been trying to stay out of trouble," I tell him.

"Since when do you care?"

"Since Coach told me I'm off the team for good if I don't fall in line."

"That sucks."

He throws back the last of his burger.

The diner is humming tonight, but I'm not really feeling it. It's Friday night, and everyone is talking about a party on tomorrow night, but there's no way I'm going near that.

I lean forward a bit farther to grab some fries off his plate and my ribs scream in protest. Every time I think they're starting to feel better, I'm reminded that my luck isn't that good.

It's going to be a long while before I'm back to one hundred percent.

He's quiet again, which is normal for him, but it feels like a different kind of quiet. He's glancing at something behind me every few seconds.

I turn around to look and then I know what's up his ass.

Soph and Tonks are enjoying a romantic meal for two.

Bryson looks like someone pissed in his cornflakes.

I don't get the guy. Seems like he's been quietly pining away over her from a distance for years, but he never made a real move.

He's a good-looking dude. I'm sure he could have got any girl he wanted. And judging by Sophia's reaction to him, and the kiss they had at the house party a while back, I'm pretty sure she was into him too.

"Want me to talk to her?"

Soph and I have become friends since Berlin came into the picture.

It occurs to me in that moment that she's my cousin. She's my family. So is her younger brother, Toby. Her dad is my uncle. They're my blood.

Fuck. I have people. Not that they probably know I'm part of their family tree yet.

Other than Cull and the women who raised us, I've never really had people. Ma's family disowned her when she got pregnant with me and wouldn't name a father. I don't think I've even met the people.

"Nope," he answers, reminding me that I asked him a question.

"You should just tell her how you feel."

He doesn't acknowledge that I've spoken. *Whatever.* Not my problem.

"I've got to take a piss," I say as I get to my feet.

I can't be fucked with his whole tortured wallowing. I've got enough of my own torture going on. He can handle his shit.

I push open the door to the men's bathroom and head for the urinal.

I hear the door open behind me and I glance to see who it is. I'm sure as hell not expecting to see Eve standing there.

"Are you lost?" I smirk at her.

She shakes her head, a devious look in her eyes.

Shit, I know that look. She's down to fuck.

She looks pointedly between me and the stall in the corner. Fuck me, she wants to do this here and now.

"If that's what you want," I reply. It sure as fuck

doesn't bother me. I'll get my dick wet if she's willing and eager.

I head for the stall, and I can hear her following me.

She locks the door behind her and drags me to her in the next second.

I kiss her hard, banging us both against the door, not giving a shit about being subtle or quiet.

I drop my head to her neck, kissing her roughly.

I've got no interest in going full foreplay on it. We're in a fucking bathroom stall. So she better be ready.

"Just fuck me already." She moans, reaching for my shorts.

Thata girl.

She lifts her dress as I pull down my shorts.

She tries to climb onto me, but the pain in my ribs nearly kills me.

"Ow, fuck." I clutch at them, stepping back.

"What's wrong?"

"Injury." I grunt.

There's no way in fuck I'm going to be holding her up against a door right now. Not a shot in hell.

"I'll have to bow out. Sorry."

She pouts, but then I see her expression change into a devious smirk.

"Maybe you deserve a little treat."

Before I can even figure out what she's getting at, she's on her knees, and my dick is in her mouth.

Fuuuuuck. That feels insanely good.

Eve might not be girlfriend material, but the girl knows what she's doing on her knees. Even on the floor of a men's bathroom.

I let my head fall back against the door as she takes me deeper in her throat.

This is the dream outcome for me, all the results with none of the effort.

She bobs her head up and down, but I want it deeper.

I hold her head in my hands and thrust deep, in and out, until I feel myself getting close.

She's a fucking trooper, I'm not being gentle and she's just taking everything I'm giving.

She reaches through and cups my balls, and I grunt.

I'm so fucking close and that's going to push me over the edge.

She's like a fucking shark in the water – it's like she can smell how close I am. She plays with my balls again and that's all it takes. I blow my load into her mouth, hammering the back of her throat as I keep thrusting.

She swallows until it's all down and I've stopped slamming my dick in and out of her mouth.

My eyes are shut, my body laxed against the door.

Fuck me, that was exactly what I needed. Nothing like a bit of stress release.

I let go of her head and she gets to her feet and licks her lips.

I pull my shorts back up as she slips around me.

"You're welcome." She smirks before opening the stall door and walking out.

I don't know what the hell just happened, but that was the most fun I've ever had in a fucking toilet.

I wait for her to definitely be gone, before taking a piss – the thing I actually came in here for – and then leaving.

Bryson has probably been sitting at the table wondering where the fuck I've gone.

Actually, the guy doesn't miss a thing, so I'm sure he would have seen Eve follow me in here. I may as well just own it.

I stroll back out into the restaurant and head back to our table.

He glances at me as I sit down but doesn't say anything.

"What? No round of applause?" I grin.

He lifts an eyebrow and smirks. "You're a dog."

"But I'm a satisfied dog."

Eve catches my eye across the restaurant and makes a show of wiping the corners of her mouth with a napkin.

She's a dirty bitch, that one.

I shouldn't play with fire like this. I've slept with her a few times now, and I know full well that if I don't cut it off, she's going to start getting attached.

For now at least though, she knows the score.

Bryson chuckles, once again, not having missed a thing. "Satisfied or not, you're still a dog, bro."

NINE

Pax

"Honey, I'm home!" I call out into the empty classroom.

I really should behave myself, but at this point I'm probably not capable. I spent the rest of my lunch break yesterday sitting out here alone after she evicted me from the back lab.

It was boring, but I found a way to entertain myself.

I smirk as I think about it. She's going to regret leaving me out here with nothing better to do with my time.

"Pax?" she calls out. "I'm out back."

I head back there, intrigued to see what she'll be doing today.

This is my first after school session, and I've got no fucking idea how long we'll be here, but luckily for her, I brought snacks.

"No white coat today?" I ask as I find her sitting at a bench with a laptop in front of her.

"Not today."

"That's a shame, I'm partial to a bit of science role play."

She rolls her eyes at me, the action exaggerated and dramatic. "Are you off your meds or something?"

I grin and clap my hands together. "It's a mystery. What are we doing today, Lily-boo?"

"For starters, we're going to figure out how to get you to stop calling me that."

"No can do." I smirk. "It's endearing, just embrace it."

She shakes her head at me. "You're a real-life moron."

"Said with endearment. I like it. Way to jump on board."

"There was quite literally not one ounce of endearment in that sentence."

"It's okay, brains, you don't have to play coy with me. The science girl and the rugby boy might just be the power couple the world needs."

"Do you ever get sick of the sound of your own voice?" she asks me.

I shrug. "Hasn't happened yet, but you'll be the first to know if it does."

"*Wonderful,*" she says sarcastically.

"You know what else is wonderful?"

"You know what, I'm almost afraid to ask."

I chuckle. I like this girl. She's fun to wind up.

"It's just a bit of gossip that found its way to me. Wanna hear it?"

She sighs heavily. I think she'd like to protest, but

she's a smart girl, and it's pretty obvious by now that I can't be stopped.

"It's kind of a secret, but...." I say, leaning in closer to her, "I heard that Carbon and Hydrogen went on a date. Apparently, they really... *bonded*..." I deliver the punch line, waggling my eyebrows at her.

"Did you just make a *chemistry joke?*" she deadpans.

I wink at her. "I like to hear chemistry puns, *periodically*."

"Oh, sweet Jesus, this is going to be the death of me," she mutters under her breath.

"Wait, are all my jokes too basic for you? Because I'm seeing no... *reaction*."

She groans, tipping her head back. "Make it stop."

I bust out laughing. "Oh, c'mon, Lily-boo, that was funny, you've gotta give me that."

"I don't think I'm your target audience, because I absolutely will not be laughing at that."

"You're *exactly* my target audience, and that sounds like a challenge to me."

"That can sound like whatever you like, Ace, but right now, I've got work to do, if you don't mind giving me some peace and quiet."

She's pushing shit uphill with that request, but I can probably manage to shut my trap for a few short minutes, at the very least.

I watch her potter around, doing whatever it is she does best. I can hear her talking to herself quietly, sounds like she's listing things off. She seems too sweet and innocent to survive in a place like this for long. Schools like this chew up and spit out sweet little things like her.

"Are you new here?" I ask, ignoring her request for silence. "To this school I mean?"

I can't place her at Westlake. She's pretty, but kind of normal looking; not a girl you'd probably notice in a crowd. But she's got a little something about her. I think I'd have remembered if we'd been in the same classes. I'm sure I'd have remembered that ass, if nothing else.

"Nope."

"Then why don't I recognise you?"

"Probably because we're from completely different worlds. I don't run around shaking a pair of pom poms, and you *clearly* haven't spent any time in a chem lab."

A devilish grin spreads across my face. Now that she's drawn my attention to it, her ass isn't her only defining feature.

She points a finger at me in warning. "If you even *think* about saying something stupid like you'd like to see *me* shake *my* pom poms, I'm going to douse you in cleaning bleach."

"Careful, I'm starting to think you're hitting on me, Lily-boo."

She scowls. "Are you actually okay? Like, seriously... have you had a few knocks to the head lately? Do you need a ride to the hospital or something?"

I chuckle. She can't stand me already, but this is fun, I'm enjoying myself. Something I haven't done in a while now.

"Can you just go and wash some of that equipment please? I swear to God, you're hindering my work more than you're helping it."

"You just want me all soapy and wet, I get it. I'll wear

a white t-shirt for you next time. Really spice things up in here."

She closes her eyes and breathes in deeply through her nose. She's probably absolutely cursing Mr. Evans for this whole saga.

"The test tubes, Pax. Just wash the damn test tubes."

I salute her, but I can't help myself, I've got one more as I stroll across the room towards the sink.

"Hey, Lily-boo... what do you call an acid with an attitude?"

"*What?*" she asks warily, already rolling her eyes before she's even heard the punchline.

"A-*mean*-o acid."

"*Never* try your luck as a comedian," she tells me, but that time I'm sure I saw the hint of a smile on her lips.

I'll crack her one of these days, there's plenty more cringey chemistry jokes where that came from, and I'm going to get a laugh out of this chick if it kills me.

I TWIRL AROUND and around in circles on the stool. I'm starting to get dizzy, but it's a price I'm willing to pay to see how long it takes her to demand I stop.

It's Friday today, and while I've managed to avoid Ma, Mum, Cole, and most of my friends all week, I've shown up to this chem lab, every day – on time even.

Who even am I?

I've also brought snacks every day, and every day, she's declined them. There's no impressing this girl. I know she's not going to be able to turn down what I've got today. Only an unhinged sociopath can resist a big bag of crispy M&Ms.

"Honestly, I know you're looking for a reaction, and it breaks me that I have to give you one, but if you don't stop that insistent spinning, I'm going to puke. Please stop before your next job is cleaning up my vomit."

I chuckle but do what I'm told for once and stop spinning. Mostly because she asked, but also a little because I seriously feel like I'm about to spew too.

Being a pain in the ass has its price.

"You know, if I'm going to keep hanging out in here, I think I might need you to teach me a thing or two about chemistry, because I really don't know what the hell is going on half the time."

She shoots me a look.

"Okay, fine, I don't know what's going on *any* of the time. I'm meant to be helping you or something, right? I feel like a dead weight, and a dipshit. Teach me, Lil," I whine as I jump off my stool and walk towards her, a little wobbly on my feet from the fifty million rotations I just did.

"I appreciate your enthusiasm, I really do. But this is meant to be you helping me, not me turning into Professor Wilder and –"

"Wait, your last name is Wilder?"

"Yeah... why?"

"Nah nothing, it's just a bit ironic."

"Do tell," she deadpans.

I feel that grin creeping onto my face again. "Well, there's not much *wild* about you, is there Lily-boo?"

She stands up a little straighter. "You know, it's cute you think you know me at all."

"It's cute you think I don't," I reply.

She narrows her eyes slightly, but she doesn't look away. We just stand there, looking at one another across the room. This is probably the longest she's held eye contact in five days.

Five days. It's hard to believe that's all it's been.

What's even harder to believe is the fact that I feel sort of disappointed I won't see her again tomorrow.

It does give me two days to find more terrible chemistry jokes though, so that's something at least. I'll be coming in hot by lunch time Monday.

We're still in our silent stand off when I hear a voice.

"Paxikins, science suits you."

I spin around and find Berlin lingering in the doorway. I'd know the voice anywhere, but I certainly wasn't expecting to hear it here of all places. I wasn't even aware she knew where I was spending my time.

Out of anyone who could have shown up at that door, I'm most glad it's her.

"Ice! Come in for a minute. I swear your IQ goes up from just walking in the door."

"Not hard for you though, is it pumpkin? That thing's only got one way to go."

Smart bitch.

I laugh and she looks at me in surprise.

"What are you doing here anyway?" I ask as she strolls through the door.

"Cull told me you had your prison sentence today,

and I thought you might want a ride home after, since it's just free study periods this afternoon."

It's then that Berlin notices Lily, over in the corner.

"Oh, sorry, I didn't see you there. No offence with the prison sentence thing."

Lily smiles shyly. "That's okay, I'm well aware he's here against his will."

"Ice, Lily, Lily, Ice," I say, gesturing between the two of them.

"My name is actually Berlin; you can ignore his ice queen bullshit."

Lily laughs. "It's fine, I know what your name is."

Ice eyes her curiously. I think she forgets how totally and utterly noticeable she is. Everyone in this school knows who she is, and she's only been here five minutes.

"So, do you want a ride? I might go get a milkshake and then do some drawing if you want to come over?" Berlin asks me.

I nod my head. That sounds a lot more productive than trying to score some weed and getting stoned does. Probably better for my dignity too.

"Yeah, I'm down, can I meet you at the car though? I've got to help Lily-boo for about another twenty minutes."

"Honestly, it's fine, you can go now," Lily says. She sounds relieved at the idea of getting me out of here early.

"Come on now, brains, you're not getting rid of me that easily. If I have to do my time, it's only fair you do too."

"At this point, I'm not sure whose punishment this arrangement really is," she grumbles.

She's probably wondering what she did to piss off Principal Evans.

"I'll meet you at the car," Berlin says. "It was nice to meet you, Lily. Good luck with him," she says as she strolls out of the room.

"You too," Lily replies.

It's all very polite for two sassy chicks.

I watch Berlin leave and then I slowly turn back to Lily. The silence kind of hangs in the air between us. It's weird.

"So, is she your girlfriend or something?" she asks as she busies herself with some equipment in front of her.

I smirk. "You already know she's Cullen's girl. You don't have to pretend you're immune to high school gossip for my benefit, Lil, I love good bit of tea as much as the next person."

She blushes.

"She's my friend." I pause for a second. "Actually... she's my sister."

Her brows rise in surprise.

"Well, that was weird. I haven't said that out loud to anyone yet."

I don't know what possessed me to say it now, but I guess the sooner the better. It's not exactly a well-kept secret at this point, so may as well get the rumour mill churning.

"I have to admit, that's one piece of gossip that hasn't reached the science block."

"I don't think it's made it anywhere yet. It's kind of... new information."

She sits down, facing me. "New information, as in, you only just found out you're related?"

I nod. "Yeah. I've never known who my dad was. Figured he was some druggy loser or something, and my ma was keeping it a secret to protect me. I found out the other day that Cole Davids is my dad. Him and Berlin moved back to New Zealand now that his pro rugby career is over, and my mother decided it wasn't a secret that she could keep anymore."

"Well, shit."

I huff out a laugh. "Well, shit, indeed."

"So that explains why you're going around raging and throwing hands."

I run my hand through my hair. "I guess I haven't taken it all that well so far."

"At least you have a reason for acting like an asshole I suppose. It's good to know that being a dick isn't just a defining characteristic of your personality."

I smirk at her. "Might be a little bit of column A, a little bit of column B."

My smile quickly fades though, the reminder of my fucking circus of a life has killed my mood a little.

"You're mad at your mum, right?"

I nod my head slowly, watching her. I don't remember telling her that's what I was most pissed about, but maybe it's obvious... I guess she's a smart girl and all.

"Do you think you can forgive her?"

"I don't know."

"I know your mum has messed up, Pax, and I'm not saying it's okay, but there's a lot worse out there. Trust me on that."

I don't really have a response to that.

"Must be cool finally knowing your dad, though? And Cole... he's a legend. How's he doing with finding out he has a secret son?"

I feel like a total prick in that moment, for one, because she's right – Cole *is* a legend. He's a good man. And two, because I haven't got the slightest idea of how he's doing – because I'm a self-centred little prick who hasn't thought to ask.

"Honestly, I don't know. I haven't talked to him."

Her expression changes, just slightly, and I somehow wind up feeling a little like I've disappointed her.

"Well maybe it's time you did."

"I don't know what to say to him."

"Then give him a chance to talk."

She's right again. I don't know about this hanging out with a smart chick shit. She knows things. She's observant. She's paying attention to things I never would have even remembered.

"I haven't met the guy, but I hear he's a good man. You should see what he has to say."

I'm trying to swallow the lump in my throat, but it won't seem to go down. I decide to steer the conversation in another direction.

"He was kind of a big deal in his day."

"I know who Cole Davids is, Pax. I actually really enjoy watching rugby."

"*Really?*"

"Really. I even watch all the school games."

"So, you've seen me play?"

"I've seen you play." She nods.

"Huh. Can't say I would have picked that."

"Yeah, well you do seem to love to peg people with your stereotypes," she mutters, sounding like maybe it might have actually hurt her feelings.

I feel a little bad.

"You can't tell me you haven't done the same thing to me, Lily-boo."

"Maybe." She shrugs. "But in my defence, you're here under the instruction of the principal, as a punishment, because you got sloshed at school and tried to beat up some random guy. I think my assumptions about you aren't too far off."

Harsh but fair.

But how did...

I raise my eyebrows at her. That was definitely more information than what I gave her. Lily-boo has been doing her homework.

"You been asking around about me, brains?" I chuckle.

She rolls her eyes. "Don't flatter yourself. Everyone is talking about how you got your ass kicked."

I groan, mockingly. "Ass kicked? You wound me."

"Sounds like that kid was the one who wounded you."

"A double shot." I clutch my chest. "Science genius and sniper rolled into one."

"You think I haven't noticed the way you clutch your ribs every time you laugh or cough, and how you're breathing shallow? They broken?"

That does catch me off guard. I had no idea I was making it so obvious. No one else has commented on my ribs, not Cull, Mum, or even Berlin. The fact that Lily has so clearly seen through my act is worrying. The last thing I need is coach getting wind of this.

"Just bruised," I tell her, even though I have no real clue how bad they are. "I thought I was doing a good job of hiding that."

She laughs humourlessly. "You're about as subtle as a slap in the face, Pax."

"Noted."

"And I'm going to go out on a limb here and guess that you haven't even had them looked at..."

I look back at her sheepishly.

"Just what I thought. You should get them checked out. You're not going to be a hot shot rugby player again any time soon if you're injured."

She's right, I know she is, I'm just not sure what to do with her concern. I also like hearing that she thinks I'm a good player. I'm not sure what to do with that either.

"Want to see what's on the menu today?" I ask her, changing the subject.

She laughs lightly. "I keep telling you, I'm not hungry."

I stroll over to where I dumped my backpack and pull out the huge bag of crispy M&Ms. She watches me saunter over, then drop the bag on the table in front of her.

"No one can resist these."

She shakes her head at me, her lips turned up in amusement. "*I* can."

"They're little chocolate circles covered in colourful goodness, Lily-boo, get a grip."

She laughs, and seeing a smile on her face makes me smile too. It's nice to see her relax.

"You get a grip. What are you, a toddler?"

"Maybe I am, but I'm a toddler with a big bag of chocolate."

I pull the bag open and scoop out a handful of the delicious treats. "They're *crispy*, Lil. You can't say no," I say around a mouthful of chocolate.

She rolls her eyes but sticks her hand into the bag and pulls one out anyway. She pops it into her mouth, and I'm just about to lecture her on how only crazy people eat them one by one, when she gets in first.

"You can go now if you want. Your sister will be waiting for you. I'm done here for the day anyway."

"You sure?"

"I'm sure." She shoves the bag towards me, but I push it right back.

"Nope. They're for you. You need some kind of reward for putting up with me all week."

I can tell she wants to argue, but I'm already grabbing my bag and heading for the door, I'm not going to hear it, and she should be aware by now that arguing with me is pointless.

"Hey, Lily-boo, before I go..." I catch her eye, smirking.

"Don't do it," she warns me. "If I have to hear another one of your jokes, I'm going to flush my ears out with acid."

"You know you want to hear it," I reply smugly.

"I *strongly* disagree with that statement."

"You know I'm going to tell it anyway, right? And

honestly the way you kick up a stink kind of turns me on." I wink at her.

She makes a fake gagging motion, and I lose it laughing. She's quick, this girl, and I dig it.

I take a few steps towards the door but turn back before I reach it. "Why can you never trust an atom?"

She doesn't even reply. She just stares at me, with no shit, not a *single* fucking emotion on her face.

I don't even care. I know she's listening, and if she thinks her lack of response is going to stop me finishing my joke, then she's sorely mistaken.

"Because they make up literally everything."

She stares.

I wait.

She shakes her head at me, but this time I'm about ninety percent confident that she's hiding a smile.

I'm wearing her down. It's only a matter of time before she breaks.

I stroll the rest of the distance to the door. "Have a good weekend, Lily-boo, I hope you can manage without me for two days."

"It'll be tough going, but I think I'll survive," she calls dryly after me.

My chuckle echoes around the halls.

TEN

Lily

Keke blows a giant bubble with her bubble-gum and then lets it pop half over her face. It's gross. She's the only person I know above the age of six who still chews bubble-gum, but she loves the stuff. Judging by the smell of it, this week's favourite is grape.

"So, how's babysitting duty been treating you? That's a classic stitch up from the boss there, eh? Like what was he thinking giving you some shit head soccer player to look after?"

"He's a *rugby* player." I sigh, although I don't know why I bother correcting her; Keke's knowledge of rugby and soccer is limited to the fact that they're both sports. She just, quite simply, does not give a shit. "And it's hard work, seriously, all he does is make a mess, touch everything, and distract me from my experiments by making stupid jokes."

"Sounds like hell."

I nod my head in agreement, although a teeny tiny part of me is enjoying having someone in the lab with me. It gets pretty lonely being by myself all the time, and having Pax there, as annoying as he might be, at least means I'm not all on my own.

"You spend too much time in there anyway, you should ditch him tomorrow and we can go get our nails done."

I don't even bother giving her any feedback on that idea. We both know it's not going to happen. She's always trying to get me to ditch school with her, and I'm always turning her down. At this point, I'm sure she's just doing it out of habit. If I agreed, she'd probably nearly fall off her chair and then tell me I can't actually ditch my studies. Not now, not when I'm so close.

It's become my whole life.

I was embarrassed to admit it the other day when Pax asked me why he didn't recognise me, but the truth is that I spend pretty much all my free time studying. Especially this year and last. I've got goals. I want big things for myself. I want to go to university, and the only way to get there is with a scholarship and student loans. My grandmother certainly doesn't have spare cash lying around. The programme I want to get into doesn't take just anyone. I have to prove myself. Those goals mean I rarely socialise or even leave my classrooms. I'm basically a hermit.

I'm a nobody in this school. I'm invisible. Especially

to people like Pax. I'm not a 'hot girl', I'm not a cheer-leader, I'm just a nobody. I blend in, and I've learnt to love it.

Keke, on the other hand, does anything but blend in.

She doesn't care what anyone thinks of her. One time, she dyed her hair dark as night and wore nothing but black goth style accessories for six months straight, all because some girl told her that her black nail polish was out of style. Then she got bored of that, bleached her hair white blonde and turned up looking like a barbie doll.

Her hair is currently purple. I've never known someone to have so many different hair colours. It's a wild ride.

"Where's Grammy today?"

"Book club with her friends from the walking group."

"Fuck she's just the cutest thing I've ever seen." Keke swoons. All her grandparents have passed away, some before she was even born, so she loves my grandmother like she was her own.

Everyone does, really. She's the most chill older woman I've ever met. I guess having a crack head for a daughter really made her loosen up the reins on normal teenager shit.

Not that I get up to anything outrageous anyway. I never go to parties; I've barely been drunk in my life, and I don't smoke or take drugs. I don't date – not because I don't want to, but because no guy has ever asked.

I guess you have to go out into the world and meet people if you want to get asked on dates – who would have thought?

"She'll be back in about an hour if you want to stay for dinner?"

"Obviously," she says, flipping her hair, before settling back onto the couch in my bedroom and opening a magazine.

I've already read that thing front to back and then once more through again for good measure.

Celebrity gossip is my guilty pleasure, but I refuse to seek it out online. There's something nostalgic about flipping the pages of a magazine.

"I hope she's making that roast meat I like."

"It is Sunday, so I'd say you'll be in luck."

Keke always hangs out here. We rarely go to her house even though I love her family. They treat me like one of their own. They're the classic, perfect family next door. Loving parents, three kids, two girls and a boy. They've even got a golden retriever. Keke seems far too wild to have come from a family so... *normal*, but they love her to death. Sometimes it makes me jealous. My parents are losers, and I know I'm better off without them, but that doesn't mean I don't sometimes wish things were different.

She tosses the magazine on the table, and I scowl. She didn't even look at it long enough to get to the good stuff. I'd kill to have someone to dissect the latest tea from *The Kardashian's* with, but it's not going to be Keeks. She'd probably ask me if Kim Kardashian was the president's wife, or something equally as stupid.

She's insanely smart, and if you wanted to talk to her about native insects, or marine biology, you'd never shut her up, but if she's not interested in something, then to her, it just simply doesn't exist. She could also chew your ear off for hours about eighties rock music, but that's another topic entirely.

"So, I've been researching universities for next year," she says.

This gets my attention. I've been hounding her to start filling in the forms for ages now.

"*And...*" I prompt.

"And I was thinking that if you wind up down in the South Island, maybe I just might as well."

I shriek and dive at her, wrapping her in a hug she won't have a shot of escaping from. She's not really a hugger, but I am, and she can suck it up just this once.

"Oh my god, get off me," she moans, but her arms tighten around me, squeezing me.

I get a few more seconds of forced affection in, and then decide to quit while I'm ahead. I don't want her flinching when I enter a room or something.

"What changed your mind?" I ask as I roll into the spot next to her.

"Well, I know I said I wanted to just stay here and get a reputation as being a weird bug girl, but that idea doesn't sound all that fun if you're not around to make fun of me for it."

"And your idea of joining the anti-whaling expeditions?" I ask, brow raised, amusement poorly hidden.

It's not that I don't think it's a great cause, but it's also not a career path I ever saw really taking off for her.

She couldn't dye her hair fifty-five times a year from a boat out in the middle of the ocean.

She pouts. "I forgot I get seasick."

I can't hide my amusement this time.

She shoves me playfully in the shoulder. "Shut up. Annnnnyway... they have a really good marine biology programme down there, so I think I'll apply to that. My parents are thrilled, obviously."

"I'm sure they are. Not that 'weird bug girl' isn't every parent's dream for their child."

"Ungrateful bastards." She sniggers.

The funny thing about her parents is that even if she didn't go to uni, even if she sat around the house for five years collecting weird plastic insects and had bright pink hair, they'd still probably be proud as punch. It's quite sweet really.

"So, what's your new side kick going to do next year then?"

I frown at her for a minute, until I realise she's talking about Pax.

I shrug. "How would I know?"

"I just figured you'd know what your future boyfriend had planned for his life," she says casually.

Smart bitch.

"He's *not* my future boyfriend, and if I had to guess, I'd say he'll be in jail, if he carries on like he has been."

"Oooh a bad boy. I approve. You should climb that."

"Keke!" I groan.

"You're going all red."

I know I am, I can feel the heat in my cheeks. She's going to have a field day with this.

"Do you want to climb him?" she asks me seriously.

"No! He's hot, but he's a mess. He's a hot mess."

"Oh. My. God. You *like* him. I shouldn't be surprised;

you've always had a soft spot for those athletic types. All those balls being thrown around and whatever else they do."

I can't even focus on her ridiculous description of 'athletic', I've got bigger problems.

"I do *not* like Pax."

She lifts a brow. "Oh cool, so we're lying to each other now, are we? That's great, Lily, just great."

Her feigned theatrics make me roll my eyes. "Stop being so dramatic."

"Stop being a dirty little liar."

"Oh my god, Keeks, I promise, if I fall in love with this guy, you'll be the first to know, okay?"

"I damn well better be, I better know before you even do, got it?"

"Makes *perfect* sense," I deadpan. "But you can relax, I'm not about to begin some sordid affair. A guy like him isn't going to be interested in a girl like me."

"Oh yeah, because guys never like pretty girls who actually have something going on between the ears. You're right, *you nasty*," she teases me. "And besides, the deal was you'll tell me if *you* like *him*, not if *he's* in love with *you*. Which he totally should be – FYI."

"There's plenty of pretty girls around, and I'm sure at least half of them are smart. I'm not the kind of girl the rugby team date. I'm not skinny and bleach blonde. I'm mousey with a fat ass, and I'm okay with that."

She rolls her eyes at my comment about my butt. We have this argument weekly. "At least you've got tits, hips and ass, I look like a pancake."

"Can we save ourselves the time and just finish this

disagreement now? I already know how it goes, I say I'm chubby, you tell me I'm totally insane, we argue, neither of us changes our opinion, rinse and repeat in another seven or so days... that about round it up?"

She nods at me. "Pleasure doing business with you."

I WALK into the bathroom and immediately curse myself for having a functioning bladder. This is the last place I want to be as five blonde girls turn to glare at me, simply for walking in the door.

One of them has tears streaming down her face, Bianca I'm pretty sure her name is, and the rest look like they're rallying around her like some kind of cheerleader team meeting.

I don't know what they've got going on in here, but it's not something I want to be present for, I know that much.

A popular girl AGM is not something I need to be part of.

I realise I'm frozen on the spot while they're all standing there, shooting daggers at me.

Shit.

The last thing I want is to draw attention to myself.

I look at the ground and move quickly towards the cubicle on the opposite side of the bathroom, but it's too late, the damage has been done. I looked a little too long. Lucky me.

"Can we help you with something?" I don't know which one spoke, but my money is on Liana.

Everyone in school knows who she is, especially since

the war between her and Berlin started. Even *Keke* knows who Liana is, and that's saying something.

She's the queen bee, and the rest of these girls are her minions. She's got a big mouth and balls the size of coconuts.

I shake my head, eyes still firmly set on the floor. I'm nearly to the safety of the cubicle when I see a shoe step in front of me, cutting me off. I should have just turned around and left again.

Here I was, thinking I was meant to be smart.

My palms start sweating.

I don't want any problems. Certainly not with these girls. Truth be told, I'm terrified of them. Always have been.

I clutch my chemistry books closer to my chest, like they're somehow going to protect me.

"What are these, nerd?"

I see a perfectly manicured hand reach out and tug the books from my hands.

I watch as she takes hold of one and the other three fall to the ground, my handwritten notes slipping out and floating to the ground with them.

I hear a series of giggles and sniggers.

God, girls are the absolute fucking worst. I can feel tears pooling in my eyes, and they haven't even been that mean to me yet. I say *yet,* because I know it's coming.

I crouch down to pick up my books, but she stomps her foot on my hand, pinning it to the ground.

"Don't," she sneers.

Well, if I wasn't about to cry before, I sure am now. I

blink frantically, trying to stop myself from giving her the satisfaction of knowing she's causing me pain.

She twists her foot, and a whimper escapes.

It really fucking hurts.

"Ouch," I cry as she presses more of her weight into her foot before finally stepping off my hand. I cradle my sore hand in my good one, and the first drop of moisture escapes my eye.

"Advanced Chemistry," she drawls. "Classic dork bullshit."

I try to ignore her.

"Stand up when I'm talking to you."

I suck in a harsh, ragged breath, but it does nothing to calm me down. I don't know what to do. I don't want to be weak, but I don't know how to be strong either.

I slowly stand, deciding to just face her and get it over with, maybe she'll get bored quickly if I just do what she asks. That's probably the most naïve thought I've ever had, but at this point I'm out of options.

I finally look up at her. I was right – it *is* Liana running the torment. The other four girls are just looking on with wicked glances at their latest bit of entertainment.

I'm the sacrificial lamb and Liana is holding a shot gun.

She's such a beautiful girl. Clearly that doesn't extend to the type of person she is, but on the outside, she's stunning to look at.

She slowly circles around me, my advanced chem book open in her hands as I just stand there like an idiot.

"What do you want, nerd?"

I don't answer, I just keep standing there, eyes wide, body frozen.

"Answer me, peasant."

"I – I ah... I needed to pee," I stutter quietly.

The pack of hyenas all laugh again.

"This is a private conversation," she says, pausing directly in front of me. She's so tall and well put together, she makes me feel like a child caught eavesdropping on her mum.

"I didn't know," I whisper.

"Well now you do."

"I'll get out of your way."

I crouch down and start hurriedly collecting my books from the ground around her feet.

I stand up and look at the book in her hands. I don't have the balls to ask her for it, but I can't leave it either. That textbook cost over one hundred dollars and there's no way we can afford to just go out and buy another one.

She notices me looking at the book, and a scary looking smile spreads across her lips. She can see it's important to me. I don't like this.

"You want your book back?" she asks me.

I don't know what the right answer is. I just want to take my things and go somewhere where I can cry in private.

I nod my head. I don't know if I could speak right now if I tried.

"How about I give it back to you, page by page?" she says, I see her hand move and hear the unmistakable noise of paper being torn.

I feel the colour drain out of my face.

She's going to stand here and rip my book to pieces.

"Please don't," I whisper, tears streaming down my face now.

"What was that? I couldn't hear you," she taunts, as she rips page after page out of the book and lets them fall to the floor.

"Stop!" I cry.

But she doesn't stop, in fact, she comes closer, knocks the other books out of my hands again and keeps on ripping.

The girls are all hysterically laughing now, and I'm glad they're having fun, because this is quickly turning into one of the worst days I've had in a long time.

I drop to my knees and desperately try picking up everything, but it's too much, the pages keep on floating down around my head and I'm crying so much I can barely see what I'm doing.

I'm close to lying down on the floor and waiting for it all to be over.

"What the fuck is going on in here?!" I hear a voice yell.

I didn't even hear the door open, but it's pretty clear someone has just walked in and is now witnessing my torment.

Lucky me.

I want to tell her, whoever she is, to run, because next thing she'll be bawling over a textbook too, but I can't find any words.

It takes me a moment to notice, but the ripping of pages has momentarily ceased.

"You're a vile piece of shit, you know that? Can't you just leave people the fuck alone?"

I blink back the tears and can finally see clearly now. Another set of shoes come to a stop next to me.

I look up, and much to my horror, realise it's Berlin who has come to attempt to save me.

I'm both mortified and hopeful at the same time. She's a total bad ass, if anyone can get Liana to stop destroying my most valuable book, she can, but she's also looking at me sobbing on a bathroom floor, surrounded by the remains of my belongings.

It's not exactly how I want to portray myself.

"What do you care about this chubby loser?" Liana sneers, her finger tugging on another page of my textbook.

"Rip one more page out of that fucking book and I'll stick your head down that toilet and flush," Berlin warns her.

I quickly pick up everything I can get my hands on and stumble to my feet. I might have a chance to escape here, but I can't leave Berlin alone. These bitches are crazy. I wobble a little on my feet and Berlin reaches out and presses me backwards, so I'm half behind her, like she's protecting me.

"Are you really going to get all spicy with me over some geek?"

Berlin laughs. "She's not *some geek*, she's my friend, and if you ever lay a finger on her again, you're going to have me to deal with. And trust me, *bitch*, you've got no idea how spicy I can really get."

Liana laughs, but I can tell some of the confidence has been knocked out of her. I don't know exactly what's gone on between these two – there's been plenty of rumours, but it appears that Berlin is one up in this battle, and that gives me a tiny bit of hope.

"You're out numbered, whore," Liana sneers.

"Do I look worried?" Berlin claps back.

Truthfully, she doesn't. She doesn't seem in the least bit fazed by the blonde demon in front of us. I'll have to ask her how she does that.

I hear the door push open again, and my head snaps in that direction. I don't know who it's going to be, but I hope to God it's not any more of these popular bitches.

Five on two is already not great odds.

I almost start crying again, but in relief this time, when I see four of Berlin's friends walk through the door.

"Are you taking a shit in here or something, we're going to be late." One of them asks. "Oh," she adds, as she takes in the scene in front of her.

I don't know her name, but she's got red hair and she's beautiful.

"Oh *no*," the little blonde girl with them mutters as she sees the scene in front of her. I know who she is, she's Sophia – Berlin's cousin. She looks like she'd be about as useful in a fight as a helium balloon, but I can appreciate that's probably a bit rich coming from me.

Her gaze quickly slips over the popular girls and finds me, where it softens and morphs into the most sympathetic face I've ever seen.

Wonderful. I must look like the total loser I am.

None of these girls look particularly happy to be involved in whatever the hell is going on right now, but credit to them, they gather around behind me and Berlin, no questions asked.

"Guess those numbers have swung back in my favour," Berlin drawls, drawing my attention back to her.

Liana looks like she's just sucked on a lemon, but she doesn't back down.

"I can't wait for the day that I wipe that smug attitude off your face," Liana spits. "You think you can come to my town, to *my* school, and take over? Keep dreaming, skank."

Berlin steps forwards quickly and Liana flinches, and stumbles backwards a step. I hate to say it, but it makes me so happy to see. I've never supported violence or bullying, but there is something oddly satisfying about witnessing this awful girl get a taste of her own medicine first hand.

Berlin snatches my book out of Liana's hand while she's caught off guard. The book is probably completely ruined by now, but I still feel ten times better once it's out of her hands.

Liana tries to recover from her stumble backwards, but she doesn't nail it gracefully.

It's obvious to everyone in the room in that moment that Berlin is in charge and on top.

Liana finally stands tall again, sticks her nose in the air like she's been watching too many shitty cliché teenage movies from the nineties, spins on her heel and marches towards the door.

"It isn't over, bitch, I'll get you back for this," she calls over her shoulder as her little blonde shadows fall into step behind her. They may as well be hissing; it'd go nicely with the death glares they're sending.

"Look forward to it," Berlin mutters.

The bitch brigade files out, and when the door shuts behind them, I actually hear the breath rush out of me. My legs feel weak underneath me, and I'm pretty sure they're barely holding me up anymore.

"Woah, I got ya," the red head says as she grabs my shoulders to steady me.

"Oh my god, Lily, are you okay?" Sophia rushes towards me.

I had no idea she knew my name, but it's not really the time to ask questions about that. I just nod my head and do my best to not fall down.

"Fuck I hate that bitch," Berlin says as she turns around to look at me. "Are you alright? What the hell was that all about?"

I shrug my shoulders. I probably look like a deer in the headlights. "I don't know," I whisper. "I just came in to use the bathroom and they were in the middle of something, and I guess I just pissed them off."

"That's such bullshit. Someone needs to get her expelled," another girl says. I'm pretty sure her name's Laura.

"I'm working on it," Berlin drawls.

They're all looking at me with such kindness. Well, except Berlin. She sort of looks like she's planning on setting something on fire, but it's in my honour, so I guess that's kind of sweet... in a deranged way.

"We need to go and show a teacher what she's done to your book," Sophia says.

I shake my head quickly. "No. I'll just tape it back together. It's okay."

I reach out to take the book from Berlin. She flips it closed, glances at the state of it, and hands it to me. "I don't think there's any saving that, Lily."

I shrug my shoulder and blink back another wave of tears. I don't know how I'm going to use this book after this, but I'll just have to manage.

"Thank you for helping me," I tell her.

She waves my gratitude off like it was no big deal. I don't even think it *was* a big deal to her. She doesn't even look shaken.

"No, seriously. I don't know what would have happened if you hadn't stood up for me."

"Give me your phone. I'll add you on Instagram and snap. You can message me if she gives you any more shit."

"I don't have Instagram or snap," I admit.

One of them gasps in shock.

That gets a giggle out of me.

"*Girl.* We have some serious work to do. Lunchtime tomorrow, we're getting you on social media," Berlin tells me.

"I'll be in the lab at lunchtime tomorrow."

I can feel my cheeks heating. I sound like such a loser. What eighteen-year-old doesn't even have basic social media, let alone spends lunch in a lab.

"Well, I'll see you there then." She smirks.

"Me too," Sophia pipes up. Then she gives me a hug. I don't know where it came from, but I think she needs to give it to me as much as I need to receive it.

"I'll meet you girls out front in a sec, okay?" Berlin tells her friends. "Just give us a minute."

They all give me sad smiles and goodbyes and leave the two of us alone.

Berlin grabs the last few random pages of my book off the floor and hands them to me. "So, are you really okay?"

"I'm not sure," I tell her honestly.

I'm not naive enough to think stuff like that doesn't go on at high schools, but it's never really happened to me.

Ignorance is bliss.

"Liana is a bitch, but she's not going to lay a finger on you again, I'll make sure of that."

She tosses her long, dark hair over her shoulder. She's so confident and beautiful, I wish I could be more like that.

"You wait until Pax and Cullen hear about this shit, they'll skin her alive."

"Oh my god, please don't tell Pax about this, he'll think I'm such a loser."

She frowns at me.

"I'm begging you, *please* don't say anything to him."

The last thing I need is him knowing my business – that she found me crying on a filthy bathroom floor like a total failure.

"Fine. I won't say anything, but you don't need to hide anything from him. He's the one who has shit to be embarrassed about, not you. Liana being an unhinged sociopath isn't anything new. And besides, Pax can't stand her."

At least I know the guy has one thing right in his brain.

"Come on, let's go," she tells me.

I go to follow her, but I'm reminded of why I came in here in the first place.

"I still really need to pee," I admit.

She laughs but gestures for me to go ahead, and when I come back out of the cubicle, she's still there waiting for me.

ELEVEN

Pax

I've managed to stay out of trouble for the whole week so far, but when I saw Lily's hand all wrapped up in a bandage and her spirits looking crushed, I was more than willing to start throwing hands at whoever was responsible.

She told me nothing happened – that she *fell* – but I also didn't miss the state of her textbook all ripped apart and taped back together.

Must have been some fall.

And then Ice and her girls turned up and started setting up a gram page and fuck knows what else for Lily.

I don't know what the hell is going on, but I don't like it.

Something happened yesterday, and no one is telling me shit.

I even told one of my better chemistry jokes today, and she didn't even tell me to get out of her lab. Barely even rolled her eyes.

"What's on your mind, cupcake?" Cull lightly punches my arm to snap me out of my trance.

"Nerd problems," I mutter.

"The science girl making your life hard?"

I shake my head and swing my feet up onto the coffee table. "Nah, she's got about as much bite as a new-born baby."

"So, what's up your ass then?"

I sigh heavily. If only I knew.

"I think she's getting bullied or something. I dunno, man, but Ice knows what's up."

He thinks for a minute.

"Oh, is she the little brown-haired thing that B helped out the other day? I thought she was into maths, but it could have been science. Lola or something?"

What the fuck?

"Lily," I correct him.

"Yeah, that was it. Berlin and the girls looked after her or something."

"What the fuck happened, and how do you know about it?"

"B told me. I was only half listening though because she kept doing this thing with her legs, but I'm pretty sure Berlin and the girls cleaned up Lola or whatever. I think I heard something about seeing the nurse. Maybe something about a wrecked book. Dunno the details, bro."

"Lily," I snap.

"Lily. *Whatever*. Sounded like Liana saw and was a mean bitch or something."

Fucking Liana. She's the biggest bitch on the face of the god damn planet. She looks down on everyone at Westlake like they're dipped in shit. If you're not her friend, you're a peasant.

I can only imagine how Liana would view a girl like Lily. Especially if she was handed material to make fun of on a silver platter.

"That girl is like a feral cat that needs to be locked in a cage and forced to have behavioural training."

Cull is flicking through TV channels, only half paying attention to me.

"Yeah, but fuck getting close enough to get scratched," he mumbles.

Rich coming from him. He stuck his dick in that. Fucking head case.

"What else did Ice say?"

He shrugs. "I dunno, man, I was only half listening... what's it to you anyway?"

Isn't that the question of the century.

"I want to make sure Lily is okay. And I'm sick of Liana's shit. You never should have given that girl the time of day, Cull. She's like the gift that keeps on giving. You fucked her over and we're all paying the price."

"Tell me something I don't know."

I'm in no position to be giving lectures about fuck ups, but I reached my limit with Liana a long time ago.

We both stare at the TV screen, and I don't know about him, but I'm not taking any of it in. I can't quite pinpoint why I feel so wound up about this Lily stuff.

There's something about her that makes me feel like she needs protecting.

She's so... *soft*. I can't imagine she's had to experience too many harsh realities of the world, and bitchy little mean cheerleaders aren't what a girl like Lily would be used to dealing with.

I can barely look after myself right now, let alone look after her, but I'm sure as fuck not going to just sit by and let Liana make her feel like shit.

I saw what that girl did to Berlin, but Ice, she can handle it. She's tough. Lily isn't like those girls. She's different, and at Westlake High, different makes you vulnerable.

"Did Ice say anythi –"

"I'm gonna stop you right there, bro, and say that I don't know. If you're so interested, ask Berlin yourself. Or better yet, ask your little lab boss."

"She won't tell me shit."

"Then maybe you should take the hint and mind your business."

I flip him off.

I'll mind my business when I'm dead.

"Berlin coming over tonight?" I ask him.

He shakes his head. "Nah, not tonight."

I nod and get up out of my chair. "I'm going to call her."

"Lucky her," he drawls.

I go into my room and shut the door behind me, calling Berlin as I do it.

"Brother from another mother, whatever do I owe the pleasure?" she answers.

I haven't found much about this situation very entertaining lately, but that gets a laugh out of me.

"Can't you just say *hello* like a normal person?"

"Nope."

"Fair enough."

"What's up, Paxikins, calling me to bitch about Cullen again?"

I chuckle. "Not today, but if he'd spend more time listening to you talk and less time looking at your legs, I probably wouldn't have needed to call anyway."

"A girl has to have her superpowers." She sighs. "What's on your mind, princess?"

"I wanna talk about Lily."

She pauses for a second. "What about Lily?"

I roll my eyes. "Don't even try it. I know she had an accident or something... and I know Liana was giving her a hard time and you're going to tell me the rest of the story."

"I don't know any story."

"Stop trying to play coy with me, it's not your strong suit."

"Can't you just follow her on Instagram and relax?"

"I'll look her up, after you tell me the story."

"You know what I think?" she asks, ignoring my request.

"I'm sure you're going to tell me."

"I think you like her."

"*Of course* I like her, she's a sweet girl. She doesn't need to get caught up in any drama. There's no hidden agenda, there's no scandal, I just want to make sure she's okay."

"Whatever you say, Pax. But rest assured, I have the situation handled. Lily is a little embarrassed, but fine. Everything is right in the world."

"You're seriously not going to tell me what happened?"

"Nope. Girl code, Pax, it's a thing."

"What about sibling code?"

"We're only half-siblings, you only get half the commitment."

"That's bullshit."

"That's life, Paxikins."

"Can't you just tell me? I won't say anything to her."

I can almost hear her eyes roll. "Oh yeah, because you're so well known for your discretion."

"*Ice.*"

"It's not going to happen, give it a rest. She specifically asked me not to speak to you about it, and I'm not going to turn around and be a little bitch who can't keep a secret."

"She asked you not to tell me –"

"Dad's calling me, I gotta go. Oh, and Pax? It's nice to have you back."

I don't even get a chance to reply before the line goes dead.

Well... that was interesting.

Lily specifically asked Berlin not to tell me about whatever the hell went on, and that only makes me want to know even more.

I'd pay good money to know why I, specifically, am not allowed in on this secret, but I'd pay even more to know exactly what happened between my little science nerd and the biggest bitch in town.

I KNOW I probably shouldn't be eavesdropping out here again like some kind of creepy fucker, but some of the most vital information I know has been overheard from this hallway, so when I hear Cole's voice coming from my dining room late at night, there's no way in hell I'm going to sneak back into bed like an obedient little kid.

I don't know what he's doing here, but it sounds like he and Ma are arguing.

"I don't care, Julia, the kid hates me. The least I can do is ease the burden from another angle."

"I can't take that money from you, Cole. It's too much."

"Then I'll give it to Pax and he can blow it on whatever he wants, and you and Hannah can keep working ridiculous hours to make ends meet."

"We've managed just fine for eighteen years," she snaps.

"Jesus Christ, Julia." Cole sounds exhausted. "I know you've done fine. I know the two of you don't need me. You've raised our son better than I ever could have, I'm not trying to take that away from you, but the way I see it, I owe you a lot of child support, and I'm going to do this, whether you like it or not. He's my son, you've taken his entire childhood from me, and if all I can do now is throw some money at it, then I'd like to see you stop me. I can afford it and he's going to get it, one way or another."

Ma is quiet.

They both are.

I'm about to stick my head around the corner and see if he's gone, when he speaks, his voice cracking.

"I'm so fucking disappointed in you, Jules."

Fuck.

I feel his pain right now. I don't know what to do with it, or how to let it in, but I *feel* it. Right deep inside me.

I'm so fucking disappointed in her too.

"I know it doesn't mean anything to you, but I'm so sorry, Cole. I made a call and it was the wrong one. I can't take it back, but I do want you to have a relationship with Pax if I haven't completely destroyed that possibility."

"He's my son, I'll have a relationship with him if it kills me."

"He's so mad," she says quietly. "He's acting out, getting into trouble. He can't even look at me. I don't know if you'll be able to get through to him, but you're welcome to try."

"I will *never* stop trying," Cole tells her, and there's something in his tone that sends tingles down my spine.

I can hear Berlin in the way he's speaking. I can hear *me.*

The loyalty. The fierce undertone that's impossible to doubt.

Cole Davids isn't going to give up on me, and while that does make me feel some weird kind of fuzzy shit down deep, it also makes my head want to explode. I don't know what to do. I know what I need to do, what I *should* do, but getting my head in the right space to do it is another thing entirely.

"Cole, I... I really don't know how to fix this," she tells him.

I don't know if she *can* fix this. That might be what worries me most.

"I think it might be time for you to accept there's a possibility that this can't be fixed." He says, mirroring my thoughts.

"Don't say that." It's a horrified whisper.

"I need to go. I'll get in touch with the bank tomorrow and we'll go from there.

I've heard enough.

I don't know how much money he's trying to give Ma, or how he can bring himself to do anything for her after everything she's done, but I'll find out one way or another.

I sneak back down the hallway and quietly close my door behind me. I get into bed, but I know fucking damn well I'm not going to sleep after that.

I grab my phone and start going through my notifications – anything to take my mind off the shit show that is my life.

There's nothing of any interest there.

A few DMs from some chicks from school that I haven't even bothered opening. Those girls are crazy – they started popping up like some kind of toxic cancers after I got in that fight – Eve was the first, but she certainly isn't the last who's tried. Girls like that, they're all about the drama. That might have got my motor running once upon a time, but not anymore. I've got no space left for that shit. I've got enough going on with my own fuck ups, without sticking my dick into another one. I'm done with that shit. Eve included.

Something that Ice said earlier pops into my mind, and I search up *Lily Wilder* on Instagram.

I grin as I find her. She's private, so I request to follow her.

Her profile pic is her in the science lab; she probably looks embarrassed but it's too small to really tell. There's no bio, just her name, which she's clearly not living up to.

Out here living life on the *wild* side.

I should be saving my puns for Lily.

I sit there staring at my phone, willing her to respond to my request, but she doesn't. I scroll through my own profile, checking there's nothing lame or embarrassing for her to see when she checks it out.

I spend ten minutes overthinking like a little bitch, before going back to her profile. Still no response.

Oh well.

I open my internet browser and start googling more chemistry jokes. It's good value and an even better time waster, and right now, taking my mind off everything is exactly what I need.

TWELVE

Lily

"I've been trying to get you to get on social media for years now, and these girls get you there in a day. What are they? Magic?"

"Chill out. I don't even know how to use it."

"You *followed* me on Instagram."

"I don't even know what that means!"

"Next thing you'll be making viral TikToks. I don't even know who you are anymore."

I flop back on my bed and throw my arm over my eyes, just so I don't have to look at her gleeful grin.

She's so smug.

I don't know why she's so big on this stuff; she doesn't care about what anyone is doing. She's probably only using social media to look at weird fish shit or something equally as strange on there, so I have no idea why she's so thrilled I've finally jumped on board.

"They didn't exactly give me a choice about it," I grumble. "And I don't have TikTok – I wouldn't know what to do on there."

She rolls her eyes dramatically. "Instagram is a solid start I guess."

I don't mind, really. It's not like I'm going to use it or anything. It's just a harmless little app icon sitting on my screen. And it got them off my case and me back to my work, so it was a small price to pay as far as I'm concerned.

"So I'm told," I reply dryly.

"Well, I don't know who these chicks are, but I like them. Maybe they could get you to spend time outside of that lab for once. I'll tell them that's their next mission."

"I don't think we're all going to be hanging out like friends all the time. I'm sure they'll get bored soon and go back to whatever it is they normally do with themselves. They just feel sorry for me after the shit that went down."

"Stupid cheerleader bitches," Keke mutters at the reminder of the *incident*. "I made five blonde voo-doo dolls and stuck pins in them all, you know."

"I appreciate that, Keeks," I tell her as I bite back a laugh.

I don't really know if she's kidding or not. It really could go either way with her. Regardless, I'm entertained.

"Show me your profile."

I mutter a string of pointless protests and sit up, reaching for my phone on my nightstand and opening the app to show her my tragic profile that'll never see the light of day. It's not like there's anything there to see at least.

Oh shit.

I have a notification.

Pax Benson has requested to follow you.

"Oh god, make it *stop*."

She raises an eyebrow at me in question.

"Pax requested to follow me," I explain.

I groan as her eyes light up. "I hear wedding bells," she says in a sing-song voice.

"Stop talking."

"Can I be your maid of honour?"

"Stop it," I tell her again as I get to my feet and start collecting up all my stuff for school. "We're going to be late for class."

"You say that like it's a bad thing."

"You have biology first period," I remind her.

"*Shit.*"

I knew she wasn't about to miss her favourite subject.

"You better accept that follow request." She points a warning finger at me as we grab our stuff.

I sigh heavily. This sounds like a good way for things to get out of hand.

I could delete the app and be done with all of it, but I know Berlin will check, and for some reason I want her to like me. I don't want to be the loser who couldn't handle one friend request.

Grammy – the legend that she is – drives us over to school, while Keek's fills the car with mindless chatter and Grams nods and smiles. I do nothing but think about the request sitting on my phone. I have no idea why a guy like Pax would want to be associated with me. Maybe he just wants another way to be able to torture me with horrendous science jokes.

It's certainly not going to get him any popular points, that's for damn sure, especially not now that I'm an enemy of Liana and her friends. Pax probably doesn't need any help in that area anyway though I guess. He's Mr. Popular already.

I hate to admit it, but when we pull up outside the school and I see a group of blonde girls waiting by the gate, my anxiety levels skyrocket, and Pax Benson's social media is long forgotten.

My chest feels tight, and my breathing is getting shallow.

"Ready, Lil?"

The girls turn around at the same moment Keke speaks to me, and I see they're only juniors. It's not Liana and her shadows.

I'm out here getting my heart rate up over a few fourteen-year-old girls.

"Lily?"

"Yeah, sorry, let's go," I say, trying to shake off the awful feeling in the pit of my stomach. "Thanks for the ride, Grammy, have a good day."

We walk together to the science block, Keke is going on and on about some marine species that's nearing extinction, and for once, I'm happy that absolutely nothing is required from me for her to carry a conversation. I don't think I'd have much to contribute at the moment.

She heads off to biology, and I make my way into my

lab to distract myself for my study period.

I hang up my bag and shrug on a lab coat, and I'm about to pull out the work I was finishing up last night when a book on the table catches my eye.

It's got my name on a sheet of paper on top of it, and when I slide that out of the way, a brand-new copy of the book Liana tore up, is looking back at me.

I HAVE no idea where Berlin and her friends sit at lunch, because I'm always hiding away in my lab every lunch break.

I feel kind of like a vampire wandering around out here in the sun – a rare occurrence for this time of year. It's still fucking freezing, but at least it's not raining. I'm so used to being willingly stuck indoors; I'm not familiar with the hum of chatter that fills the air at this time of day.

Keke, as per usual was less than no help when I asked her if she knew where the girls might be. I swear she's even more on her own planet than I am. I actually have absolutely no idea what she gets up to every day at lunch.

I love her to death, but she's an interesting girl that one.

I keep looking around hopefully.

I want to thank Berlin for the book.

I still can't believe she did that. I don't think money is a big deal for her and her dad, but still, she didn't have to do that for me. It was a very sweet and unexpected gesture.

I wander around for a bit longer, but I'm not having much luck here. I can't seem to see any of them.

I find myself around the back of the art block and I'm about to give up and turn around to head back to the lab when I hear a couple of guys talking. Sophia's name being mentioned gets my attention, so I stop and listen.

"Sophia Davids," one of them says. "Innocent little blonde thing."

"No idea," the other guy replies.

I don't know if it's just the two of them there or what, but I only hear two voices.

I tuck myself against the wall and stand still to try and catch every word I can.

"You know that new chick that Cullen is fucking losing his shit over?"

"Yeah, Berlin."

"Yeah. Soph is her cousin."

I hear the flick of a lighter and a long inhale. This must be where the smokers hide out.

"Innocent sounds like code for boring."

"Yeah, you're not wrong. She's nice and shit, but she's not going to put out any time soon."

"Why are you fucking around with her then?"

"I'm not. I'm just thinking about it."

"*Why?*"

"You know I love a challenge."

I can't figure out who I'm listening to here, but it doesn't sound like this guy gives two shits about Sophia as a person – he just wants to get into her pants.

I guess this is nothing new for teenage males – or

probably males in general. You tell them something is off limits and they're just going to want it more.

I wish I knew who these guys were, I could at least give Sophia a heads up about who to avoid.

"She might be like her cousin once she gets going."

"Berlin is fucking hot."

"That chick definitely knows how to fuck I reckon."

I grimace. I'm not sure I want to eavesdrop on this conversation anymore. It's got the potential to get a bit grubby from here, and I'd rather eat a jean jacket than listen to these two basically jack each other off while talking about how hot the girls are.

I abandon my mission and slink away from the back of the building.

I don't really like being out here like this.

Not only do I have no clue where Berlin and Sophia sit, I also don't know where Liana and her feral mates hang out, and the last thing I want is to accidentally find the wrong group of females.

I've still got a sore hand and bruised ego from the last encounter.

Just the thought of that makes my heart race and my breathing ragged. I need to get out of here before I have a panic attack.

I turn the final corner, thinking of nothing much else than making a beeline for the safety of my lab, when I run directly into someone.

I put my hands up to catch myself, and find my palms planted against a broad chest.

"Lily-boo!"

A relieved breath slips out of me.

I'm shocked at how just the sound of his voice is able to calm me down.

I might not know all that much about Pax, but I trust him. I know that he wouldn't let something bad happen to me.

Part of me wants to wrap my arms around his middle and hold on tight, but the functioning part of my brain has more sense – thank fuck. I get my balance and step back away from him.

"Hey," I reply.

He glances behind me and frowns. "What are you doing back here?"

I look over my shoulder, as much as I'd love to know who was talking back there, I hope I'm not being followed by two guys – that'd look dodgy as hell.

There's no one there.

"I was trying to find Berlin and the girls, I just needed to thank her for something."

He looks between my face and the corner of the building.

"You're not going to find them back there, brains."

Well I know that now.

I feel myself turning red. "Yeah, I don't really know where to look." I shift my weight from foot to foot. "I don't exactly get out much."

He chuckles and throws his arm over my shoulder, leading me away from the building.

I'm not sure how I feel about this. I feel kind of like his loser little sister. But on the other hand, he's warm and smells good, so I can't complain too much.

"That's where the local drug dealers hang out," he informs me.

I feel my mouth fall open.

Oh my god.

Fuck, I am such a loner loser.

I literally know nothing about life around this school. I've come here for years, and I had no clue that we had local drug dealers that hang out behind the art block.

"Oh, sweet, innocent little Lily-boo."

I jab him in the ribs with my finger. "Shut up, okay. So, I don't have any street smarts. It's whatever."

Something dawns on me then, as he steers me clear of the art blocks. "Wait a minute... if that's where the druggies chill, why were you going around there?"

He chuckles. "I was just looking for a mate."

I twist my neck to look up and raise a brow at him as he strolls along next to me, casual as hell, his arm still around my shoulders. "That's my line."

"Two people can be doing the same thing at the same time, you know. We just happened to bump into each other. It's called a meet cute. You can Google it."

"I know what a meet cute is, and that was *not* one."

"Ours could have been cuter if I'm being honest."

I shrug off his arm and stop walking so I can glare at him properly. "Were you going to buy drugs?"

He just laughs again. It's infuriating.

"*Well?*" I demand.

"Chill, brains, I'm not buying drugs. I was just trying to find Eli, and sometimes he hangs out around there with Tonksy and some of those boys, but I think Cullen said something about a team gym session, so they're probably all there. I'm just the loser outsider these days."

I don't know if I believe him or not, but it doesn't really matter to me. As long as he's not snorting coke off my lab benches, we're good. It's not like he's my responsibility.

"Whatever, I'm going back to my work."

"I thought you wanted to find Berlin?"

"I'll just message her. It's not safe out here," I reply as I rush off in the direction of the science block.

He howls with laughter but doesn't follow me.

"Accept my follow request, nerd, you know you want to," he calls after me.

I turn and flip him off.

"I'll see you after school!" he yells, a giant grin on his face.

I have to try *so* hard not to smile, which concerns me greatly. He's wearing me down, and letting this boy make me smile too much would be a very, very silly thing for me to do.

I knew I shouldn't have left the safety of my geek zone.

Research concluded. It's too risky out here.

THIRTEEN

Pax

Lily Wilder has accepted your follow request.

Lily Wilder has requested to follow you.

Well damn. Lily, Lily, *Lily*... who would have thought?

I bet that is the ballsiest move she's ever made.

I click accept and go straight to her page to check out what she's posted, but there's no posts. Not a single one.

I wasn't expecting any raunchy selfies or anything, but I thought she'd a least have one picture of something nerdy to show.

Berlin has probably forbidden it. Wouldn't want to ruin her image or some shit like that.

She's not giving me much to go on here. I was hoping for some content that would give me some clues about what she's into, other than science.

I doubt she's going to be posting any stories, so I'm not going to be able to get any interaction out of her that way.

Fuck it. I'll just have to take the bull by the horns.

I click on her message button and attach a picture of a chemistry joke, it says, "chemistry puns? I'm in my element!" with a cartoon drawing of a test tube with a smiley face.

I'm grinning like an idiot as I press send.

She's going to hate it and love it at the same time. I wish I could see her face when she opens it.

I wasn't expecting to hear back from her, since it's stupid o'clock, so when I see the little typing bubbles on the screen, my grin widens.

Maybe my little nerd is an early riser.

I actually laugh out loud when her reply shows up on my screen.

Lily: Please, for the love of all things holy, stop with the chemistry jokes.

I type out a reply.

Pax: Ah Lily-boo, I've missed you bossing me around

Lily: I saw you yesterday.

Pax: Yeah but you didn't even tell me off once. It was kind of disappointing

Lily: I apologise. If it makes you feel better, you were just as annoying yesterday as every other day before it, and I despised every second of your company.

I chuckle. Such spicy attitude for such a little nerd.

Pax: That was rude and hurtful

Lily: Good.

Pax: I didn't ask for the attitude

Lily: I know. It's on the house.

I like this side of Lily. Being ballsy suits her.

Pax: Lucky me

Lily: Go play with a ball or something

Pax: Why are you thinking about playing with my balls?

Lily: *deep sigh*. You're bad news.

Pax: Live a little Lily-boo… maybe you like it bad

Lily: I don't think you're reaching your target audience here.

Pax: It turns me on when you talk nerdy to me.

Lily: Alright, Ace, that's enough excitement for one morning. I'll see you at lunch

I'm cracking up by the end of our little exchange. I love the way she pretends to hate the banter, when I'm fairly certain she quietly loves it.

The morning flies by – drawing with Berlin, PE and a study period, and then it's time for lunch and my 'punishment' with Lily.

I barely walked in the door, and she dragged me over to the table and had me 'observing a chemical reaction'. I still don't really know what that means, but I must be moving up in the world if I'm allowed to do something other than hand her stuff, wash things and type numbers into documents.

"Lily! This shit is bubbling, and I don't like it," I call out to her.

I still can't tell if this is a genuine experiment or if she's ripping the piss out of me and having me sit here watching vinegar and baking soda or something.

"That's good," she yells back from the main classroom. "Just keep watching, I'll be there in a minute."

I take a cautious step backwards but don't take my eyes off the glass jug bubbling away with purpley-pinky liquid inside it.

It rises slightly closer to the neck of the jug.

"Lily-boo!"

"Calm your tits, I'm coming." She shakes her head at me, but there's a pretty smile on her face. "Why are you standing so far away? It's not going to jump up and bite you."

"I'm not willing to find out if you're telling the truth or not," I mutter.

She looks thoroughly amused.

"What is this thing meant to be doing anyway?"

"I want to test it at different stages of reactions so I can determine the outcome of another experiment I'm working on."

"I don't get it."

She laughs, actually laughs, just a little, but it's the most beautiful sound.

I just stare at her blankly like an out-of-his-depth fool.

She sighs and then spends the next fifteen minutes telling me all the details of what she's trying to achieve with this extended research programme. I don't understand even a quarter of it, but she talks with such excitement and passion, there's no way in hell I'm going to interrupt her to ask what I'm pretty sure would be dumb-ass questions. I just nod and smile and act like I know what it all means.

She's dipping stuff into the test tubes now and rattling off information I can't even begin to try and understand while I sit at her computer and wait to be told what to do.

She keeps stopping and telling me what numbers and times to type into columns on the document – something I can actually manage to get right.

None of it means shit to me, but I make sure I do a perfect job.

It's clearly important to her and I don't want to be the idiot jock who fucks it all up.

She eventually turns off the Bunsen burner and comes over to look at the rows of numbers that I'm sure are meant to signify something. Maybe to someone intelligent they would.

"Huh," she muses as she reads it over my shoulder. "Then that would mean that..." She trails off, muttering elements and numbers and shit that sound so foreign to me, she may as well be speaking Chinese.

It's been like this for weeks. In some ways, I feel dumber by the day, but somehow, every time I walk through that door, she's making me feel a little bit more like myself again too.

I never thought I'd enjoy this punishment. I never thought I'd enjoy spending time with her. I never thought I'd catch feelings. I sure as hell didn't expect to learn anything.

Maybe old man Evans knows what he's doing after all.

"Have you been going to training lately?" she asks as she moves to sit opposite me, pulling me out of my little moment of realisation.

I shake my head. "Nah, not really. They train on a Tuesday and Thursday after school, and I'm here with you."

Plus, I'm pretty sure I'm still banned, but I don't really want to bring that up and sound like a dickhead.

"We should change the arrangement then. Your ribs are better, you should be out there."

It's not until she says it, that I realise she's right. My ribs *are* better. I don't know how the fuck she knew that before I did.

"Where do you get off on being so observant? Anyone would think you enjoy watching me."

She rolls her eyes dramatically and tries to busy herself in a book, but I can see the red cheeks she's trying so hard to hide.

I can't quite figure her out. Every now and then I could swear she wants me to kiss her, but then she'll put half a room between us like she can't get far enough away. Talk about mixed messages.

"You're incredibly self-indulgent, you know that, don't you," she mutters.

"Don't accuse me of knowing big words."

"God you're *impossible*." She groans.

I chuckle.

My phone makes a beep and I pick it up off the table next to me.

Eve: We still need to finish what we started in that bathroom.

I look at the message for a while.

It'd be so easy to reply and tell her that I'm all healed up and I'll climb in her bedroom window tonight.

But fuck that.

I look over at Lily, and meeting up with Eve is the last thing I want to do.

I clear the notification, smile, and put my phone back down where it was.

Lily isn't paying me one scrap of attention, but something changes for me in that moment.

I don't want all that toxic shit anymore. All I want, is to sit here and talk shit with this crazy smart girl for as long as she'll let me.

THE LAST PERSON I expect to see on my front porch when I head out this morning is Cole, but there he is, in all his rugby legend glory.

He looks surprised to see me, but he composes himself quickly.

"Hey, kid."

"*Dad,*" I reply dryly.

I don't know what the fuck my problem with him is, but I've got one apparently. Doesn't help that he's caught me at a bad moment. I ran into Coach after school yesterday, and I was feeling brave – which is code for stupid – when I asked him if I could come back to training yet. He didn't even let me down gently. I haven't earnt that right yet. He made that perfectly clear.

I know it's all my own fault, but that didn't make it sting any less. I've been in a shitty mood ever since.

"I thought you'd be at school."

"Had study periods this morning. Gotta head into the chemistry lab for lunch," I mumble.

He nods as though that makes perfect sense to him. Maybe Ice told him about my punishment.

I glance at my watch. I don't know what he wants, but I hope it's not going to take long. I don't want to be late for Lily.

I don't quite know when it happened, but at some point, turning up to that lab every day to see her stopped becoming a chore, and started becoming the highlight of my day. I think I'm seriously falling for that girl.

"Ma isn't here, she's at work."

"I didn't come to see her. I ah..." He rubs at the back of his neck like he's nervous. "I just came to drop something off. I didn't expect anyone to be home."

I look at him expectantly. "Okay then... well, do you want me to put it inside, orrrr...."

He looks sort of sheepish. I don't know what he's doing here.

"It won't really fit inside," he finally says.

I frown at him. I've got no fucking idea what he's talking about.

He exhales deeply and then tosses whatever he's got in his hands to me.

I catch it, look down and see it's a set of keys.

The Land Rover logo looks back at me.

"I don't get it."

He points behind me, and I turn to see a shiny black Land Rover sitting in the drive. I swear it's brand new., That thing must have cost a small fortune. Cole has more money than sense.

"Nice ride," I say.

"Glad you like it. Berlin picked it. It's yours."

I spin back to look at him.

It's fucking what?

"Excuse me?"

"It's yours. Signed the paperwork yesterday. It's already in your name and the insurance is paid."

My jaw feels like it's on the fucking ground. I must look like a cartoon character with my eyes bugging out of my head.

I don't know what to say, I don't know what to do. This car probably costs more than our house.

It's too much.

"I can't drive a car like this while Ma and Mum work themselves into the ground to pay the bills."

A guy like Cole wouldn't understand that. Clearly he's short on sense, but not on cash, apparently.

He crosses his arms across his chest. "I've taken care of it."

"Taken care of *what?*"

I know I'm being a prick. I've just been given a car that probably cost over one hundred and fifty grand, and I haven't even said thank you.

"The bills. The mortgage."

This is what I overheard him talking to Ma about the other night.

I know I should be grateful, but I just feel... angry. I don't know if I'm angry at him, or at Ma, or just at the whole world.

I just know I'm angry.

"You can't just buy your way into my life."

Hurt flashes across his face. "I'm not trying to buy my way into anything, but you're my son. Berlin is my daughter, and I got her a car for her eighteenth birthday, it's only fair that I get you one too. Sorry it's late."

"And the mortgage? The bills? Is that meant to make up for eighteen years of not knowing you?"

I know I'm way over the line. My anger is so far in the wrong direction that it's almost laughable. None of this is Cole's fault – other than his inability to wrap his dick, but I can't stop the rage bubbling inside me.

Cole looks hurt, and it's fair enough. If that were me, and some punk-ass little shit who shared my DNA was talking to me like that, I'd probably want to knock his head in, but not Cole. He just stands there looking at me with disappointment.

"Look, you're my son, and I think you're a good guy. My daughter certainly thinks a lot of you, but I'll be honest with you, kid, you're making it real hard to like you right now. I know you're hurting. I know you're angry, but it's about time you got your head out of your ass and realised that you're not the only one in pain. This isn't yours exclusively, Pax. You don't get to sling shit at the people who care about you. Your Ma, Mum, me, Berlin, Cullen, we all care about you, and none of us are going anywhere. I'm doing my best here; I'm trying to at least make up for all the struggles you've had. If nothing else, I can ease that load. If you don't want to know me, then it'll kill me, kid, and I'll never stop trying, but only you can decide how you handle that."

"You practice that in the mirror?"

He just shakes his head and walks down off the porch, leaving me there with nothing but disgust for myself.

He stops about halfway down the drive.

"I'm really sorry that you're dealing with this, Pax, I am. I'm sorry I'm dealing with this too. And I know it's eighteen years late, but I want to know my son. I hope you'll let me."

He turns around then and leaves. He must have driven here in the Land Rover, because he doesn't get into another vehicle, he just strolls down the street, and eventually breaks into a run. I hadn't even noticed he was kitted out in running gear. No rest for the wicked.

I stare at the car in the drive.

I don't know what the fuck to do. I don't know whether I should drive it to school or let it roll off a cliff.

With the douche bag attitude I just displayed, I wouldn't be surprised if he shows up here later to take the thing off me again.

God, I'm a total cunt sometimes.

I'm starting to spiral – I can feel it.

My phone vibrates in my pocket, and I already know it's my reminder to get to the lab for Lily.

Lily.

She's like a shining beacon of light in the darkness.

I just need to get to Lily.

FOURTEEN

Lily

I can tell just by looking at him that something's wrong. There's no smile on his face, no mischievous glint in his eye, no swagger in his stride.

He looks broken.

"Pax?"

His eyes don't even flicker to mine, there's no acknowledgement that he's even heard me speak.

This is bad.

"Hey, Lily," he finally replies, just as I'm about to repeat his name.

"Are you okay?"

"I have a brand-new Land Rover," he states, his tone flat.

Ummm. I'm confused.

"You have a brand-new Land Rover?" I question, hoping for further elaboration.

He offers nothing but a nod of his head.

"You didn't steal it, did you?" I ask, genuinely concerned now.

He hasn't exactly been on a great trajectory behaviour wise, lately, and he's looking all kinds of unhinged right now.

He laughs a humourless laugh and shakes his head again. "I didn't steal it."

I don't remember moving, but I've crossed the room and I'm standing in front of him now. "I think you should come and sit down."

He doesn't answer, but he also doesn't argue, so I lead him over to the bench and pull out a stool for him. I take a seat next to him and wait patiently for him to be ready to talk. It doesn't take long.

"Cole – *my dad* – he bought me a Land Rover. Said it was for my birthday. Apologised for it being late even."

Score. I wish some guy would show up and be my dad and buy me a fancy-ass car, but given the reaction from Pax right now, I'm going to guess he's feeling somewhat conflicted.

"Okay... do you... not like Land Rovers?" I take a stab in the dark.

"Who in their right mind doesn't like Land Rovers?" he half snaps.

I take a deep breath and remind myself to be patient. "I'm going to need you to tell me what's going on in that head of yours, Pax."

"I'm sorry. I wish I knew. I'm so *angry*. I feel like he's trying to buy me."

He sounds like a broken little boy. My heart aches for him.

"He's probably just trying to make up for lost time. Maybe he thought buying you that would help make up for all the years of things he couldn't buy you." I shrug my shoulders.

"I don't even know him and he's on my doorstep trying to give me a car worth a small fortune, and he's paying off Ma's mortgage... it's too much. I'm so fucked off. I don't know how to handle it and it feels like he's making it worse."

"I get that, Pax, but he's making an effort. That's all he's doing. Would you rather he did nothing? Maybe you should stop being so stubborn and give him a chance."

"Never mind. You wouldn't understand," he snaps at me. I don't like his tone, but instead of shrinking back like I usually would, I snap back for once. I'm not going to sit here quietly and let him tell me what I do and don't understand.

"You know *what*? You've really got to stop thinking that you know me. You don't know *anything* about my life outside of this room. You don't know what I've been through. You don't know what I've seen." I rein myself in – I'm getting frustrated and emotional, neither of which I want to do. I know he's hurting, and I want to help. The last thing I want to do is argue. "I know a little something about missing out on parents, Pax," I add softly.

"Like what?" he asks, his tone still harsher than it needs to be.

"My parents left me when I was two, okay? I've lived with my grandmother ever since."

The frustration on his face dissolves instantly and morphs into a soft, sad expression.

"*Lily.*"

"Yeah, well... I told you that you don't know me."

"I'm sorry, it's a bad habit of mine."

He shuffles his seat closer to mine.

"What is?" I whisper, momentarily shocked by his closeness.

He picks up one of my hands and places it in his. "Underestimating you. You're so much stronger than I give you credit for. You're a hell of a lot stronger than me."

I don't know about that at all, but he's looking at me like I'm the strongest person alive.

"Your parents... where are they?"

I don't usually talk about them to anyone, but for whatever reason, I want to tell him.

"They're still around. My dad has never spent more than about six months out of jail, and I don't think he's had any other kids, but my mum definitely had another one. A girl. Her father's family took her on as a baby when my mum couldn't keep her. They moved to the South Island. She's my half-sister and I've never even met her."

"Where's her dad?"

I shrug. "He's probably a crack head like my mum. I can't imagine she got knocked up by an upstanding citizen."

His eyes widen.

"And your dad, is he in jail now?"

"I honestly don't know. Last I heard, coke was his drug of choice, but I wouldn't know. I haven't seen the man in about fourteen years."

"Fucking hell, Lily."

Reactions like this are why I don't like to talk about my fucked-up family much. I'm fine really. I know I'm better off with Grammy, always have been, but I do worry about what happens when she's gone. I know I'm nearly an adult now, but I still don't feel ready to tackle the world alone and she certainly isn't getting any younger.

"I'd give anything for a decent man – a man like Cole to turn up on my doorstep and tell me he was my father. I'd be over the moon if I had a father who actually *wanted* to know me in the right way. You need to find a way to channel all this anger, or it's going to eat you alive, Pax. Cole seems like a good man. You should let yourself have a relationship with him."

He lets my words soak in for a few moments.

"You're right. I know you're right, but I don't know if I know how to do that."

I squeeze his hand. "I think you just have to make like a proton and stay positive."

He's silent for about thirty seconds, just staring at me.

"Did you just make a cringey science joke?"

I wince. "I think I did. Honestly, I'm embarrassed by my behaviour. I guess that's how much I want you to cheer up."

"*Shit.* You really do like me, huh? Way to come on strong, Lily-boo." His lips creep up into a grin.

I roll my eyes hard, but I can't deny that I like my hand in his. I also can't deny the speed of my heartrate with him sitting here next to me. It's *so* fast, and every time he leans towards me it speeds up even more.

I *want* him to lean in closer. I want him to lean in close enough for his mouth to touch mine.

Fuck's sake. Keke was right. I *do* like him. I like him a whole lot.

"Don't flatter yourself," I mumble as he shifts his body ever so slightly, so it's facing me even more than it was a few seconds ago.

His thumb skims over my skin, sending tingles racing up and down my spine.

"Have some composure, you're practically throwing yourself at me," he teases softly.

I can feel myself blushing as his thumb moves back and forth over my hand. All I can do is watch the action, my stomach flipping like crazy. I feel like I'm about to get kissed, but that *can't* be what's happening here.

No way.

Pax is a god. He's ripped to shreds and he's got a jawline that looks like it could cut through glass. He's got gorgeous eyes; so dark they're nearly black. He's got no business kissing a chubby, mousey brown, science girl.

Those two things just don't go together. I'm a smart girl – I know my place, and it's not with Pax.

"*Lily.* Look at me," he whispers.

His mouth is so close to me now that I feel his breath on my ear. I have to stop myself from shuddering.

I'm pathetic. I'm sure Pax is *more* than experienced and then here I am, over here getting flutters from an exhale. *Honestly.* I need to pull myself together.

"*Lily.*"

I tilt my head up and finally face him. I can feel how ridiculously flushed my cheeks are. I don't even know what I'm embarrassed about, but I am.

The corners of his mouth turn up into a smile.

"You are the sweetest girl I've ever met."

He slowly raises his hand and grazes the back of his fingers down my cheek.

My eyelids flutter shut at his touch and there's nothing I can do to stop them.

He cups my jaw with his palm and I'm looking at him again in a flash.

Breathe. I remind myself. I'd never live down the humiliation if he really did try to kiss me and I fainted.

He leans in closer.

"Pax, you don't –" I try to tell him that he doesn't have to do this, but he doesn't give me the chance to say anything more.

He silences me by pressing his lips to mine in a kiss so sweet and tender it makes my knees weak. It's incredibly lucky I'm sitting down already, or I think I would have fallen over.

I can't believe this.

Pax Benson, Westlake High's star winger is kissing *me.*

Me. Boring Lily Wilder.

I can't believe it.

He pulls away but doesn't go far; his nose is still touching mine.

"I've been wanting to do that for weeks."

"Really?" I whisper.

"Since the day you kicked me out of this lab... All that

confidence and attitude." He makes a humming noise deep in his throat. It speaks a thousand more words than a picture ever could. "You've been on my mind ever since. Can't seem to get you out of it."

"Maybe you hit your head in that fight."

He chuckles. "My head is perfectly fine, thank you."

"You've had an emotional afternoon, maybe you just needed someone for comfort."

He looks amused by my attempts to give him an out. To my utter shock, he doesn't seem to want one.

"Stop trying to talk me out of the way I feel about you."

My heart rate picks up again hearing him say that he feels something for me.

I don't know what to do about this. Yes, I've been crushing on him, I'm willing to admit that now, but it was meant to be one of those harmless crushes that never goes anywhere.

I never for a second imagined that he'd even so much as look at me twice. I never imagined I'd be kissing such a bad boy.

"Well, it makes no sense, Pax, you shouldn't be feeling *anything* for me."

"Maybe you shouldn't be telling me how I should feel." He smirks. "I knew you were bossy, but it's really getting out of hand. You should probably let me kiss you again to make it up to me."

I open my mouth to argue his smart-ass comments, but snap it shut again when I realise that I don't want to argue with him. I want nothing more than for him to kiss me again.

"Well, I wouldn't want to be known as bossy, now would I..." I reply playfully.

He grins, pulls me closer and kisses me again. This time isn't nearly as sweet, but it's even better than the first time. It's hot and steamy and it somehow feels forbidden.

He kisses me until I feel lightheaded.

"You make me *weak*, Lily," he rasps, his breathing heavy against my face.

The irony of that statement. I know what he means, and it empowers me to another level that I can make a guy like him feel vulnerable, but the way he makes me feel is quite the opposite.

Right now, I don't think anything could take me down. I feel invincible.

"*You* make *me* feel strong."

I think he likes the sound of that.

"ALRIGHT, let's hear it. What's today's joke?" I ask him the second he walks through the door. I've decided to take the bull by the horns and get it out of the way early. Not that it'll probably stop him from going for the next hour anyway, but it's worth a shot.

He looks confused for a second before a grin spreads across his face. "Well hello to you too, beautiful."

"Save your hellos. I might make you leave again... depends how bad the joke is."

He mulls it over for a few seconds.

"You wanna hear a potassium joke?"

"Sure."

"*K*," he replies.

I wait. He stares.

"K. Get it? *K*. Potassium. K."

I just point at the door, fighting a smile the whole time.

"Oh, come on! At least let me tell another one. You've got to give a guy a second chance."

I cross my arms across my chest and tap my feet.

"Did I tell you my chemistry experiment exploded?"

"You didn't."

"Yeah... but it's okay, *oxidants happen*."

I shake my head at him. "Did you Google 'lame chemistry jokes' or something?"

"I had to make these bad chemistry jokes, because all the good ones *Argon*."

He looks at me expectantly, his brows raised and the goofiest looking grin on his face. I can't help it, I finally crack and burst into laughter.

He's so unbelievably lame and it's somehow the cutest thing I've ever seen.

"Yesssssss!" he cheers, jumping around, fist-pumping and making an absolute racket. "*Finally!*"

"Shhhhh." I giggle. "You'll get Mr. Higgins in here next."

"I don't even care. I'd be proud to tell him my achievements. I made you laugh over a stupid science joke. I am elite. I am the king. My work here is done."

I'm still laughing.

He rushes across the room towards me and sweeps me up into his arms. "I knew I could do it."

"Congratulations." I giggle. "It's quite the achievement. Now put me down."

"Nope."

He smashes his mouth to mine, kissing me so passionately my whole body tingles. I forget that we're standing in an open classroom where anyone could walk by and see us. I forget that I'm far too heavy for him to be holding up. I forget that this is crazy. Instead, I just fall into the fairy-tale for a moment and kiss him back.

At least he's quiet while he's kissing me.

His tongue slips into my mouth, and I have to stop myself from groaning. I fail and it slips out any way.

"Jesus, Lily," he growls, his voice gruff and strained. "You can't be making noises like that."

He rests his face against my neck, still holding me up in his arms. I wiggle a little in an attempt to get down, but his grip only tightens, his broad shoulders flexing under my palms.

He's just so *hot*.

He starts kissing my neck, his lips lightly brushing across my sensitive skin. I shiver as he gets closer to my throat.

He trails up towards my ear lobe and another moan slips out. I can't help it. It feels so good.

He makes a noise deep in his throat, and before I can even register what's happening, we're moving. He strides out of the classroom and into the back lab, kicking the door shut behind him.

I don't know how he makes it feel so easy, but he certainly doesn't seem to be bothered by carrying me around.

He heads for the small couch in the corner of the room that no one ever uses and sits himself down, so I'm in his lap.

I try to tug at my skirt, which is riding up far more than I'm okay with, but he just grunts and grabs my hands and pins them behind my back.

I feel so embarrassed, I'm sure I'm blushing like crazy.

"You are so beautiful, Lily," he says as he looks me over.

He looks at every part of me with as much appreciation as the last part. Even the parts I hate.

He grips my wrists in one of his big hands and brings the other around to my thigh. He skims his fingers up and down my exposed skin, setting me on fire and making me crazy.

I feel like I'm about to explode. I'm so insanely turned on by this boy, I don't even know what to do with myself.

I'm barely holding onto my self-control as he trails his fingers higher and higher until they reach the hem of my skirt. He lets them linger there a while, tickling my skin, before heading back down towards my knee. I exhale heavily in the anticipation of him going higher – of him touching more.

It scares the hell out of me, but I want him to touch me there. I want him to touch me everywhere.

"So fucking sexy," he murmurs.

I never thought I'd hear the day *I* was called sexy.

Part of me thinks this is just a dream. Or that he's involved in some kind of bet. But right now, I don't care, I want to feel like this forever.

I shift my weight a little bit, and I'm shocked to feel that he's rock hard in his shorts.

Pax Benson is turned on by *me*. Even if this all were a big joke, if his buddies were making a bet with him – the fact that he's turned on makes me feel incredible.

He lets go of my hands and I wrap them around his neck, bringing him closer to me.

He skims his fingers over my skirt, and to the hem of my school blouse.

I inhale sharply as he slides his hands under and onto my bare stomach.

Breathe, I have to remind myself.

He pulls his face back from mine to watch me as his hands slide higher until they're touching my bra.

"Is this okay?" he asks softly.

I nod my head. It's so much more than okay. It's amazing. He cups my tits in his warm hands, and I lean into his touch.

I've never been overly happy to have larger boobs – they weren't exactly fun when I was fourteen and too embarrassed to ask Grammy to buy me a proper bra, but with Pax's thumbs rubbing over my nipples through the thin fabric, and his big hands full, I finally feel like maybe they're not so bad after all.

"Fuck," he says on an exhale, so quietly I almost miss it.

"I wish I was adenine," he mumbles. "Then I could get paired with *U*."

I arch my back as my eyes close, my breath heavy. "Don't ruin this with lame jokes."

"Those lame jokes got me you." He pinches my

nipples, and I feel it between my legs. I groan at the rush of blood as he releases them again.

"You got me in *spite* of those lame jokes," I reply, my voice barely recognisable.

"God, I want you so fucking bad," he growls, his hips lifting slightly.

My eyes fly open again and look right into his. "You do?"

He nods and kisses my neck again.

"You have *no* idea, Lily."

He lifts his hips again, but slower this time and far more deliberately, pressing himself into me.

"But not here. Not now. You deserve so much more than this, and I'm going to give it to you."

"What if I don't care about more?" I breathe as he keeps kissing me, driving me crazy. I think that's the only reason I'm not freaking out, because I know we're not really going to do anything here in this lab. I can be confident and bold here without too much risk.

"That's how you want our first time to go? Hot and heavy with the periodic table setting the mood and the smell of metal in the air?" He chuckles, his voice raspy and his breath warm on my face.

Little does he know, it wouldn't just be my first time with him, it'd be my first time. *Ever.* I'm a total virgin.

And he's right, we don't need to be doing that on a couch in the corner of a classroom lab. Certainly not on a cream-coloured couch.

"About that..." I say.

I've been meaning to tell him that I've never been with anyone, but I feel like a loser every time I try.

He slips his hands from my bra to my side and runs his hands slowly up and down my skin. It feels so nice. I never imagined feeling so comfortable with a guy's hands on me.

"What about it, beautiful?"

I hear the door swing open loudly and Keke's voice fills the room. I try to scramble off Pax, but I'm too slow.

"Well, well, well, this is an interesting little experiment you two have going on here. Are we calling it 'the making of a teenage pregnancy'?"

"Oh my god." I try to get off his lap gracefully and fail spectacularly.

"Keke, what are you doing here?" I demand as I stumble to my feet.

"Witnessing free porn, apparently."

"Keke!" I smooth my skirt out over my legs and look over at Pax.

"I think I'll stay seated for now." He smirks, gesturing to his crotch.

I feel my eyes bulge. "Good call."

"You dirty little horn dogs," she cries. "Getting it on in the science lab, what a risky little game."

"We weren't getting it on."

"Maybe not yet, but you weren't far away."

"Keeks!" I warn her.

"Oh, don't go getting all high and mighty with me, I'm just glad you weren't naked. Put a hat on the door or something next time, would you?"

"Oh my god." I cover my face, which is bright red, with my hands.

"I'll wait outside. I'd hate to stand in any bodily fluids.

But you and me will be having words, missy, you were meant to tell me when you fell in love."

Oh for the love of all things holy.

If it's possible, I go even more red. She exits the room as quickly as she entered, taking my dignity with her.

Pax's phone starts ringing.

"Oh my god, now what?" I groan.

Pax laughs and answers the call, on speaker.

"What's up?"

"Paxikins, I need a favour."

"Hello, Pax, how are you? I'm good thanks, Berlin, yourself?"

"Oh, shut up and listen."

"With manners like that, how can I refuse," Pax drawls.

"Look, just give the old man a break, would you? He's emo all the time and I'm sick of living with a moody prick. He's pretty cool if you get to know him. As far as parents go, I wouldn't trade him for anyone, so can you just give it a chance, *PLEASE?*"

"And he's like, stupid hot," someone in the background chimes in.

I cover my laugh with my hand.

"Yeah, I'll keep how hot my dad is in mind when I talk to him next, thanks, Carissa."

"Just think about it," Berlin sasses him. "Gotta go."

The line goes dead, and Pax adjusts himself in his shorts as he grins at me.

"Well that was a pretty chaotic five minutes." He smirks.

Chaotic doesn't even begin to cover it.

FIFTEEN

Pax

When Cole pulls into the parking lot for training, I'm already there waiting for him. I told Lily I wanted to go and talk to him, and she was only too happy to let me off my lab bitch-boy duties for the afternoon.

She shoved me out the door so quickly I'm starting to think she doesn't really need my *help* at all. She better watch herself, she'll give me a complex. I chuckle as I think about how I nearly set her lab coat on fire a few days ago. The girl really should feel lucky to have such a capable sidekick.

Cole's face lights up when he notices me there, leaning against the fancy-ass car he bought me. I've been driving it every day, much to Cull's delight, and fuck man, even if I didn't want to know my dad, there's no way I'd be giving this thing up.

I've tasted luxury and it sure is sweet.

I'm surprised he looks so happy to see me though, after I was a grade A prick last time. For all he knows, I might be here to chuck another tantrum and throw the keys at him.

At the moment I wouldn't put that past me. I'm kind of a douche.

I wanted to catch Cole before training, and before the whole team was around to watch the show. It's not like the news of Cole being my dad hasn't spread like wildfire anyway, but I still don't need an audience for this conversation. I'm not a fucking dancing monkey. This isn't a zoo.

"Pax," he says warmly as he steps out of his ute – which I can't help but notice, is far older than what he's got both me and Berlin rolling in. "I didn't expect to see you here."

I didn't expect to see me here either, but all the important women in my life have been steering me towards this moment for a while now, so I figure if they're willing to lead a horse to water, the least I can do is take a drink.

I can't quite figure out what I want to say. I open my mouth, but nothing is coming out. I've never tried to make peace with a dad I didn't know I had, so this is all new to me. Maybe I should have brought beers. Or chocolates. Or flowers.

I'm fucking lost and barrelling towards getting wildly off track.

Cole doesn't seem to mind the silence.

"How's it driving?" he asks me as he approaches, nodding towards the Land Rover.

"Good." I nod. "Like, next level good."

"It's smooth, huh? I took it for a burn before I gave it to you," he admits, "might have to get myself one." He runs his hand over the ass of the car.

"You should. It's got a shit load of go."

I'm sure he knows I'm not here to talk about the vehicle's top end speed, but he's giving me time to man up and work myself into it, and I appreciate that.

I take a deep breath and finally find my balls.

"Thank you, for the car. And for the money for Ma. I know a thank you isn't enough, but I appreciate it, Cole, it's too much, but it means a lot to me that you wanted to do it anyway."

He nods his head in a way that makes me feel like those words are soothing his soul. They're probably the first respectable words I've uttered to him since I learned I was his son.

"And I'm sorry for the way I acted. I was way out of line, and you didn't deserve it. I directed my anger in all the wrong places."

"I appreciate the apology, and I'm sorry if I handled things wrong. I've never had an illegitimate child pop up before; I don't know what the proper etiquette is."

It's good know it's not just me fumbling it. We're like the blind leading the blind.

"I heard it was customary for illegitimate sons to get *two* vehicles, but I guess I can make do with one," I joke.

He chuckles. "You here for practice?" He tilts his head towards the warmup fields.

I turn to look and see Cullen standing on the field, dressed for training, watching the two of us. He nods his head at me. I raise my chin in response.

"Nah... I haven't really talked to Coach again yet. He told me no the last time I asked. I don't know if he'll ever want me back after all the shit I pulled."

I wouldn't want me back. I'm a fucking embarrassment.

"I've talked to Coach Green. He said you can come back to the team if you think you're ready. And Principal Evans has called time on your community service, science thing. It's time to get your head back in the game. If that's what you want?"

No fucking way.

I'm back...

I'm surprised by how much I *do* want that. I miss my mates. I miss my team. I miss the thrill of hauling ass down a field and diving with the ball over the try line.

I miss a group of sweaty dudes having my back.

I miss my body moving.

The only part that doesn't sit right with me, is giving up my time with Lily. I don't want that. I don't want to be freed from that 'responsibility', not yet; maybe not ever. I know I'm probably still hindering her more than I'm helping, but I'm *needed* there. I'm valued. It gave me purpose when nothing else could. It's given me Lily.

"I'm ready," I tell him quickly. "I want back in."

"I know. I already told him you were." He smirks. "I'd have come to talk to you over the weekend if you hadn't shown up here today."

I don't know whether to be shocked or impressed by his ability to read me.

"How'd you know?"

He shrugs. "You've just got that look in your eye.

You're craving the drive that rugby gives you. I may not know you very well yet, but we share the same DNA, and I see a lot of myself in you."

That makes me feel all warm inside and shit. I could do a hell of a lot worse than being like him. He's a legend of the game. He might just be an all-round legend from what I'm seeing and hearing from him.

"Can I ask you something?" I shift my weight from foot to foot. I don't know why I feel nervous, it's a fair question.

"Fire away."

"Why didn't you ask Ma for a paternity test? She just turns around, after all these years and puts a kid on you, and you just believe her, no questions asked?"

It's been bugging me for a while now. I thought maybe Ma had my hair tested without telling me or something, but no one has ever mentioned anything about it being proven that Cole is definitely my father. The last thing I need is to finally figure out how to let him in, and then have it all ripped out from under me. Ma might be lying – she's probably an expert at that by now.

He chuckles. "If you saw some photos of me at eighteen, you'd understand. You're a chip off the old block. I hate to break it to you, but there's very little doubt that you're my son. Me and Berlin were flicking through some old albums the other week. I can't believe I didn't see the resemblance sooner."

"It'd probably be pretty weird to be eyeing up teenage boys thinking that they might look like you did back in the day."

"You make a good point," he agrees with a laugh.

"And besides, Julia doesn't want anything from me. You're legally an adult now. She's got no reason to tell me I'm your father if I'm not – it certainly hasn't made her popular with anyone."

I guess he's right there too. Ma has made herself enemy number one, and she doesn't want anything for it. I overheard that loud and clear when her and Cole were talking in the kitchen.

"It'd be cool to see some of those photos of you when you went to school here and stuff... if that's all good with you."

I swear his eyes glass over. "That'd be more than all good with me. You just come over to the house any time. You're always welcome, Pax. I mean that. And I'm just a phone call away if you ever need anything. And I mean *anything*."

"Ice – ah, *Berlin*, might not be so keen on the open-door policy," I say with a grin.

"I know she acts like a hard ass, but that girl would have you move in tomorrow if it's what you wanted. You all mean so much to her in such a short time. I never expected that she'd make such good friends here."

"Don't go getting all sentimental in your old age," I joke.

He laughs loudly, from down in his belly. "You sound just like her."

I guess Berlin has had a solid influence on me too.

"Seriously though, she was pissed about it at first, but moving back here was the best decision I ever made. This is home. Even more so now that you're in my life."

"I'm sorry I've been acting like such a dickhead. I know I've been stressing her out."

"She's just worried about you. She's worried about *me*. I wish she'd worry about herself instead."

"I'll try not to give her anymore reasons to worry."

He nods his head. "No more fighting, eh."

"No more fighting," I agree, embarrassed.

I don't know what I was thinking, starting a brawl at school like a dickhead. Actually, I do, it wasn't *me* thinking, it was the rum. The rum ain't so smart.

"Coach told me you were wasted that day."

"Snitch," I mutter. "I haven't touched a drink in a while now," I say loudly.

Now that I think about it, it's been weeks since I touched drugs too, and I haven't even noticed. Talking to Lily has become my new drug of choice.

"Good. You've got talent on that field. I think you could go places, you and Cullen.Hell, probably even Bryson if he wanted it bad enough. Every guy getting paid to play would kill for the natural talent you've got. If you want to pursue it, you can make a career out of it."

I like that he's telling me what he thinks without telling me what to do. He's encouraging without being controlling. Cull could learn a few things from him.

I know I'm a good player. I know I could make something of myself through rugby, I just don't know what I want.

"Do you think I should?" I ask him, shifting my weight from foot to foot.

I don't care much about what anyone thinks, but I

care about his answer to this question. It's different when there's shared DNA invested.

"It doesn't matter what I think. What matters is what you want."

"I'll think about it."

"Good. And for now, just get back into the game, have fun and enjoy whatever you choose to do, that's all that really matters. You blink and all this will be over, and you'll be old and washed up like me, so enjoy it while it lasts."

"Shit man... Apologies and life advice, bit heavy for a Tuesday afternoon."

"Next time we'll go for a quiet beer and talk about the weather."

I chuckle. I know he's kidding, but I actually think I'd like that. I never thought I'd get to have a beer with my dad, but maybe it's not so out of reach after all.

"Alright, kid, you got some training gear in there?" He points to the boot of my car. "You're about to get thrown in the deep end."

I grin excitedly. I'll probably be on the verge of spewing in about fifteen minutes, but I don't even care. It'll be worth it.

I lift open the boot and grab my gear bag, which has barely been touched for weeks now. It'll probably stink, but I haven't exactly had any use for rugby boots in the science block.

That reminds me...

"Hey, Cole... can you do me one favour?"

He nods.

"Don't tell anyone that I don't have to go into the lab

anymore? I think maybe I might want to keep doing that..."

He huffs out a laugh and looks at me knowingly. "Sure thing, kid, mum's the word."

I smile, satisfied. "Thanks."

"So, what's her name?"

"What's who's name?"

"Come on, don't try and tell me this isn't about a girl."

I give him a look. "It might be."

He laughs and shakes his head in amusement. "Oh, to be a teenager again. Seems like a lifetime ago."

I'm not buying it. He's a good-looking man, I can't imagine his dating life has slowed up at all with age.

I bet Cole Davids in his prime got some epic women. He could have had them eating out of the palm of his hand if that's what he wanted. I don't know how he balanced that life with raising Berlin, but she turned out pretty good, so he obviously managed okay.

We start to head over to the warmup fields, a comfortable silence between us, when he stops suddenly and taps my arm.

"Hey, while we're asking for favours, can you do one thing for me too?"

"I guess so." I shrug, eyeing him curiously. I can't imagine what *I* would be able to do for *him*, but I probably owe him at this point. "What is it?"

"Talk to your mother? I don't know if you've noticed, but she's looking thin. I don't know if she's eating or sleeping well. And I know she fucked up, but she's the only mum you've got. Well, other than Hannah, but you know what I mean."

We both exchange a laugh at the weird home life I've grown up to find normal.

"No sense in gaining one parent only to lose another," he carries on. "Life's too short. I'm not saying you should forgive and forget, but you could try it on for size."

"I'm not sure anything I have to say to her is going to make that situation any better. I actually might even be able to make it worse."

It's a real concern of mine. I've got a temper sometimes and I don't want to lose my shit again.

He lifts a shoulder. "Well, you won't know until you try."

PAX: **Lily-boo... how'd you feel about swapping our lab days around?**

Lily: You're back on the team?!

Pax: I'm back on the team baby

Lily: Yaaaaay! I'm going to show up to practice and yell cringey rugby jokes at you the whole time.

Pax: I always knew you had secret ambitions to be a cheerleader, you'd look hot in the uniform too

Lily: Asshole

Pax: #followyourdreams

Lily: This is your weekly reminder that I'm totally capable of exposing you to chemicals that could kill you and not leave a trace.

Pax: Message received my little sociopath

Lily: So did it go good with your dad?

Pax: Yeah itt did. He's cool. He's going to show me some photos of him at my age. He reckons I look just like him

Lily: I'm really happy for you, Pax

I'm pretty happy for me too, if I'm honest.

None of this is easy, but maybe that's the point. Character building and all that shit.

Pax: He wants me to talk to Ma…

Lily: He's a smart man, if only someone else had been saying the same thing for weeks…

Smart ass.

Pax: I don't know what to say to her. I don't forgive her

Lily: If you got a call in the morning to say she'd been killed overnight, what would you wish you'd had a chance to tell her?

Jesus. Morbid turn. That's not at all what I was expecting her to say, but I think I see where she's going with this.

Pax: That I love her and she was a great mum

Lily: Then I'd start by telling her that

She's makes a solid point. I might not forgive Ma, but I do love her, and she's still the woman who raised me. It doesn't count for everything, but it counts for something.

Pax: Her car just pulled into the drive

Lily: Well then, I'll talk to you later. Don't be a wanker, I know that'll be a real effort for you x

I chuckle. Smart bitch.

I peek out the window and see Ma is unloading grocery bags out of her boot. I jog to the door and out front to help her.

I must have been a fucking nightmare lately because when she sees me grab the rest of the bags out of the car, she almost falls over in shock.

I guess I haven't been pulling my weight, which means Cull has probably been pulling it for me. No wonder he's such a grumpy fucker. I haven't touched the lawn mower in God knows how long.

I really am a prick.

"Thank you," she says as she watches me hulk the bags up the path.

I drop them onto the kitchen bench and grab an apple off the top of one of them.

Ma starts fussing around the kitchen, putting shit away in all its special little spots. She's got that kind of OCD that isn't actually real OCD, but it's where the rules are the rules and the system can't be fucked with.

I bite into my apple and just watch. I'd help, but we both know I'd do it wrong, and she'd spend the next ten minutes redoing everything I put anywhere.

This feels like old times, normal times. It's kind of nice.

"That silly cow. Who would put the bread rolls at the *bottom* of the bag," she mutters to herself as she pulls out a pack of squished rolls. "Go back to school, sweetie."

I can't help but laugh. Mum is definitely the more compassionate parent in this house; Ma is slightly more savage.

I take another bite of my apple, and then talk around it. "I talked to Cole today. And I got back on the team."

Her eyes light up. "You did? That's great news. When can you play again?"

"I'll probably be on the bench for the next game, but hopefully I'll be back in the action the week after that."

"You must be happy about that."

I nod. "Got my ass kicked at practice today, but I'm back on the horse now."

She stops and just looks at me for a few seconds, her expression warm. "I'm really happy for you, Pax. It's been missing from your life."

I don't know what to say to that. I don't know how I feel about the fact that it's right. I never thought of myself as someone who needed rugby; I'm not Cull, but she's right. It has been missing. I take another bite instead of replying.

"How did it go with Cole?" she asks warily.

"It was fine. He's a good dude. I apologised for being an ungrateful little prick."

"I think that's probably fair enough, given the flash car he's got you boys driving around in."

I feel kind of bad cruising around in that while Ma is out there driving an old Toyota Corolla, but now that Cole has paid off the mortgage, maybe she'll be able to upgrade sometime soon.

"Principal Evans said I'm done with my punishment too. I don't know if he called you or what..."

I went into his office after practice and spoke to him. I apologised for being a dick and told him it wouldn't happen again.

I'm not saying I'll never throw another punch, but I think I can manage the rest of the school year without getting wasted at school and smacking some innocent kid.

Saying sorry still doesn't feel like enough, but it's a start, I guess.

"He sent me an email. I'm sure you'll be glad to be free of that commitment."

She looks pleased. I'm sure she's far from proud, but she doesn't look like she's about to skin me alive, so that's something.

"I think I'm going to keep going actually. I like it in there."

She stops stacking cereal into the shelves and looks at me, surprised. "Since when? I thought you hated science."

"I don't love it."

She raises her eyebrows at me in question.

"The girl I've been helping... Lily. She's pretty cool."

Her expression softens into that look mothers get when they know their children are catching feelings for someone. I don't know how they know, but they do.

I remember Mum giving Cull the same look when he turned all soft and fell in love with Ice.

She completely abandons the groceries and rushes over to sit down next to me.

"*Lily*," she gushes. "Such a pretty name."

I shake my head in amusement. "What do you want to know?" I ask her warily.

"Everything."

I chuckle.

I don't know where to start. Anything I say about Lily won't do her enough justice.

"She's smart. She's *so* smart. Way smarter than me. She's pretty, and shy, but she can stand her own too. She doesn't put up with any of my bullshit."

Ma is practically beaming. "I like her already."

"Yeah, well, so do I, but I don't want to jinx it, so can we talk about something else?"

"Have you been out on a date yet?" she asks, ignoring me.

I shake my head. "I'm scared to ask."

There's part of me that thinks a girl like Lily wouldn't want to be caught dead out in public with a meathead rugby player like me. It's not like I haven't thought about the two of us hanging out, outside of the lab, in fact, I've had some fairly vivid dreams about one aspect of it, but I'm shitting my pants. Lily doesn't have a choice about hanging out with me at the moment – which is why I'm not about to tell her that I don't have to be there. She might kick me out.

"Don't be ridiculous. Ask the poor girl out already. She's probably dying waiting for you to do it."

I didn't think about it like that.

"Yeah, I'll think of something."

"When you find someone special, you have to treat them like they're special, because if *you* don't, some other guy will."

Any guy would be lucky to have Lily. She's too good for me, but I don't plan on letting that get in my way.

I just nod my head. She's right. Lily needs to know how special she really is.

Ma must sense that I've said all I'm going to say, because she stands up, looks at me gratefully, squeezes my shoulder and goes back to unpacking the last of the bags.

It feels nice.

I'm glad I talked with Ma. Cole was right, she does look thin. She might not be my favourite person right now, but I don't want to see her waste away.

It's not the same between us, it might never be the same again. But maybe that might just have to be enough for the both of us.

SIXTEEN

Lily

"Lily-boo, are you busy after we get done here? Like tonight…"

I smile to myself. I've been waiting for a week for this. We've been sneaking kisses and touches every day, giggling away like little kids who don't want to get caught, but he hasn't asked me out on a real date. Our relationship – or whatever this is, only exists within these walls.

As far as the rest of the world is concerned, we're perfect strangers.

"I'm not busy tonight."

I'm not busy *any* night, but he doesn't need to know that. Nothing makes you sound like more of an anti-social loser than saying you have absolutely no plans all week, at eighteen years old.

"Wanna get some food with me? After this... like a date?"

I turn around to look at him, and if I didn't know better, I'd swear he was nervous. He looks like he's sweating bullets.

I take my time slipping off my lab coat. "You want to take me out on a date?" I question him.

He nods, swallowing at the same time. I watch as his throat moves. I don't know how he makes that look attractive, but he does.

I'm playing it cool, but the idea of going out in public together is making my pulse race. I try not to care what other people say or think, but it's hard – people are definitely going to be talking about this.

I pick up my bag off the floor. "It took you long enough to ask." He just stares at me as I stroll out of the room in front of him. "Where are we going?"

It takes him a second to react, but when he does, his grin is blinding.

God, he's so cute.

He drives me home to change and waits in the car while I get organised and tell Grammy I'll be out for a while.

She doesn't ask me too many questions about where I'm going, or who with, which I appreciate. I love Grammy, and she's chill as hell, but I don't want to talk to her about boys right now – not while one is waiting for me in the car anyway.

Pax chucked on some clothes from his bag while I was gone, so there was nothing left to do but head to our date.

He chose the American diner in town, which

surprised me. Not because he doesn't seem like the type to hang out there, but because he *does*. I know that's where heaps of the kids from school hang out. It's like cheerleader central on a Friday night.

I expected him to pick somewhere quiet, somewhere where maybe everyone wouldn't see us, but we pull into the car park, and he jumps out like it's no big deal to be taking a girl like me to a place like this.

He ushers me to a private table down the back, where we're out of view of the main restaurant – which is pretty packed for a Wednesday night.

"Maybe we'll actually be able to hear each other talk down here." He grins as he pulls out a chair for me. I didn't expect him to have too much in the way of gentlemanly behaviour, but he's been opening doors and guiding me around like it's nineteen twenty and he's trying to court me. It's not unwelcome.

"Yeah, it's busy as. Is this the cool place to hang out or something?" I tease.

"I guess you could say that." He chuckles.

"I wouldn't know," I lie. I may not *hang* here, but that doesn't mean I don't know it's the place to be.

The closest I've come to hanging out here was when I interviewed for a job a couple of years ago. Pretty glad I didn't end up getting that job. I can only imagine how horrific it would be, waiting tables for Liana and her crew.

"I'm not exactly in the *cool* crowd."

I'm joking around – it's not like I actually care, but his dark eyes stare into mine, totally unwavering, not a hint of humour in them.

"You're the coolest person I know, Lily. My favourite thing about you is that you're *nothing* like anyone else."

I wasn't expecting that. That intensity is something else.

I can feel myself blushing. I dip my eyes to the menu on the table to avoid his intense gaze. I can't handle that much eye contact, not from him, not like that.

"Is that your go-to pick-up line?" I clear my throat, trying to lighten the mood.

He raises his brows. "Depends if it's working."

It's *definitely* working. Everything he does is working for me. I've got butterflies going crazy in my stomach.

I look back up at him, and he's smirking at me. He looks cocky, but God, it suits him.

He chuckles, and just like that he's back to being the joker I'm used to.

"What do you feel like eating, Lily-boo?"

I narrow my eyes at the use of the obnoxious nick-name. "I don't know, Ace, what's tickling your whiskers?"

He laughs lightly and picks up his menu, I do the same.

"I could *smash* a burg."

I lower my menu and peer over the top of it at him. "Did you just say *smash a burg?*"

"You bet I did."

I bite back a laugh.

I'd love a burger, but there's no way I'm going to order one, especially not in front of Pax. I skim past the list and look for the salads.

"The chicken salad sounds pretty good."

He hooks his finger over the top of my menu and

drags it downwards. "*Salad?*" He says the word like it's pure filth. You'd think I'd just said I was going to order a bowl of steaming shit.

"What's wrong with salad?"

"Nothing, if you're a rabbit."

I shake my head at him, unable to hide the smile on my face.

"Look, Lil, I don't want to be one of those guys who tells his girl what to do, but if you can't find a better order than a salad, we're going to have some serious problems."

His girl.

His. Girl.

The words echo through my head, weaving their way into my stupid, defenceless heart.

I don't know how this boy is doing it. He drives me *crazy*, he's loud, a touch obnoxious, he's rough, impulsive and reckless, and here I am, catching feelings for him like some kind of idiot.

"Seriously, at least order a sandwich and fries or something. And a thick shake. You can't come to a place like this and not get a shake."

"I'm lactose intolerant. No ice cream for me. I'm actually not allowed sugar either... meat is kind of a no go as well."

"*What?*" he demands. The look on his face is like I just told him I was into kicking puppies as an after-school hobby. Outright horrified.

I can't help it; I break out into laughter. "I'm kidding. *Relax.* I can eat dairy. You should see your face. And I'd inject sugar into my veins if it wasn't frowned upon."

That's why I can never lose the extra weight on my hips and ass. Too much sugar down my pie hole.

"Are you really a vegetarian?"

I just laugh.

"That's it. You're getting a burger. And fries. And a shake. That's the consequences of fucking with me."

"I can't eat all that," I argue.

"And that's where I earn my keep, brains. I'm like a vacuum cleaner for leftovers."

I start to tell him no, but he cuts me off. "Chicken or beef?"

"But I'm a plant eater, remember?"

He narrows his eyes at me. "You're not going to get me again tonight."

I hold a straight face for as long as I can before my smile escapes. "Okay fine. I lied."

"I *knew* you were talking shit. You seem like the kind of girl who'd really enjoy a piece of meat."

"Did you just make a penis joke?"

He laughs loudly. "I can't believe you just said 'penis' in a restaurant."

"You just said it too."

"Well played. I see I'm in the presence of greatness."

I tip my head to the side in a cutesy gesture.

"Now, chicken or beef, you savage carnivore?"

"Seriously, Pax, I don't think I should order a big meal."

He looks right into my eyes, and it's all I can do not to shiver under the weight of it. He sees right through me sometimes. I don't know how he does it.

He's oddly perceptive when it comes to me and food.

No one else has ever noticed that insecurity, and while he's never actually said anything to me about it, I swear to God, he can smell it on me or something.

"I want you to order *exactly* what you feel like eating, Lily, and I'm going to do the same, and then we're going to sit here together and eat it." He brushes his fingers over the back of mine.

There's so much he's not saying, but I'm feeling it regardless.

He's making me feel like it's okay to be me.

"Beef," I whisper without giving it another thought.

He holds my gaze, it's unrelenting, unwavering. I can't look away. I can't think about all those little things that don't matter. I don't care about my stomach or thighs when he's looking at me like that.

"That's my girl."

The waitress comes over then, and after a bit of back and forth, we get our orders sorted and she leaves us alone again.

"Can I ask you something? And it's definitely a stupid question, no doubt about it," he asks.

"Wouldn't be the first, I'm sure it won't be the last from you."

"That's insulting."

"Doesn't make it any less true," I say with a laugh.

He's fighting off a laugh and losing the battle.

"What's your question?"

"I wanted to know how it's going? Everything you're working on... obviously your assistant is doing an outstanding job, but truthfully, I'm a little concerned the lead scientist doesn't know what she's doing."

He's so cute. Always with the jokes, but I can tell he's genuinely curious about how it's going. He doesn't understand a word of it, but he's there for moral support nonetheless.

"It's going really well. I'm going to have to spend a lot of time writing up the essay, there's a lot of material and findings to cover, but I'm getting there."

"That's good." He nods.

"Couldn't have got this far without you," I tease. I think we both know I could have, but he *has* proved helpful in some respects... and a complete and utter distraction in everything else.

"You're welcome. Surely by now this project should have my name on it too?" He smirks.

"Sure, if you can tell me the title of my thesis, I'll add your name to the front," I quip.

He pauses for a few beats. "Touché."

He's got this laid-back smile plastered across his face that I love. It's fairly new, it's only made an appearance over the past few weeks since he's really relaxed around me. I think it's my favourite of all his smiles so far.

"That's what I thought." I laugh.

The waitress comes back over with two giant shakes. They look so good, but I don't know how the hell I'm actually going to eat everything. I hope he really was serious about being a vacuum cleaner.

"I'm just going to go to the bathroom." I excuse myself and get up from my chair.

I don't turn around to check, and maybe it's all in my head, but I swear I can feel his eyes on my ass the whole time I walk to the bathroom.

Wishful thinking.

I hold my breath as I push the door open.

I can't even walk into a bathroom without my heart rate spiking anymore, it's pathetic.

I always push the door open before I put my body right through the door now too. Gives me time to bail if I need to. I hate that I've let those girls make me as jumpy as a cat on a hot tin roof, but that's what's happened.

Another scar to bear.

Thankfully, this bathroom is completely empty, so I make quick work of it, and hurry to get back out to Pax.

I come around the corner, and my heart drops into my stomach when I see the cheerleading uniform and blonde hair at our table.

My step falters, and I debate rushing back into the bathroom, but it's too late, I see Pax's head stick out around the side of the girl's body, and he gives me an urgent look that makes me think he needs saving.

The girl notices him looking and turns to see what he's seeing. I breathe a sigh of relief when I realise it's not Liana.

It could be one of the other girls from the bathroom though. I didn't take my eyes off the ground long enough to look at every single one, and I'm glad about that. Having the fear of God put in me over one bitchy girl is enough; I don't need to be walking on eggshells around five of them.

She looks at me, a fake smile on her face, before turning back to Pax. He ignores her and waves me over.

I slowly make my way across the dining room, back to our table.

She leans over as I approach and says something to him, far too close to his ear.

I *hate* this.

I hate everything about it. I know she's just standing there talking, but she's beautiful, and she's a cheerleader. She'd look perfect with him, hanging off his arm. She'd look like she belonged.

Pax looks like he couldn't give two shits about whatever it is she's saying to him, which does make me feel at least a little better about it, but not enough to ease my concerns entirely.

"Whatever, Becky, go play with you friends," I hear him say as I approach the table.

She tries to talk to him again, but he doesn't even glance at her.

I look nervously between the two of them. I don't know whether to sit or stand.

I wish she'd just leave.

"This has been *thrilling*, but my date is back," he drawls to the girl – Becky, apparently.

Ouch.

I bet that hurt. He just dismissed her. *Hard.*

He smiles warmly at me, and nods at me to take my seat.

He doesn't even look at her again, so I don't either as I sit down. He just holds my gaze, amusement dancing in his eyes. I have to admit, I am finding this a little bit funny.

I eventually hear her huff out a breath and then she turns and disappears, a fruity, girly scent going with her.

"Fuck that girl is a pain in the ass." He grunts.

I wonder if they've slept together. I'm tempted to ask, but I've always been a big believer in not asking questions that you don't want to know the answers to, so I stay quiet.

"What did she want?"

He reaches across the table and plays with my hand. "I don't know. Something about a party. I don't know why she gave a shit about telling me though. I wouldn't call us friends. I appreciate the girls hyping up the crowd at games and stuff, but other than that, I don't want anything to do with the cheer hoes."

He's got that right. I'm sure some of them are really talented athletes, but more than half seem to only care about being in a competition to see who can manage to wear the shortest skirt and do the most rugby players.

I feel pretty average in my jeans and knit by comparison though, but I guess my underwear isn't hanging out for half the restaurant to see, so there's that.

I glance in the direction that she went and see there's a whole gang of 'cheer hoes'. I look away quickly. I've got no doubt Liana will be with them, and I do not want to get involved in that. I scan the rest of the room, and a waving hand catches my eye. It's Berlin.

"There's Berlin over there," I tell Pax.

He turns around and looks, then waves animatedly at his sister.

She's with Sophia and the other girls, and two guys. I know they're Cullen and Bryson, but I've never actually met them myself.

Cullen is watching Berlin; it's like he's totally unaware of everything going on in the room around him. All he can see is her.

Bryson looks like he's being subjected to a long and painful death.

I wave to Berlin and the girls and then turn back to Pax. "What's the deal with Bryson? He always looks like someone is turning a knife in his back."

Pax turns back to me and laughs. "You're not far off. He's not usually a ray of sunshine anyway, but ever since Sophia started hanging out with Tonksy, he's been extra sour."

"Is he into her?"

He makes a 'pffft' noise. "He's not simply *into her*, he's fucking obsessed. I think he's been quietly pining away for her for years. It's hard to tell because he hardly ever says shit."

"And she's dating his mate? Brutal."

"Yip. Can't blame her though. He didn't shoot his shot. Soph got sick of waiting. I think Ice might have had something to do with it all. From what I hear, the idea was to make Bry jealous, but Soph has been seeing Tonks a while now, so maybe she just likes him better."

"Sounds awkward."

"It's a circus. Monkeys on the loose everywhere. Teenage politics and dramatic bullshit."

"I don't think I'd have the energy. Or the time."

"I just couldn't be fucked," he adds in.

We smile at each other. It's nice to feel like we're on the same page.

"It's entertaining to watch though; I'll give it that." He snickers.

It does sound like it. It's like my treasured gossips columns, in real life.

"I think we had enough drama to last a lifetime with the whole Liana and Cullen debacle, though. No one needs another dramatic love triangle."

My stomach swirls uncomfortably at the mention of Liana.

"What happened with Liana?"

"Classic story. He wanted to get his dick wet, she wanted him to fall in love. Chaos ensued." He smirks like the reminder of it entertains him greatly. "I told him it was a bad idea, you know."

"I'm sure you did."

"She lost her shit when Berlin started at Westlake and Cullen took notice. There was some crap go down, Liana cut up Berlin's PE uniform and stuff."

"She *didn't?*"

I don't know why, but that makes me feel a bit better about her destroying my textbook. It's nice to know I'm not the only one she's got to.

"Oh, she did. But classic Ice, she put it on anyway and managed to get one up on queen bitch. It was pretty crack up actually."

I guess that's the difference between someone like me, and someone like Berlin. I sat on the floor in tears, where she got up and said *fuck that.*

She doesn't take anyone's shit.

"Anyway, much to Liana's disgust, she got the flick, Cullen and Berlin got together, and I guess the rest is history."

Our burgers arrive and Pax is basically drooling. I have to admit, this looks *so* much better than a salad.

I still don't think a girl with an ass the size of mine

should be eating a burger on a first date with a boy who looks like he does, but I can at least pick at it for a while.

"Yeah, so basically Bry loves Soph, Soph is dating Tonks, Tonks is an idiot, Berlin and Cullen are in love, Liana hates Berlin and anyone associated with her, she acts like she hates Cullen too, but she'd definitely put his knob in her mouth again if she was given the chance."

I almost spit out the mouthful of food I just bit.

He laughs as though he got the reaction he was hoping for.

"Oh my god, you can't be talking about knobs when I've got a mouthful."

"Oh, you'd have a mouthful alright."

Shit.

Oh, dear *god*, the insinuation alone is turning me on. I don't think I've ever really pictured myself doing anything like that with a guy, but it's pretty hard not to visualise it with him.

He's got this wicked grin on his face as he watches me blush. He knows exactly what he's doing to me.

"That's some serious confidence, I hope I don't wind up disappointed," I surprise myself by saying.

He looks surprised too. He freezes for a second, his burger midway to his mouth before he erupts into laughter. "I like you, Lily-boo."

"Of course you do. I'm spectacular."

"I see my confidence is rubbing off on you."

"You had to earn your keep sometime, right?"

He just grins, clearly loving the banter. I still feel flushed from the thought of having his dick in my mouth.

I try to think about something else, *anything* else, but it's a struggle with him sitting across from me, looking like that.

He's gorgeous. The definition of tall, dark and handsome.

We settle into an easy rhythm, eating and talking, and I surprise myself by not worrying about every mouthful of food I take.

I was right about not being able to eat it all though, and he was right about cleaning up the leftovers. I don't know where he puts it all. I'd be willing to bet he's nothing but ripped muscle under that t-shirt. I can't imagine he's got a jiggly stomach like I do.

"Oh man, I think I'm going to explode." He groans, leaning back in his chair with his arms above his head. His shirt rises up, exposing a slither of his olive skin.

I nod my head. "That was *so* yum."

"A salad," he mutters, shaking his head in disbelief at my first suggestion of order.

"Oh, you just shush," I say with a roll of my eyes.

He glances over his shoulder again, and then sits up ramrod straight in his seat before quickly turning back and angling his face even further around.

His eyes are wide like he's seen a ghost.

"What's wrong?"

He looks panicked.

I look over to where he was looking, and Berlin and that crew are all still there, the cheerleaders are gone, and there's a family at the counter. It looks like they're paying for their bill. I have no idea what could have made him react the way he just has.

"Nothing," he mutters.

"It doesn't look like nothing to me."

He peers back around behind him and seems to relax a little. I look again, the family is heading for the door, and I'm half expecting to see a zombie or something behind them, but when they move, there's nothing.

"Pax, what's going on?" I reach for his hand, and he lets me, but only gives it a quick squeeze before letting go and getting to his feet.

"Nothing, sorry, I thought I saw someone I want to avoid, but it was nothing. Shall we go?"

I'm so confused, but I get to my feet and grab my jacket off the back of my seat. I don't know what the hell is going on, and it doesn't sound like I'm going to find out either. He's freezing me out.

He presses his hand to the small of my back, leads me to the counter and pays for our food. I'm too baffled by the strange turn of events to protest too much about him paying my share.

He starts leading me towards the door, and I realise he's trying to escape without even talking to his friends.

I don't know why, but that makes me feel like I want to cry. I feel embarrassed, even though, as far as I'm aware, I've done nothing wrong.

His sudden mood switch and the need to escape has me reeling.

"Pax!" Cullen calls out to him.

I hear Pax exhale heavily and my eyes actually do prick with tears. It's pretty obvious to me that he's trying to keep me and his closest friends separate.

"Yo!" Pax replies. We slowly walk closer to their table, but not too close. He's still vying for a quick escape.

The girls are all smiling at me, Cullen looks indifferent, and Bryson looks like he'd rather get hit by a car than sit here a moment longer.

"Can you tell Mum I'll stay at Berlin's tonight?"

"Yeah, sweet as."

"Good date?" Berlin waggles her brows at me.

I don't know what to say to that. It was a great date until a few minutes ago. Now I don't know what to think.

"What are you guys doing Friday night?" she pushes on, either oblivious to the weird vibe, or ignoring it.

I shrug. I can't even register what night it is tonight. I just feel panicked. I want to go home.

"You should come to the party," Berlin tells me.

Pax answers before I can. "Lily isn't really the party type."

He's right, I'm not, but there's something about how quickly he declined on my behalf that I don't like.

"Why don't we let Lily decide that for herself," Berlin fires back at him, full of attitude.

She looks at me expectantly.

"Ah, he's right. I'm not much of a party girl," I mutter.

Berlin looks between the two of us in confusion, and then tries to catch Pax's eye, but he ignores her.

"We've got to go," he mumbles.

Pax ushers me out of the restaurant, yelling to his friends over his shoulder about seeing them at school tomorrow. It's like he can't get us out of there fast enough.

He didn't even introduce me to his two best friends.

I don't know what's changed in the past fifteen minutes, but it's not a change I'm feeling good about.

I NEED TO GET A GRIP. I'm over here getting all teary because the guy I like didn't want me to come to a party with him and his friends, and because the vibes were off when we walked out of a restaurant. He kissed me goodbye when he dropped me home, but something was different. It was like the life had been drained out of him. It's hard not to think that it's something to do with me.

I'm becoming pathetic and vulnerable, and I hate it. It's really not what I envisioned being the main problem on my mind at this point in the year.

I quite literally have my whole entire future pinned on my scholarship work, and right now, I'm not sure I could even tell you what the subject matter is.

I'm a joke. Just not a funny one.

The stupidest part is that I don't even want to go to the party. If he had asked me to go, I probably would have said no. Parties really aren't my thing, but now that I know he doesn't want me there, for whatever reason, I really want to be there.

I think I'm more disappointed in myself than anything. Especially after all the time we've spent together. I let myself believe he was different. I thought he saw me for me, and that it wouldn't matter what his friends thought.

I guess I was wrong. I'm still the chubby nerd, and he's still the ripped rugby player.

Why would he want me to come to the party with him? That's not my scene. I've barely touched a drink in my life. I've been eighteen for two months now and I haven't set foot inside a bar.

I should just stay in my lane, in my lab, and mind my business.

I sigh as I put away the last of the equipment I used.

Pax is at rugby training tonight, so it's just me in the lab. He sent me a good morning message today and a couple of funny memes, but that's it. Something is up. I can tell.

I hear voices in the corridor, and I pause to listen.

Usually everyone is long gone by now, but it sounds like a couple of girls talking.

I hear a light tap on the door of the main classroom and then a, "heeellllllloooo."

"Hello?" I call back, warily. I'm not expecting Keke yet, and she never knocks.

"Lily! It's Berlin."

I exhale in relief.

"And Sophia!" the other voice calls.

"I'm back here!"

They start talking between themselves in fast, urgent tones.

"I know, right? I can't believe that bitch, she needs to stick one of those horrendous fake nails up her nose and reset her brain."

Sophia looks horrified at Berlin's comment.

I don't see how the two of them are related at all. Physically, they couldn't be more different, tall and short, dark-haired and light, olive-skinned and pale. The only thing they seem to share is those dark Davids' eyes.

"That makes me *very* uncomfortable." Sophia grimaces.

"Good. That was the intention."

"Who needs their brain resetting?" I ask.

"Liana," Sophia provides.

That gets my attention. That girl's name alone is enough to keep me awake at night.

She'll probably be at that party. Liana's the kind of girl I'd expect to see hanging out with a guy like Pax.

She's beautiful, thin, blonde and has money. She's also a bitch, but still. She's everything I'm not.

Berlin gets a grossed-out look on her face. "That stupid bitch who gave you trouble in the bathroom. I heard her asking around about who you were. She must have seen you at the diner last night."

It's cute that she thinks I need an explanation of who Liana is, but this information is probably the last thing I want to hear right now. I can physically feel the colour draining from my face.

I don't want to be talked about. I'm happy being completely off the radar.

"Chill. It's fine. We've got her handled," Berlin reassures me. "Shit, you look pale, don't go passing out or anything. I don't know first aid."

"Why would she want to know who I am?"

"Because she's a feral bitch who hates anything that she's not in control of," Sophia offers.

"That doesn't really answer my question," I whisper.

"It doesn't even matter. It's not like it's hard to find out anyone's name in this tiny town. It's fine. *Relax.* She's not going to do shit to you again." Berlin flips her long hair over her shoulder as she talks.

I wish I had that confidence.

Berlin is made of some tough shit. I'm more squishy and soft – there's not much tough about me.

"She's not going to do anything crazy again. She'll work sneaky shit next time," Sophia says.

I'm not sure if that was meant to be reassuring or what, but I'm *not* reassured. Not in the slightest.

Sophia must read that on my face because she starts trying to back track, but Berlin cuts her off.

"Oh my god *stop*. She's a blonde little devil; it's not the end of the world."

"She drugged us, and destroyed your artwork, and your PE uniform, and God only knows what else," Sophia argues.

Clearly these two girls have different ideas of what is and isn't a big deal.

"*Drugged* you?" I gasp.

"Oh man, we have so much to catch you up on." Berlin sighs.

"Let's start with how we're fucking with her." Sophia claps her hands together excitedly.

"Which thing?" Berlin asks.

"The Instagram page," Sophia clarifies; she's clearly enjoying whatever this is.

I don't know how I feel about them skimming over drugging and destruction of property, but I'm well out of my depth here. I'm just along for the ride. No doubt this story will loop around at some point.

Chaos tends to go around in circles.

Berlin snorts and turns back to me. "So, I'm completely going to hell, *but...* I made this fake Instagram page for this guy I used to go to school with, added a bunch of his pics and stuff, and I've been talking to her, as him, for like, *months.*"

"Oh my god."

I think I'm actually scared of Berlin. She seems like the kind of girl who deserves a healthy amount of fear.

"I know," Berlin replies, crossing her legs on the stool she's parked herself on. "I never intended to make it go on this long, but she keeps admitting to all this horrible shit she's doing to other people, and she even sends me photos for evidence. It's wild. I'm screenshotting it all and keeping it so when I take her down, she goes all the way to hell where she belongs."

"What are you going to do to her?" I ask, bewildered by the shit going down in this school that I had no idea about.

Berlin flips her hair again. "I haven't quite decided yet, but it's gonna be big. She's tried to ruin me since I set foot in this town, she's messed with Cullen, Pax, *you.*" She points at me. "I'm not going to just let that slide."

"I don't know how you find the time to be an evil genius," I tell her.

"Not all of us hide out in a science lab every second of our spare time," she teases.

Touché.

"Speaking of, got anything I could slip in her drink to give her the runs or something?"

I laugh. "Everything in here is slightly more toxic, but

I'm pretty sure an over-the-counter laxative would do the trick."

"Not just a pretty face, are ya?"

They carry on telling me everything I could want to know – and even shit I absolutely do *not* want to know, about Liana, her minions and the chaos that has been swirling since Berlin arrived at Westlake.

We talk about all of it, and I even get in to it, throwing in some suggestions here and there.

I don't know Berlin well, but she seems fairly intuitive, and I'm thankful she seems to understand that I don't want to talk about Pax. She doesn't bring him up once. We don't speak about his odd behaviour, or his rejection of the idea of me joining them tomorrow night. We just act like it never happened.

As crazy as this all is, it's nice to feel like a 'normal' teenage girl, hanging out with my girlfriends and gossiping.

I love Keeks, she's my best friend, but she doesn't give two shits about any of this, and while it's not something I'd want to do every day, sometimes it's nice to feel like everyone else.

SEVENTEEN

Pax

"Bro, we gotta go!"

"Yeah, I'm coming."

I chug down the rest of the beer I opened earlier and shove my phone into my pocket. I've been staring at my messages to Lily for about half an hour, but I've been too chicken shit to send another one.

I want to come clean and tell her everything, but I can't. She'll think I'm a total loser if I do. It's bad enough she knows I got into trouble for fighting at school, but that's not even the half of it.

It gets so much worse.

I thought I was done for when the bottle store owner was in the diner last night with his family. I was sure he was going to look across and see me, then start yelling that

I was the one he was looking for. The one who trashed his counter and fled the scene.

I swear to God, my heart has never beat so fast in my life.

Lily was right there, all sweet and perfect, and I was on the other side of the table, a complete and utter fucking disgrace.

It was a serious reality check.

She doesn't deserve to have to deal with me and my shit. She's kind, and innocent and trustworthy, and if she knew everything I'd fucked up, she'd probably never want to talk to me again.

"*Pax!*" Cullen yells again.

Fuck's sake.

A party is the absolute last fucking place I feel like going, but it's not like the boys are going to let me stay behind.

I need something to take my mind off everything anyway. I can't keep sitting here in these four walls, sulking because the girl I've fallen in love with is too good for me.

I've got to get out of here. I grab my shit and follow along with the boys, barely contributing to any bullshit chat as we go.

We arrive at the house, and it's exactly what I was expecting. Classic high school house party.

I don't know if it's my messed-up head or what, but this doesn't excite me anymore. It's the same party I've been to a hundred times. Same people, same crowds, same bullshit.

Hanging out with Lily has made me crave substance.

I love my mates, I really do, but I'd rather have stayed home with them, and had a few quiet beers than come here and talk to a fuck load of people I couldn't give two shits about.

I follow the boys through the packed living room and into the kitchen in search of a beer.

If I'm going to have to endure this thing for the next few hours, then I'm at least going to get myself a little tipsy.

I watch a couple of games of four kings, and talk to a few people, and before I know it – a little tipsy is replaced with drunk as fuck.

I didn't really pay much attention at the time, but now that I think about how much I've had to drink, it's obvious that every twenty minutes or so, one of the cheer squad popped up and passed me another beer.

It's pretty obvious now that I've arrived at shit-facedville, that they're trying to get me plastered, but I'm too drunk to care why.

Drunk me doesn't care about much. Lily is still front and centre in my mind, but even she's a little blurry and soft around the edges now. She's numbed. It's actually fucking nice. Everything was starting to feel all sharp and pointy again. I was starting to feel like I was losing control.

I get up off the stool I've been sitting on for the past hour. It's a fucking mistake.

I'm not just drunk, I'm *hammered*.

I eye up the couch across the room and make my way towards it. A few guys from the team are over there. I might be able to hide out for the rest of the night with a bit of fucking luck.

They start talking to me as I approach, but I'm too fucked to say anything more than a few muttered words back.

I just sit my ass down and shut my eyes.

I don't know if I fall asleep for a while or what, but when I snap back, a few of the girls have joined the group. Eve is sitting right next to me, talking to someone across the circle.

I don't know why she's sitting so close to me, or why her leg is touching mine, but she smiles at me when she sees I'm conscious again.

"Ah, he lives."

I grunt out a reply, but it's not even words. Fuck, I'm a mess. I need to snap out of it.

"We were starting to get worried you might have been out for the count."

She's batting her lashes at me and all that kind of shit. I know how she works; we've hooked up enough times for me to realise she's keen. I'd have to be run over by a truck to not be able to pick up what she's putting down.

Eve's a beautiful girl. A little nutty, but beautiful. She's nice enough, but she's one of Liana's pawns, and that fact alone is enough to make her unattractive to me. There was a time when she did it for me, but that time has long passed.

She puts her hand on my chest. "Are you having a good night?"

I'm having a fucking shit night, but I doubt that's the

answer she's looking for, because we both know she doesn't actually care.

I close my eyes again for a few minutes.

"Here, Pax. We're all doing one."

I open my eyes and she's handing me a shot of something brown. She's got another one in her hand, presumably for her.

I might not be the sharpest tool in the shed, but I can sense this isn't the best idea, but like the dipshit I am, I take it from her anyway.

Fuck it, may as well do a thorough job of drowning my sorrows. It could be worse, I could be sucking on a bong or popping pills.

A hangover I can handle. I'll just sleep it off and worry about my problems when the room stops spinning.

"Cheers," she coos, clinking her shot glass against mine. I toss it back. It slides down my throat with a burn.

I feel the warmth of it spreading to my arms and legs. It feels good.

I can kind of feel her right next to me, but I'm not really with it.

"Pax!" someone yells, and I sit up suddenly.

"Woah, look out." Eve's now right in front of me somehow, and I reach for her. I nearly knocked the silly bitch backwards.

"Sorry," I mutter.

Shit I'm smashed.

I look around for who said my name, but no one's there looking for me.

I fall back against the couch, my arms going limp at my side.

Eve leans in, whispering something in my ear, but it's lost on me. I can't hear shit. She's just an annoying buzzing noise at my ear like a fly locked in a room.

"Oh, absolutely fucking *not*."

Ah shit. I hear *that*. I know *that* voice. I also know I can't ignore that voice. I feel more sober already.

"Get your grubby little hoe mitts off him."

Hoe mitts? I look down and sure enough, Eve's hands are all over me, not just her hands in fact, half her body is on me.

Fuck. What the fuck?

"What's it got to do with you, Berlin? Can't you just mind your own business for once."

"He's my brother, *sweetie*, that makes him my business. Now go play on the road, the grown-ups need to talk."

I'd laugh if I wasn't so wasted. Ice is on form, as per.

Eve huffs but does what she's told, scrapes herself off me and gets to her feet. I feel the couch move next to me, but I don't even bother looking.

"And tell your little queen bitch to go fuck herself. And to have some creativity, for the love of God. It's pathetic."

I don't know what the fuck that last bit was about, but I'm too drunk to care.

I sigh.

"You know what? You're a real loser, Pax."

"Slipper... Cinderella fits," I mumble. That's not what I meant, but the words won't go together the way I want them to.

"Eve? *Seriously?* That's just great, dickhead."

I feel like I should know what she's so pissed off about.

"What are we going to do with this tosser?"

"What's your *problem?*" I slur.

"That's it, pick him up," I hear Berlin instruct. Fuck. That's the *I'm done with your shit* tone I've come to know so well. "Get him out of here."

Someone pulls me to my feet and basically drags me across the room.

I don't know where we're going, but I know it's not going to be good.

BERLIN SHOVES me in the chest so hard that I fall backwards into the armchair.

Fucking convenient that was there or I'd be on my ass.

I look around and try to remember where the hell I am. I don't know whose room this is, but it's not mine. That sucks. I'm tired. I'd be pretty keen on my bed right about now.

Bryson is watching from the doorway. I think the prick is enjoying himself. He's the one who dragged me away and now apparently his work is done. I think I might have blacked out. I don't remember the trip in here. I don't even know if we're still at the party.

"I'll leave you to it. I think you've got things handled here," he says to Ice before he shuts the door behind him.

Good. At least I won't have an audience for the absolute ripping I know I'm about to get. I flip him off, but by the time I get my hand raised, he's already gone.

"What in the ever-loving *fuck* are you doing?" she demands.

"Having *fun*. You should try it some time." My eyes half close.

She flips me off. "Maybe I *would* be able to enjoy myself every now and then if I wasn't constantly running around trying to stop my dipshit brother from ruining everything good in his life."

I flip her off in response.

"And newsflash, getting written off and acting like a drop kick, *isn't* my idea of fun anyway. You look like an asshole."

I am an asshole, so I guess that's fitting.

"Just when I thought you were finally back on track, that you were *finally* sorting your life out... then I see some silly cheerleader bitch draped over you, when you should be hanging out with Lily."

Fuck. Lily.

Just the mention of Lily's name sobers me up. It's like I haven't touched a drink all night.

"Nothing happened," I snap.

"Yeah, and you're fucking lucky it didn't because you will break that girl's heart, Pax. She's not built for bullshit. She needs something real with someone who will take care of her. If you can't be that guy, then you need to let her down easy and stay the fuck away."

"You think I don't know that? The last thing I want to do is hurt her."

"Then what the fuck is all *this*? Why didn't you invite her to come? Why isn't she here? Why are you acting like such a colossal douche?"

She rapid fires the questions at me. I might feel a hell of a lot less drunk, but my brain is still on the go slow and I can't find answers for any of them.

"Are you *embarrassed*, Pax? Is that what this is about?"

I open my mouth to tell her *no*, but nothing comes out. I falter. She's right. I *am* embarrassed. If I'm being one hundred percent honest, I don't want Lily here, because I'm embarrassed as hell.

"Oh my god," Berlin whispers, horrified. "You are, aren't you? You're embarrassed of Lily. You don't want all your 'super cool' friends knowing you're dating a chick who actually has a brain."

Jesus Christ.

"I'm not embarrassed of Lily," I snap at her.

"Seriously? Sure seems that way. That's what you're trying to hide, isn't it? That you're hanging out with a smart girl? And you're embarrassed for her to meet your halfwit friends?" she carries on, ignoring my objections and the rising rage inside me.

She's looking at me with disgust.

She's fucking wrong though. She couldn't be *more* wrong.

My brain clicks into gear and finally co-operates with my mouth.

"I don't want her here with everyone because I'm embarrassed of *me!*" I yell at her, getting to my feet. "Fuck's sake, Ice, I'm not embarrassed of *her*, she's *incredible*. She's smart, funny, beautiful, she's good all the way through, and I'm terrified that if she finds out what I'm really like, she'll run a mile. That girl makes me *feel* again, and I don't know if I can lose that. I love her, and I *need* her." My chest is heaving, I don't feel like I can get enough air.

Her expression softens in understanding.

We just stare at each other for a long while.

"She can't be all that smart if she's falling for a big dummy like you," she finally says.

I sigh heavily and fall back into my chair, letting my eyes close again. "I'm fucking it all up."

She sits down in the chair next to me. "You sure are."

"That's not very encouraging."

"I'm not going to lie to you to make you feel better. It's like you don't even know me at all."

I groan and hold my face in my hands.

She scoots over so she's sitting closer to me and wraps an arm around my shoulders.

"Here's a thought, Pax... Maybe don't act like an idiot. Don't be the guy we all saw tonight. Be the guy she deserves instead."

It sounds so simple when she says it like that. Unfortunately for me, making good choices seems to be where I'm screwing up most lately, but I can do better – *be* better, for Lily.

I can at least try. I have to. I can't lose her, not without a fight – even if the only thing I'm fighting is myself.

EIGHTEEN

Pax

It hurts to open my eyes. Actually, it hurts to even have eyes.

I don't think I've ever been particularly aware of the roof of my mouth before, but right now it feels like it's made of sandpaper that someone set fire to and then put out with a bucket of chicken shit.

I haven't been this hungover in a long time. I'd hate to know how it smells in this room.

My door swings open wildly, slamming into the wall.

Fuck, my head.

"You're an asshole," Cullen grunts.

"Tell me something I don't know," I mumble.

"Get out of bed. Going for a run is your punishment."

I almost throw up just thinking about running. He

can't be fucking serious. But he's out my door again, and I can hear his fucking running shoes on the floorboards.

I think that motherfucker is serious, and that does not bode well for me.

"What's it to you anyway?" I yell after him, making my head pound and my throat scream in protest.

Jesus. I regret doing that.

"Fucked if I know, I don't give a shit about your love life. But it's got Berlin all wild, and if it's important to her then it's important to me, and that makes *you* an *asshole,*" he calls from down the hallway.

Fair enough. I can't argue with that logic. Happy wife, happy life.

I already know I'm an asshole, everyone's individual reasons about why I'm an asshole are irrelevant when it comes down to it.

I half open one eye, and it feels like someone is sticking pins into it.

This has got to be the worst I've ever felt after a few too many beers.

I don't know who I think I'm fooling, it was way more than a few too many. It was about a dozen too many. I'm going to have the hangover from hell.

At this point I'm probably made of ninety percent beer. I'm probably still half-drunk too.

I reach around blindly, knocking shit over until I come up with my phone.

I feel like I'm going to spew from the exertion of that. Cull is fucking dreaming if he thinks I'm going for a run.

I'd rather not die today, and I have no doubt that if I actually attempted it, it'd probably kill me.

I manage to keep my eyes open long enough to see that I've only got six percent battery. *Lovely.*

I've also got a message from Berlin on Instagram. I tap on it and see that she's sent me Liana's story.

This doesn't seem like a good sign.

I tap on the story and a photo from the party shows up. A photo that has me in it.

Me, with Eve basically in my lap.

Posted fourteen hours ago.

Fuck.

Fourteen hours is a lot of hours.

Everyone in the school will have seen that by now.

I hope like hell that Lily is the exception.

I doubt my luck is that good. It never is, but if there's anyone who's going to be out of the social media loop, it's Lily.

Berlin is bound to know the verdict on that, but I'm too scared to ring her and find out. I feel like I'm spiralling again, but this time it's not just me I'm taking down, it's Lily too, and out of everyone in my life, she's the one who deserves it the least.

Fuck it. I have to know.

I could call directly – that would be the grown-up thing to do, but I'm terrified. I wouldn't know what to say.

Instead, I'm going to act like the pussy I am, and text my sister.

Pax: Has she seen it?

Berlin: She's a smart girl, what do you think?

My mouth feels like it has way too much saliva in it.

She is a smart girl, and she knows something is up with me. I'm sure she's already gone looking for evidence to confirm her fears. That's what she does – she researches things. And by the looks of this, she'll have found it.

Liana is public. Lily is suspicious. That's not a good mix.

I'm such a dumb prick. All I had to do was talk to her, and now I've probably done too much damage for her to even listen to me, let alone understand and forgive me.

Play stupid games, win stupid prizes.

There's no way I can ask Liana to take this down. She'd probably post it again every day for a week, just to spite me. The best I can do is own my fuck ups and beg for forgiveness.

Pax: Fuck.

I don't know what else to say.

Berlin: Yip.

I don't know what to do.

It's fucked.

I'm fucked.

If I've ruined this – if I've stuffed up one of the best things in my life, I'm never going to forgive myself.

NINETEEN ·

Lily

Well, this must be what heartbreak feels like.

My chest feels like it's been ripped wide open, and a woodpecker is tapping away at my heart, destroying it piece by piece.

I look at the picture for the hundredth time. Pax, sitting back on a couch with Eve – one of the cheerleaders, draped around him, basically on top of him. He's not looking directly at the camera, but you can see his face. He doesn't exactly look like he's having a good time, but they're *together* – it couldn't be more obvious.

I want to screenshot the image, to torture myself further, but I don't know anything about Instagram, and I don't want Liana getting some type of notification that I've done that. The last thing I need is her knowing I've been snooping on her profile. That'd only embarrass me further.

I knew social media was only going to cause me a fucking headache and this just proves it. To be fair, it's not exactly social media that has hurt me – it's Pax, but still.

All these stupid, skanky girls and their public profiles and their tempting stories. Damn them all.

I should have known better. I shouldn't have gone looking, but I couldn't stop myself, and once I started, it was a deep, dark rabbit hole.

In a way, I'm glad I did. I'd rather be an idiot who knows about it than an idiot who doesn't. I'd hate to think that everyone in the school knew something about me and I didn't have a clue what was going on. Now *that* would be embarrassing.

Keke stayed over last night, and I'm so grateful she's here. She's still asleep, but there's going to be a serious counselling role for her when she wakes up. My hands are shaking.

Nothing good comes of waking up at five in the morning. It's seven now and all I've done for two hours is torture myself.

Pax posted one picture to his story last night, of him, Cullen and Bryson at the party. Just the three of them, but I could see all the cheerleaders all in the background. That's what started the early morning search.

I haven't heard a word from him for about twelve hours. It's unnerving. I half expected to wake up to a drunk voicemail, or at least a message, but there was nothing. Radio silence.

My mind is running wild, wondering if he's in bed

with her. Are they waking up together? Did they have sex? God, I really hope none of that is true.

Keke makes a loud snoring noise, and I look at her hopefully, but she just rolls over and goes back to sleep.

Shit.

I don't know what to do. I can't just lie here, looking at this picture over and over. I'm going to lose my mind. I think about blocking Liana and all her friends, but I don't even know how to do that, or if they'll be able to see that I did.

I should just delete the whole app and be done with it. That'd be the smart thing to do.

My finger hovers over the icon, but I can't do it. I don't think I'm quite finished punishing myself just yet.

My phone vibrates in my hand, and I get such a fright, I drop it onto the floor next to my bed.

I scramble to pick it back up, and I hate the way that my head goes straight to Pax, hoping it's him, even though he's hurt me so much.

I swipe the screen and see it's not Pax, it's Berlin. I'm both sad and happy at the same time. as much as I want to hear from him, I'm scared about what he'd say. I wouldn't know what to do if he just carried on like nothing was wrong – or worse yet, confessed to things that I'd never be able to scrub from my memory.

Berlin: Are you okay?

There's no doubt about what she's referring to.

Loaded question. I don't really know what to say, so I decide to answer her question with a question.

Lily: How'd you know I saw it?

Berlin: Because I'm a female and I know how we operate when we're hurt. I would have gone looking too.

Lily: I don't think I am okay.

Berlin: Fair enough. For what it's worth, I ripped him a new one.

Lily: Thanks. I think.

Berlin: He really isn't all bad.

Lily: I know he's not.

Berlin: I'm not saying you should forgive him, but shit on social media isn't always what it seems, and Liana is the master at manipulation. Just keep that in mind.

I don't doubt that, but it's not like she posted that picture there exclusively for my benefit, she just happened to capture the moment that would destroy me and share it with the world.

Such fun.

Lily: I know he's your brother, but I really don't think he cares about me forgiving him. He's made it pretty clear that he's not interested.

Berlin: Just talk to him when he comes knocking, okay?

I know she probably wants to think the best of her brother, and for whatever reason, she seems to like the idea of him and I together, which is flattering, but at this point, a pipe dream.

If Pax wanted to be with me, he'd have taken me to

that party with him. He'd have had *me* draped all over him, not Eve. He wouldn't have put himself in a position where any of this could happen.

I know we haven't had the talk about being an official couple, but I don't care. He called me his, and if we're not on the same page about what that means, then I don't want anything to do with him anyway. I'm not out here hooking up with anyone else. Not that they're exactly lining up, but even if they were, that's not what I'm about.

I expect the same from someone I let in. He knew that. We've spent countless hours together. We've talked about everything and anything. He knows me. I know him.

At least I thought I did.

His name flashes across my screen and my heart goes into overdrive.

There's this thick lump in the back of my throat, making it hard to breathe. I can't make myself move. I just sit there, staring at his name as it rings through.

The screen goes black, and I suck in a deep breath. I've never had a panic attack before, but I can imagine how scary one must be right now.

A notification pops up after about thirty seconds. He's left me a voicemail.

There's no way I've got the balls to check that.

Another minute later a message arrives. I swipe it off my screen before I'm tempted to try and read it.

Thirty seconds after that, he calls again.

That's how the next hour and a half goes. He calls, again and again. Every time I feel like my chest gets tighter. The messages pour in, one after the other, but I can't bring myself to look at a single one.

"Why do you look like you're about to cry?" Keke's groggy voice gives me a fright.

I clutch my chest as I look at her, one eye open, hair at every angle and a grimace on her face.

That's all it takes for the water works to start.

"Oh shit," she mutters as she tries to get up off her bed on the floor. She's still half asleep so it's not particularly graceful.

"What happened?"

I answer by crying more. Super helpful.

"Bitchy girls?"

I shake my head. Sure, they're involved here, but they're not what's hurt me. He is.

"What'd that soccer dude do?"

"Rugby," I choke out between tears.

I don't even bother to ask her how she knew Pax was involved. I've never cried over anything much, certainly not in front of other people, it's bound to be about a boy.

"Rugby, whatever. Same shit, different-shaped ball."

Even mid break down I can find amusement in Keke's ignorance.

"What'd he do?"

I can't even speak with how upset I am, it's pretty embarrassing really, but I'm in too deep now, I just have to roll with it until I'm all cried out.

Keke half crawls, half stumbles across the millions of blankets on her makeshift bed and wraps her arms around my waist.

She's so patient, bless her.

I finally run dry and compose myself long enough to pick up my phone and find the photo to show her.

"That *motherfucker*. Who's the slut?"

I normally wouldn't condone calling a girl a slut, but in this case, it's fact, and you can't argue with facts.

"Eve. She's a cheerleader."

Keke is sitting next to me on the bed now, and she's moved on from the original offending picture and is snooping all over Liana's profile.

"Make sure you don't push anything you shouldn't."

"This isn't my first rodeo," she replies with a smirk. "I'm a master stalker."

I don't even have the energy to ask who she'd deem worthy of stalking. The girl is a mystery.

"Paints a pretty picture, huh?" she says as she looks at a photo of Liana and two other girls. They're all dressed up and the picture is perfectly posed and edited. "I bet their parents are so proud."

Her whole profile reeks of entitlement. I should know, I've been through it about one hundred times already.

I've been all up in this girl's business.

"Have you talked to him?"

I shake my head. "He keeps calling and texting, but I haven't even looked at the messages and I've been letting the calls go to voicemail."

"Good. Let him suffer."

I think the only person suffering is me, but that's beside the point.

"Speak of the devil," she mutters, holding my phone so the screen is facing me.

He's calling again.

I groan and cover my face with my hands. "Turn it off. I can't take it anymore."

I'm going to have a heart attack if I have to sit here and watch these calls and messages come in all day.

She doesn't waste any time, and powers my phone down. I feel like I can at least kind of think straight again with it turned off. At this rate I may never turn it back on ever again.

"C'mon." She slaps her hands down on my mattress and pushes herself up to her feet. "No more being a sad sack. Let's go make him into a voo-doo doll."

Her answer to everything.

I huff out a laugh. I knew I could rely on Keke to cheer me up.

TWENTY

Pax

She must have turned her phone off. It won't even ring through anymore.

I can't say I blame her. I've called about five hundred and seventeen times already and every single one has gone straight to voicemail.

I've sent her almost as many messages, telling her that I'm sorry and I want to explain, but she hasn't even opened them.

It's pretty fucking clear she doesn't want to talk to me.

I'm going crazy over here and it's exactly what I deserve.

I need to see her, but I can't fucking drive over there. Cull took my keys off me and I'm actually quite glad he did – I'm pretty sure I'm still half cut.

Last thing I need is a drunk driving charge to go along

with all my other indiscretions, and I don't need to make an even bigger tit of myself by saying something stupid to Lily.

There's enough stupid in the air already without me adding more to it.

I need a shower and a strong coffee. I also need a massive kick up the ass, but what else is new.

"Still no answer?" Cull asks before chugging back half of a hydration drink in one go.

He did force me to go for a run with him, but I only made it two houses down before I hurled in Mrs. Conners rose garden, so he left me half dying on the grass and went on his own.

He's really got his shit together lately. His grades are good, he's looking fit as fuck and he's staying out of trouble. Hanging out with Ice has done wonders for the guy.

It really highlights what a fuck stain I've turned into though, which is a shame for me, although totally self-inflicted.

I'm so disappointed in myself. I was back on track. I've been *killing* it at training lately. I'm back into my gym and running routine, and I'm drawing again. I might still be barely passing maths and English, but a pass is a pass. Lily has been a good influence on me too, and now I've only gone and shat all over that.

I'm such a fucking winner.

"Not a fucking word from her." I grunt.

It's not like I expected her to hear me out. Lily isn't like most girls. She's not the type to yell and scream and make a scene. She doesn't thrive on drama and bullshit. She isn't going to put up with my crap just because I'm in the first fifteen. She doesn't give two shits about how well I play rugby – not if I can't treat her right while I do it.

She's not toxic, she's not crazy, she's not stupid – and there's no way she's going to let my behaviour turn her into any of those things.

"Suppose you asked for it," he replies. "You deserve to be ignored."

"Yip, I'd say I've thoroughly fucked that up."

He bites into an apple and looks at me as he chews.

I know I look like death. It's a real fucking sorry state of affairs around here.

"You really like this girl, huh?"

"And the rest." I groan.

The bastard laughs at me. "*Shit*. Didn't know you were out here falling in love."

"Bit fucking rich coming from you."

He grins at me. "Never said there was anything wrong with it, princess. Don't go getting all defensive."

"What the fuck am I meant to do, man? You got Berlin to forgive you for all that shit Liana caused. Tell me your tricks."

"Magic dick," he says around another mouthful of apple.

Well played. That gets a laugh out of me.

"Anything serious to add?"

He gestures to his crotch, smirking.

"We've lived together our whole lives, bro, I've seen it. It's not that magical."

"Write her a letter," he suggests. "Worked for me."

"I suck with words."

"Yeah, you're right. You'd fuck it up."

I flip him off.

He's right, but he's still a prick for pointing it out.

He's got me thinking though. There's one thing I'm good at with a sheet of paper and a pencil, and maybe it just might be the answer to a couple of my problems.

I'm way too hungover to even think about starting right now, but tomorrow, when I've got a clear head and a steady hand, that's when I'll start.

"Will you drive me over there?" I ask him.

"If you're too much of a sack of shit to even drive yourself there, do you really think it's the best call to go? Seems like a dumb-ass move to me."

Fuck.

He's right, but it still kills me that I'm not doing anything. Feels like the clock is ticking and I'm sitting here watching the hands move.

"Take a shower, get some sleep, and tomorrow you might be up for some grovelling."

He's right again.

"When the fuck did you get to be so sensible?"

"Probably around the same time you lost the plot."

"Convenient."

"*Necessary*," he replies, his expression serious.

God I'm a let-down. What an anticlimactic piece of shit.

"I guess Lily isn't the only person I need to say sorry to."

He tosses the now empty bottle in the rubbish bin. "Nah. I've fucked up plenty of times and you've covered my ass. We're brothers."

"I'll do better," I mumble.

"I know you will," he says as he walks out of the kitchen.

I hear the shower start and I lay my head down on the table.

I need some food. I definitely need to change my clothes and I need to get some rest.

I'm fairly confident the sleep isn't going to happen, but I'll give it a crack. Maybe I won't be such a flaming hot mess with a few hours of sleep under my belt.

No more phone calls, no more messages. I look like enough of a sociopathic stalker for one day. I'll try and make it right tomorrow.

TWENTY-ONE

Lily

Shit.

I was expecting an Uber Eats driver, so when I open the door wearing my shittiest trackpants and a massive hoodie, and see Pax standing in front of me, I almost slam the door shut again.

"Lily, wait."

Just *perfect*, not only has he crushed my hopes and dreams, but now he's seen me doing a pretty accurate impression of looking like a potato.

Far out. "Unless you've got a bag of wontons and chicken fried rice, you've got no business being here." I cross my arms across my chest. One, because I think it makes me look tough, and two, because it hides my shaking hands.

"Sorry I'm not the Chinese delivery guy."

Keke and I are comfort eating. Well, I'm comfort eating. Keeks is just going out in sympathy like the good friend she is.

I go to shut the door, but he reaches out and stops it with his palm.

"Wait, *please*, just let me apologise."

I really don't think I want to hear this right now. I'm embarrassed, my pride is destroyed. I don't need a sympathy apology because he wants to make himself feel better about all this shit. It's not my job to make him feel better.

It's not like I don't know the score. I'm not stupid.

I'm just the nerdy girl who he slummed it with for a while until he picked his favourite cheerleader and got back to life as usual.

"You don't have to. I get it. Let's just save ourselves the hassle and end this conversation here."

"What do you mean, *you get it?*" he asks, scowling.

"I *get it*, Pax. You don't have to apologise. I'm not stupid enough to think this was something real with us."

"*Lily*," he says, his voice cracking. "Don't say that."

I know I shouldn't look at him, and maybe I'm not all that smart after all, because I do it anyway. His eyes are so dark, they look black. He looks like shit. Well, as shit as a guy like him could look.

I doubt he's had a lot of sleep.

"That's not true, it was real. It *is* real. It's the most real anything I've ever had."

He reaches out for me but winces and lets his hand fall when I step back out of his reach, not allowing him to make contact.

I don't need him to touch me. That's only going to make it harder to pretend that I don't remember how he sets me on fire.

"Why are you here, Pax?"

"To say sorry, to beg for forgiveness, to explain."

"There's nothing to explain."

"There *is*. I know it sounds lame and like some made-up bullshit line, but that picture... it's not what it looks like."

I huff out a laugh. "That's funnier than all your lame jokes put together."

He shifts his weight around, clearly uncomfortable.

"I know you don't believe me, and I don't blame you, but I swear on my life that it's not what you think. I've acted like an idiot, and I know I've hurt you, but I'm not a cheat. I just want a chance to try and explain."

"I don't think I'm up for this conversation right now, Pax." I sigh heavily. I really didn't think he'd come here at all, but I definitely didn't think he'd come today.

"Neither am I, but the only thing that could make me feel worse than having it, is not having it."

"I don't know how to say this nicely, so I'm just going to say it how it comes... right now, I couldn't give a shit about how *you* feel."

I can tell that hurts him by the pained look on his face, but he looks like he respects it too.

I think it's fair enough. He clearly hasn't spent a lot of time worrying about how something might make me feel, the least I can do is return the favour.

"I'm sorry, Lily."

It feels like he's only sorry because he got caught, but

I don't even have the energy to get into that at the moment, maybe ever. I just want to forget the whole thing. I just want to not hurt anymore.

I don't need him to be the bad guy.

This story doesn't need a villain. It just needs to be over.

Close the book and put it back on the shelf.

I'm not going to sit around with my girlfriends and bitch and moan, cry and scream and make him out to be the devil. I'm not going to start rumours and spin lies. Yes, I'm hurt – *he* hurt me, but I have to take some of the responsibility for this too. I knew what I was getting myself into. I knew that he and I weren't built to last.

I was just the girl he was forced to hang out with, and he was just the boy being punished by spending time in my presence.

I want to chalk it up to experience and move on with my sad little life. Maybe I'll have more luck with the opposite sex after high school. It's not like I need the distraction with half a year to go anyway.

"I know I don't deserve it, but one day, if you're ready, I want you to hear what I have to say, because I know what you think of yourself, Lily, and I'm sure I can figure out what you think about me... and you're not seeing any of it clearly. I'm an idiot, maybe you've got that part right, but you... you're incredible. There's no one like you."

Tears pool in the corners of my eyes. I just want him to go before I cry in front of him. I've been humiliated enough without adding that in.

He's breaking me with those big dark eyes and those softly spoken words.

He sounds so truthful, so sincere, and I'm a stupid, stupid girl, because I'm letting it get to me.

"I need you to go now." I don't know how I manage to get the words out, but I do. They even sound strong.

Go me.

He nods his head and turns to leave, but pauses and comes back at the last second, leaning in close to kiss my cheek.

I don't know why I let him do it, but I can't deny it feels nice.

Idiot.

I'm going to pay for that later. I'll replay it over and over and let it fuck with my head.

I shut the door as soon as he's moved clear, and lock it just for good measure.

As though something like a door could protect me from my feelings. No slab of wood or metal is going to keep him out of my head.

I'm leaning against the door, tears rolling down my face when Keke finds me.

"Where's the food?"

I shake my head. "Not here yet."

"No need to cry about it," she teases gently.

A laugh splutters out of me, sending tears flying. "Pax was at the door."

"Oh, Lil," she says before she hugs me.

I let it all out, crying until there's another knock at the door.

This time it is our Chinese food – I make Keke check before I let her open it.

We sit in my bed with *Friends* on in the background,

eating Chinese food and pretending the past twenty-four hours haven't sucked total ass.

I DON'T KNOW why this shit happens to me. Monday's suck, but this is a new low. Maybe Keke accidently made *me* into a voodoo doll and cursed it or something, because no one should have *this* much bad luck.

Especially all within one God damn bathroom.

I came back to this one specifically because, like a moron, I figured lightning wouldn't strike the same place twice.

Well, I was wrong. I seem to be making a habit of being wrong lately. Love that for me.

"It was *epic*."

I'd recognise that voice in my sleep. It fucking haunts me.

Liana. And her bitchy little mates. The combo that I, of all people, did *not* need today.

Thankfully, I'm inside the stall at least, and as far as I'm aware, they have no idea I'm in here, but still, it's *way* too close for comfort. This whole thing feels like Déjà vu.

Just the reminder of that day is too much for me, let alone actually having to re-live it live action. No fucking thank you.

I grab my phone out of my pocket and check it hasn't somehow been turned on loud for the first time in three years.

I can't save myself right now, but maybe Keke can. I'm

meant to be meeting her in five minutes, so hopefully she'll have her phone on her.

Lily: I'm in the bathroom stall, and Liana and her cheer hoes are in here. I can't get out. Help.

A few seconds pass and I'm starting to freak out.

Keke: What is it with these chicks and the bathrooms?! They need a board room or something to hold these meetings

Lily: Not helping Keeks

Keke: I'm on it. Which bathroom?

Lily: The one by the lockers

Keke: You've really got to find a new spot to pee

Once again, not helpful, but she's right. I won't be coming back into this bathroom for quite some time after this.

"It was so funny, you should have been there."

That's still Liana talking.

"It *was* funny, until Berlin dragged him out of there and ruined it," someone else says. "She's such a pain in the ass."

"I actually like Pax. I think he's cool." That's another voice again. "I'm glad he got home okay. He was wasted."

My ears prick up at the familiar names. I don't know exactly what they're talking about, but I'm determined to find out.

"Pax used to be cool, until *she* showed up. Jealous bitch is just sticking her nose in everything."

"They're siblings, Li, I don't think Berlin's jealous, I think she's just onto us."

Whichever one that is, she actually sounds like she might have half a brain.

"Whatever, I don't even care. I got the pic and we know that little nerd saw it," Liana brags.

The hair on the back of my neck stands up.

"How do you know she saw?" one of the other girls asks.

"Oh my god, *please* tell me you know that story views are a thing," Liana drawls.

"Her name showed up on Li's view list," the other, less bitchy girl says. I wish I knew which one that was. She keeps questionable company, but there still could be hope for her.

"Lily Wilder. It was right there in black and white."

Dammit. I had no idea that was a thing. All this social media bullshit is too much for me. All this personal validation crap where you can see everything and anything that goes on. My life was a lot simpler before I downloaded that stupid app.

"Yeah, so she *def* saw it."

"Do you know what happened? Did they break up?"

"No idea, but *surely* shit has hit the fan."

"She's kind of a loser though, maybe she'll just let him get away with it."

"Look, I don't care if she keeps dating him or what. I saw an opportunity and I took it, and thanks to Eve playing dirty, her pathetic little spirit will be crushed. Job done."

I can't believe what I'm hearing. Well, I probably can, if I really give it a minute, but right now, I'm still in shock.

"So did Eve actually hook up with him or what?"

"Nah, she couldn't get him to crack, not even with all the alcohol she loaded him up with."

My heart is beating so loud I can hear it whooshing in my ears.

Pax *was* telling the truth. He was stitched up. Liana co-ordinated this entire thing. Nothing happened with him and Eve.

It doesn't explain his bizarre reaction on our date, or why he didn't want me to come to the party in the first place, but maybe, just maybe, he has been telling me the truth about that night, at the very least.

"Yeah anyway, I don't even care what happens with those losers, the damage is done. I warned that bitch Berlin not to mess with me, and she didn't listen. Then when I saw him with that little pet nerd of hers in the diner, it was just too good of an opportunity."

This girl is seriously fucking evil. I've never come across someone so rotten to the core. She's done all this, orchestrated this whole thing to hurt me and Pax, and to fuck with Berlin. She doesn't care about anyone's feelings or the collateral damage she's causing. I don't think this whole group of girls has a set of morals between them.

It's *bullshit*.

I'm over it. They can't keep getting away with this crap.

It's so far past being okay.

They thrive on fear and I'm not willing to give them what they crave anymore.

I don't know where the fuck my spine of steel came from all of a sudden, but before I can think it through enough to stop myself, I throw my bag onto my shoulder and unlock the stall door, it swings open and hits the door next to it with a loud thud.

Five sets of eyes all swing in my direction.

I barely even glance at them, I just walk to the sink, flick on the tap and wash my hands.

I can feel them all staring at me, and they must be in some serious shock, because not one of them has said a word.

It's pretty funny really. They act so tough, so unshakable, but you catch them off guard and suddenly they don't know what to do. Must be tough to figure out a plan when you're all trying to run off a single brain cell at the same time.

I catch Liana's eye in the mirror, smirk, and turn off the tap.

I don't know what the fuck has come over me, or who this sassy, strong girl is, but the look on Liana's face is priceless. If I get out of this unscathed, I'm going to be so proud of myself for being brave.

I hold her gaze as I shake the water off my hands, and then I turn and head for the door.

It's not until I have my hand on the handle that Liana finally snaps out of it and starts yelling after me. I have no idea what she's barking about, and I'm not about to stop and find out.

I'm brave, not sadistic.

I step out into the corridor, and I'm nearly bowled over by Keke, who is closely followed by Berlin. Their cheeks are flushed, like they ran across the school to get here.

"Woah." I grab Keke's shoulders. "Slow down."

Keke looks relieved to see me, but that relief is quickly replaced with exhaustion. She doubles over, sucking in air hard.

"I. Hate. Running," she pants.

Berlin's scanning the hallway. She's in much better shape than Keke, clearly.

"Did they leave?" she demands.

I shake my head and usher both girls away from the door and down the hall. They're not going to stay in that bathroom forever, and I don't need to be a sitting duck out here when they do emerge.

"I didn't have time to make a shiv, but I grabbed a pair of scissors from an art class." Keke holds them up, looking proud of herself.

"Oh my god, Keeks, what were you going to do, stab her?" I demand.

"Just wave them around a little bit, try to look kinda crazy, but it doesn't hurt to have options." She breathes heavily.

I love that she thinks she has to *try* to look crazy. I also take the scissors off her, because she's like a child – there's no way she should be running with those.

"Where are they?" Berlin asks again, her tone urgent.

"Still in the bathroom." I peer around the corner of the little doorway we've tucked ourselves into. There's still no sign of the bitch brigade. "I walked out of the stall, and they all freaked."

Berlin is still looking around too, but she does a double take when she hears what I said.

"Sorry, Miss Thang, you did *what?*"

I laugh nervously. I still can't quite believe it myself. "I got sick of hiding. They were talking shit about me, you and Pax, and I got so angry with myself for letting these stupid little girls scare and control me. I guess I snapped."

Berlin does a little celebration dance and Keke holds her hand up for a high five, from her doubled-over position. She really needs to work on her cardio.

I'm pretty proud of myself too.

"Wait." Berlin's eyes narrow. "What'd they say about us?"

That shifts my mood again, and I feel tears pricking in my eyes.

"I couldn't hear it all, but Liana was bragging about that photo of Pax and Eve and how she set it all up."

"That fucking *bitch*. I *knew* it. I knew she was behind it all. Don't get me wrong, Pax is an idiot sometimes, but that was something else. That wasn't him. He's been different since he met you."

That comment makes goosebumps break out over my skin. I don't really want to have that kind of reaction, but I can't help it. I like that he's been different with me. He's not just some little shit jock when I'm around. I see what I think is the real him.

"From what I heard, it sounds like they all kept giving him more and more drinks until he got so drunk she could basically climb on his lap without him knowing, and have a photo opportunity."

"That's disgusting. Rapey vibes much." Keke is back upright again, but her face is still the colour of a stop sign.

"He didn't touch her, Lily. Nothing happened. I'm sure he's already told you that, but I wanted you to know for sure that he's not into Eve. I was there the whole time. They didn't hook up. He's not into anyone who isn't you," Berlin promises me.

This all sounds more like the Pax that I've fallen for, but I don't know what to think anymore. I haven't known him long enough to know what to expect. We don't know each other all that well yet.

Berlin peeks around the corner again. "Queen bitch is on the move," she mutters.

I *really* hope she's not coming this way. No matter how ballsy I am all of a sudden, I'd really rather we didn't cross paths again so soon. I'm pretty sure I've used up my quota of confidence for the day.

"They're going the other direction."

I sigh in relief.

"At least she didn't tear apart any of your books this time," Keke points out.

That's a solid fact.

"Oh, yeah." I turn to Berlin. "I never thanked you for replacing that, sorry, it totally slipped my mind. I really appreciate it. You didn't have to do that."

"What?" she asks, confused.

"The textbook Liana destroyed last time... I got the new one you left in the lab."

She looks even more confused. "I'm tempted to take the credit, buuuut... that wasn't me."

"*What?* Who was it then?" Now I'm the one who's confused.

She shrugs. "I know who's dating who, not who's buying books sorry, girl."

Well shit. I'd just assumed, since she was the one who helped me that day.

I give Keke a questioning look, but she just shrugs. "I don't want to label myself as a bad friend or anything, but I don't even know which book it was."

So, if it wasn't Berlin, and it wasn't Keke, then that only really leaves one person.

Pax.

TWENTY-TWO

Pax

Never thought I'd find myself doing this. Never thought I'd ever have someone to do this *with*, but here I am.

I knock on the door and after a couple of minutes, Cole opens it.

"Pax." He grins at me. "Berlin didn't tell me you were coming over."

"She ah... she doesn't know. I'm not really here to see her. I need to talk to you."

He looks at me shifting my weight nervously. "Everything okay, kid?"

I nod, then shake my head, then nod again. Eventually I shrug. "I need some advice about girl troubles."

"Shit. Sounds serious. I think you better come in."

He ushers me into the house and into the kitchen. I

remember the first night I came here and met Cole. I was so fucking pumped to meet such a legend.

"Beer?" he asks me.

I shudder. I couldn't drink another beer after the weekend. I think it's going to take some building up to that after the hangover I suffered through. I still don't feel right, and it's been two days.

"I'm good thanks. I'll take a juice or something if you've got one."

He grabs us both drinks and sits down a couple of stools away from me at the kitchen island.

"What'd you do?" he questions.

I'm not even going to pretend to be offended by his assumption that it's my doing. He's bang on the money.

"Got drunk at a party and ended up in a photo with a chick that shouldn't have been that close to me. This other pain-in-the-ass chick posted it to her story and everyone has seen it."

"Ah yes, the great Instagram story debacle. I'm familiar with your work."

"Berlin told you?" I ask, surprised. I know Berlin and Cole are close, but I didn't think he got *all* the tea.

He tips his head from side to side. "More like she ranted on the phone about it loudly while I was in the house. Her voice carries, it's hard not to hear."

"*Great.*"

"She called you a bone head. Haven't heard that one in a while."

"I can't say it isn't deserved."

"She's firm but fair."

"Yeah, so... you know the situation."

"Your girl saw the picture, I assume?"

"Lily. Yeah, she saw it. I'd been acting as nervous as a bag of cats at a greyhound meet, and I guess that gave her reason to check up on me. She's not friends with those nasty-ass girls, but I guess she thought I was up to no good because of how sketchy I was acting."

He raises a brow at me. "Care to elaborate?"

I certainly do not care to elaborate. I'm not about to fill my dad in on all the ways I've messed up.

I rub my neck nervously. "Not really looking to throw myself under the bus here, but thanks all the same."

He chuckles. "I guess I can respect that."

"It was nothing to do with her and I though. She's... *incredible* and I'm a fuck up. I've made a shit load of stupid calls. I'm sure you're aware my decision-making hasn't been the finest."

"I'd have to be blind not to have seen that."

"Yeah... well, some of that shit felt like it was catching up with me, and because I'm dumb as dirt, I didn't talk to her about it. It's a long story, but she thought I was embarrassed of her. I hurt her feelings. But none of that is anything compared to how hurt she must have been to see some chick pretty much sitting in my lap, at a party that I not so subtly didn't invite her to."

"Berlin was right, you kind of are a bone head."

I groan and lean forward until my forehead is resting against the cool marble of the benchtop.

"You're lucky I've had a lot of practice at getting myself out of the same kind of situations. I was a bone head at your age too."

"Yeah?" I ask, my voice muffled.

"Fuck yes. I was an *idiot* when I was eighteen. Partying too hard, making stupid decisions. If it weren't for my coach pulling me aside and telling me that I had to make a choice between pro rugby and being a loose unit, I probably wouldn't have pulled my head in the way I did. I cut all that crap. Actually, that's when I started hanging out with your mother a bit."

"If you're going to start talking about you and my ma, I'm going to need to borrow some bleach to scrub that out of my brain when you're done."

He chuckles. "Wasn't going to say another word."

"Good. I hate to be an attention seeker, but can we go back to my problem with Lily? I don't know what to do."

"Have you tried talking to her?"

"Yeah, I've given it a nudge."

"Didn't go well?"

"I've had better talks."

"Text her now."

"I've already tried messaging her."

"Humour me."

"What am I meant to say?"

"Try... *I'm a moron, but I really want a chance to explain.*"

I raise an eyebrow at him.

"Say please," he adds, waiting for me to start typing.

I sigh and do it. At this point it's not like it can do any harm. She's already ignored about twenty messages, what's another one?

Pax: Can we please talk Lily? I know I'm a moron but I owe you an explanation.

I can't imagine this message with its ground-breaking content is going to make any difference, but at least I've sent it.

I sit my phone down on the bench.

"I have a good feeling about this," Cole says.

I think I lost sight of good feelings a while ago.

The phone vibrates, moving along the benchtop. I grab it.

What the fuck.

Lily: Okay. I can meet you in an hour.

"She replied. She wants to meet me in an hour," I say aloud, bewildered.

"Told you."

"How the fuck did you know that was going to work?"

"I've got a sixth sense for these things. I'm at one with the teenage girl mind."

I eye him suspiciously, and he grins.

"Heard B on the phone again earlier. She was talking about making you sweat, but she thought your girl should meet up with you and give you a chance to explain," he admits.

Fuck's sake. I feel like I'm the last person to know anything around here.

"Does Ice know you're listening into all her phone conversations?" I chuckle.

"Hey, if she wants to talk in a voice *that* loud, with the door wide open, that's on her."

"I can't believe Lily's actually gonna meet up with me."

"You're a good kid, Pax – you could use a bit of a boot

up the ass, but you're not a bad guy, I'm sure she knows that."

I hope so.

Fuck, I can't wait to see her.

I don't want to get ahead of myself; there's nothing to say this is good news. She might want to meet up to tell me to fuck off once and for all, but it's a chance I didn't have when I woke up this morning, and I fully intend to take it.

"I hope you're being safe... you know... wrapping it up and all that."

Jesus. Could have given me a heads up about the incoming sex lecture.

"You're one to talk."

"Yeah, yeah, I can appreciate that's rich coming from me, given the circumstances," he agrees. "I don't regret the way things turned out but raising Berlin on my own at such a young age; it's never been easy."

I'm pretty safe there. I'm not really in the market for becoming a single dad at eighteen, but it doesn't hurt to have a reminder of the consequences.

Be pretty hard to get someone pregnant when you're not having sex anyway.

"Me and Lily... we haven't... we're taking it slow."

He nods a couple of times, seemingly satisfied with my answer.

"She's not really like the girls I'm used to hanging out with," I add on.

He stops me there. "You know what, the less I know about you kids and your... *business*... the better. Just don't get anyone pregnant until you're a hell of a lot older, and we'll be fine."

"Suits me," I agree quickly. "I better go anyway. She wants to meet in an hour, and I need a shower."

I head for the door and come across Berlin in the doorway. I don't know if she's been listening in to this little father and son bonding moment or what.

"Well, well, well, if it isn't the devil himself," she drawls.

"No time for insults, Ice, I've got to go see my girl."

"She caved already, huh?"

"It would appear she did. Wish me luck."

"Don't tell me what to do." She grins.

It's lucky Cull is a strong man. That sense of humour would break a weaker one.

"Thanks for the talk, Cole," I call over my shoulder as I stroll out of the house, feeling surprisingly comfortable here.

"Pleasure doing business with you, kid," I hear him reply.

I HAND her the rolled-up drawing with the little note attached to it. I've been working on this day and night. It's the only thing that's kept me sane while she hasn't been speaking to me.

She reads the words on the note.

The proton isn't speaking to the other proton. She's mad atom.

I watch as she tries to fight a smile, but the corners of

her mouth turn up, giving her away. I didn't expect her to be so warm towards me.

"You are *so* lame." She sneaks a look at me.

"And you love that about me." Her gaze falters and she does a double take. It's the longest she's looked at me since before I fucked up. I just hope it's a good sign.

She holds my stare, her green eyes lighter today than they were the last time I looked into them.

I still can't believe she actually agreed to meet with me. Berlin must have been working some of her special ice queen magic on this one, because I was certain I was going to get told to fuck off, or worse yet – ignored.

"Are you going to open it?" I tilt my head towards the rolled-up piece of paper in her hand.

"I'm nervous."

I chuckle. "It's just a piece of paper, Lily-boo. It's not going to hurt you."

She probably thought the same thing about a photo until a few days ago, but here we are.

She takes a deep breath and wiggles the piece of string free until it comes right off. She slowly unrolls the sheet of paper and stares at it without saying a word for what feels like half a fucking lifetime.

"How... who? What is this?"

"It's a drawing. Of you."

I kind of feel like I'm stating the obvious here, but she's clearly confused. She looks like she's about to have a stroke or something.

"Did *you* draw this?" she whispers.

"Yeah." I nod my head.

I don't like to blow my own trumpet, but I'd give

myself a solid couple of blasts on one for this. It's the best drawing I've ever done.

"Oh my *god*."

She's still staring at it, frozen like a statue.

"It's beautiful. *I* look *beautiful*," she says, her voice cracking.

I drew her exactly as she is. The beautiful girl I'm in love with.

"You're so unbelievably beautiful, Lily. Everything about you."

She exhales heavily, and I can see her eyes are glassy. Her mouth is half open like she wants to argue with me about it.

I know she doesn't think of herself as beautiful. She's so hard on herself.

I wish she could see herself clearly – the way I see her.

She thinks I don't notice the way she picks at her food, or how she makes sure her skirt covers her thighs the second she sits down. How she wears t-shirts that are always a little too big and the way she looks down when she walks through a crowded hallway.

Hopefully this drawing will help her see the truth – that she's so, so beautiful.

"That's what I see. That's *you*. That's what the rest of the world sees when they look at you."

She looks at the drawing for a long time.

"I don't need the rest of the world to think I'm beautiful." She sneaks a look at me, and I see the rest of what she wants to say, right there in her eyes.

She doesn't need the whole world to see her beauty –
to validate her – she's happy if *I* think she's beautiful.

That's something not even I can make a mess of.

"Still doesn't make it any less true."

"I can't believe you never told me you could draw like
this."

If I'd known I was going to get this kind of reaction,
I'd have told her the day we met and drawn her the very
next one. Hell, it might have helped me win her over
sooner.

"I'm a man of many talents."

Right now, those talents mostly consist of fucking up
and digging myself into holes, but still, I do what I do,
well.

"I wanted you to know how important you are to me."

She looks like she doesn't believe me.

"You're forced to be around me, Pax. Don't act like
you're hanging out with me by choice."

"Lily-boo, my punishment ended weeks ago."

"*What?*"

"Yeah, old man Evans gave me the all-clear to ditch
you when I was allowed to join the team again."

"Why didn't you tell me?" she demands.

"I was worried you'd kick me out if you thought you
had a choice. I didn't want to give up our time together.
So, I lied. And I'm not sorry."

"I wouldn't have kicked you out," she replies softly.
She's clearly shocked by this information.

"You've thrown me out of that lab over bad jokes.
Quite frankly, you're unpredictable, and I wasn't about to
take any chances," I tease.

"*I'm* unpredictable? What about *you* and your hot and cold behaviour?"

"I thought you might have some questions about that."

I expected for her first questions to be about that night at the party, about Eve, about whether or not I'm a cheating prick, but she seems to have other ideas for now at least.

"I've got some questions alright."

"Fire away."

I've got nothing to hide now. No more lies, no more secrets. She's about to get the unedited session.

"What happened in the diner the other night? Were you embarrassed to be seen with me?"

Man, the pain in her voice when she asks that question, it kills me. I can tell by her tone that she genuinely believes that. The fact that she could ever think she was something to be embarrassed of, breaks my heart.

I don't know what's going to happen here, or if she'll ever give me the chance to be with her again, but one way or another, I'm going to find a way to make sure she knows she's something to be proud of.

"*No.* I was the one that was the embarrassment. It's a long story, but I fucked up a lot a little while back and that night I saw someone who could get me into a lot of trouble, and I panicked."

She looks confused. I can't blame her. It's not likely to be a direction she saw this going.

"I've got a lot to tell you, and I'm not proud of *any* of it."

"I guess I've got some time to listen."

TWENTY-THREE

Lily

That's not what I was expecting him to say, at all. I don't even know what's really going on here.

I don't know what kind of trouble he means. Surely it can't be worse than getting into a fight on school grounds and getting kicked off the team.

"I just wanted to get the hell out of there as quickly as I could and get you away from my mess," he explains further.

None of that makes a lot of sense to me either, but that's only my first question. We're only just getting started.

"And the party? Why didn't you want me there with you?" I demand.

He glances down at the ground and then back up to meet my eyes. "Seeing that guy at the diner – that reminder of what a fuck up I am... I knew you didn't deserve to be pulled into my bullshit. It was a harsh reminder that I don't deserve a girl like you, and I was scared that if you came with me to the party, you'd see that for yourself."

"None of this makes any sense, Pax."

He nods. "I know. That's because there's things you don't know."

"We've all got our secrets."

"I want to tell you all of it. I know nothing can make up for the way I've acted, but I want you to know everything anyway."

I don't know if I'm ready for this, but it seems like it's going to happen whether I'm ready or not, so I may as well get on board.

He starts talking, and just doesn't stop. He tells me about the alcohol, the drugs, the fight at school, the situation at the bottle store. He tells me everything he's fucked up in the past little while. He tells me about Cole, Berlin and Cullen, about his ma and his mum and how he's messing everything up with everyone who means the most to him.

He tells me about how he was finally feeling back on track, about how being around me has changed his attitude, but that it doesn't change the fact that his past mistakes are trying to haunt him.

We don't talk about the night at the party, or the photo, but I can sense he's building up to it.

"I think I need a minute to process all that," I say when he finally stops for a break.

He nods in understanding.

It's pretty wild, but I have to admit, it all makes sense now. The family at the diner the other night – they own the bottle store. The father was the one who Pax got into an altercation with. Pax saw him and panicked, and it served as a reminder that his life was a shit show. *That's* why he went all weird on me.

What a mess.

"Have you thought about coming clean? Owning your mistakes and seeing what happens?"

He nods his head solemnly. "Every day. I know I should do it, but that doesn't really make it right either. I know I need to do *something*, try and make things better, but I'm scared of making it worse. I'm skating on some pretty thin ice already and I feel like I've finally got my passion for rugby back. I don't want it taken away, even if I deserve it."

I can understand that. And he's right, him being punished doesn't make up for what he did, but maybe there's a way he can, without sinking his life further down the shitter.

"What about that kid at school? The one you smacked when you were wasted. Have you spoken to him?"

He shakes his head. "Principal Evans told me to stay away from him. I wrote him a letter, but that's not enough. I owe the kid. I could have seriously hurt him, and he didn't even do anything wrong."

"Sounds like you've got a lot of making up to do."

He nods. "Mostly to you."

Tingles run up and down my spine.

"I'm so sorry, Lily, for hurting you, for dragging you into my mess, for letting you down. Fuck, for all of it. The other night at the party... I don't know what happened. I was so drunk, and I know that's no excuse, but I swear to you, nothing went on with me and Eve."

It doesn't make any of it okay, but it does make him human. He's flawed, he makes mistakes... we all are, we all do.

"I know," I whisper.

"You believe me?"

I nod. "They set you up."

He frowns. Seems like I'm finally not the last to know something.

"I heard Liana and some of the other girls talking the other day. It was all a set up. They were trying to hurt me, and fuck with Berlin. It was all just a game to them. They got you drunk and set up the photo, posted it in the hopes it'd spread and I'd see it," I explain. "The idea was Eve would hook up with you, but she failed at that part at least."

"The *fuck*?" he growls. "*Wait*, why the hell would Liana want to hurt *you*?"

His confusion is valid, he probably really wanted to ask how Liana would even know who I was.

"You remember when I hurt my hand?"

He nods. "Yeah, you 'fell', if I remember right."

I feel my face turn red. "*Yeah*... That was Liana and some of the other girls. I don't know why they did it, but they kind of attacked me in the bathroom one day, tore up my book, and Liana stepped on my hand pretty hard."

"She fucking *what*?" he roars.

I shrink back, not because I'm scared of him, but

because I'm terrified of what he might do. I've never heard someone sound so angry.

"Pax, it's fine. I'm fine. I'm okay now."

"It's *not* fine. She *hurt* you." His chest is heaving, and his fists are balled at his sides. "She put her fucking hands on you. I knew she'd done *something*, but I thought it was a bit of name calling at worst."

I can tell it's taking every last bit of his self-control not to get up off this bench and run out of the park to hunt her down. His voice has this protective edge to it that both warms me and scares the hell out of me.

He looks like a gaming figure glitching; he's half sitting, half standing, every muscle in his body is tight and ready for action.

"*Pax.*"

I don't even think he can hear me. The red rage mist has taken over.

I don't know what to do to calm him down.

I clamber across the bench and throw myself into his lap, forcing him to sit the rest of the way down. I wrap my arms around his neck and hold him tight.

He's shaking.

Finally, after what feels like hours, I feel his body start to relax under me, and then his arms go around me, pulling me even closer. He buries his face in my hair, and I can feel him inhaling deeply.

"How'd you get away from her?" he asks me after a long silence, his tone clipped.

"Berlin and her friends came into the bathroom and saw what was happening. Berlin stood up to Liana and got them to leave. She helped me pick up all the bits of my book and get cleaned up."

He grunts in response.

I know he knew *something* had gone on, but clearly this isn't what he was expecting to hear. I still can't believe Berlin actually kept her word and didn't tell him.

He pulls me even tighter, his face nuzzling into the crook of my neck now.

"You replaced my book, didn't you?" I ask him.

He nods slowly. "I couldn't let you use that ripped-up thing. If I'd known what really happened, I'd have got the fucking cash out of Liana one way or another. Feral bitch."

"*Pax*, it was so expensive."

He chuckles. "Yeah, cleaned out my savings, but it was worth it to see how happy you were when you looked at it."

I don't know what to say.

I never would have picked him to be so sweet and considerate.

"Thank you," I whisper.

I haven't said that I forgive him, and he hasn't asked if I do, but I think we both know I'm going to – that I already do. Everything has been a mess, but we're stronger than what's trying to break us.

We're so different, yet so similar at the same time.

We're both dealing with our own demons, and somehow, we're helping to heal each other.

He pulls back abruptly, still holding me tight, but far enough that he can look at my face.

"I still haven't told you."

"Told me what?" I so badly want to hide behind my hair, my hand, my shoulder, *something*. I hate it when he looks at me so closely. I bring my hand up to my face, but he intercepts it and holds it in his. His gaze is so intense.

"Told you that I love you."

I'm caught so off guard that I think I actually gasp. "You *what?*"

He chuckles. "I love you, nerd."

I can't believe this is happening. *He* loves *me.*

What planet am I on?

"But I'm so boring."

The words come out without permission.

He laughs loudly, the last of the tension leaving his body. "You're anything but boring."

"But I'm not sporty."

He shakes his head in amusement. "Can you just stop arguing with me and tell me that you love me too."

My eyes find his. "How do you know I love you?"

"It's so obvious," he teases me.

I don't know who I think I'm kidding. I fell in love with this boy a long time ago, I've just been too chicken shit to admit it to myself, let alone to him.

"You're always throwing yourself at me and trying to impress me with those lame chemistry jokes," he carries on.

"If I admit that I love you too, will you stop with the jokes?"

He grins wide. "*Nope.*"

I roll my eyes. "I guess I'll still love you anyway."

"But I'm an idiot," he argues, mimicking my nonsense.

"Oh, I know," I agree with a laugh. "But you're pretty nice to look at."

His whole body shakes as he laughs.

"Who would have thought, eh? I guess Evans did me a real solid with this punishment after all. I should go into his office and tell him he found me the girl of my dreams."

I roll my eyes. "The girl of your dreams is not a frumpy little science girl."

"You've got no idea, brains. I'm so into you, I can barely breathe."

"Did you just quote *Ariana Grande?*"

"Yes I did and don't you judge me," he accuses.

"Oh, I'm judging you."

He looks at me with so much warmth, so much love, and a blinding smile. It's hard not to feel worthy when he's looking at me like that.

"Wait, so does this mean I've lost my assistant?"

"Fuck no. Just try and get rid of me. I'm a science genius now."

"Loose interpretation of the word 'genius' there I think."

He smirks. "Yeah, you're right. I haven't learnt sweet fuck all about chemistry, but you've taught me so much about myself."

"Are you looking for a job in motivational speaking or something?"

"You know, you've got a pretty smart mouth for such a nerd."

"Risky way to speak to your boss."

"You're right, you should deduct my wages."

"I'm halving your salary, effective immediately."

His grin is so wide, and when he kisses me, I can't remember ever feeling this kind of happy.

"SHHH, WE'LL GET CAUGHT," I hiss at him as he bangs his shoe into my wall.

"I don't mean to be rude, but isn't your grandma like eighty? She's probably taken out her hearing aids by now." He grins wickedly as he clambers the rest of the way in my window.

I shouldn't laugh, but it's pretty funny. And he's actually not far off. I could probably have a rave down here, and she still wouldn't hear a thing.

"Just get in already."

"So eager." He waggles his brows at me.

My cheeks heat. He's probably got no real idea just how eager I really am.

I've never had a guy climb in my window, let alone late on a Friday night.

It's probably all a bit ridiculous, we're both technically adults, but there's something exciting about the element of sneaking around.

I didn't get to do any of this when I was sixteen. I've always been a rule follower, not a rule breaker.

He clambers the rest of the way through and then stands there looking at me with a goofy grin on his face while I shut the window.

"What's that look for?"

He takes a couple of steps towards me, and I back up until my calves hit the side of my bed. We both know why he's here. We've gone as far as we can go without a bed and privacy. Both of which we have right now.

He lifts his brows, and I know exactly where this is going. He's found his latest lame joke.

"I wish you were a DNA helicase... so I could unzip your genes."

"Oh my god, *stop*." I groan.

He pulls me onto the bed so we're lying facing each other. "I really wish I could."

"It's not like it's hard, you just *stop*." I laugh.

"No can do, Lily-boo." He grins.

God that damn smile is going to be the death of me. He looks so cheeky and gorgeous; it makes me feel weak in the knees.

He grabs my leg and hooks it up over his.

I swallow down a gasp. I want to do so much more than this with him, and if I'm desperately trying to catch my breath all the time, he might think I can't handle it.

His fingers are playing with the hem of my t-shirt, slowly lifting it higher and higher.

I want to take it off but I'm nervous that he won't like what he sees underneath.

He doesn't seem as bothered by the idea, as he tugs it higher and higher until he eventually pulls it free of my head completely, awkwardly catching my arms and wiggling me free of it.

I lie back down onto the bed, covering myself with my arms.

"Don't hide yourself from me."

"I feel self-conscious," I whisper.

"Maybe this will help," he says before pulling his own

shirt off over his head. He even does it in that insanely hot way, using one hand to pull it from the back. I thought guys only did that in movies.

It's so hot it should be illegal.

He's lying next to me all golden toned skin and defined abs. If anything, finally seeing him without a shirt on is the opposite of helpful for my insecurities. He's *perfect*. Broad shoulders and defined chest. I couldn't have even dreamed up a sight this good. I feel insanely inferior.

He leans forward and kisses me at the same moment that his hands grip my hips and tug me towards him.

He's hard as a rock.

It seems like the only person who cares about my love handles and rolls is me.

He trails kisses down my neck and along my collar bone. His hands are all over me, and I decide it's only fair if I do the same.

I run my palms over his insane body, and he exhales heavily from my touch. He's so warm and so *firm*. He's the opposite of me.

This is the best day of my life. I never imagined I'd be touching a guy that looks like him.

"*Jesus*, Lily. I've been dreaming about you touching me like this. It feels so good."

There he goes, giving me confidence again.

I go lower, over the waistband on his shorts until I can feel him through the fabric. He moans and lets his head fall back as I gently grip his hard length.

God, I'm so turned on and he's barely even touched me yet.

"*Lily*," he says on an exhale.

His hand moves to the top of my jeans, and he undoes the button with far more ease than I'd have expected.

He runs his thumb along the top of my underwear, and as much as I want him to go further, there's something holding me back.

"Wait. I need to tell you something before we go any further."

"It's okay, I know that you haven't done this before."

As thrilled as I am to know I wear my virginity like a flashing sign on my forehead, that's not exactly what I need to tell him.

"It's not just that..."

He pushes up onto his elbow and looks at me, the picture of patience and self-control.

There's no real need for me to tell him this, and it's probably going to be a real mood killer, but I feel like I should anyway. I don't want there to be any secrets between us, and I don't want to risk that this will trigger any memories and have him not know what's going on – even though I'm sure that'll never happen. I was so young.

"Something happened to me... when I was little."

He swallows but doesn't say anything. The look in his eyes wills me to carry on.

"I was only about two, so I don't remember any of it, but my dad had some dodgy men over at the house. They were all out of their minds on God knows what. My Grammy was bringing Mum home from the hospital – I don't know what had put her in there this time, but anyway, I was there alone with my dad and the other men. Grammy came inside when they got back, and she…" I take a deep breath. "She found one of the men… touching me."

I hear his sharp intake of breath.

"He had my nappy or whatever off and was touching me… down there. My dad was in the corner, doing nothing about it. Just standing there staring – sounds like he was totally out of it."

"Lily, what the *fuck*?"

He's sitting bolt upright now.

I shrug my shoulders. "Like I said, I don't remember a thing about it. I was too little. My grandmother took me away from them on the spot, she went to the police, and I was seen at the hospital and released. Thankfully nothing worse happened. I've lived with her ever since that day. She told me the truth about why I was taken from my parents when I was about fourteen and I wouldn't drop the subject. Grammy was the only one who wanted justice for me."

"Your own mother didn't even do anything?" he replies, outraged. "She stayed with him?"

"She took my dad's side. She was too hooked on crack to get out and he was her lifeline. They didn't even fight Grammy. She was granted full custody and other than the odd letter or awkward accidental run-in downtown, I haven't seen either of them since. They don't try to visit, or even call. I'm pretty sure I saw my mum one day in the supermarket about a month ago, and she walked right past me, didn't even recognise me. She was cooked out of her mind."

"Fucking hell, baby. Are you okay?"

I shrug. "Yeah. I mean, it's fucked up and wrong, but

it's weird, because I don't remember any of it. It's like I'm telling a story that happened to someone else. I don't feel *anything* about it. I don't feel like a victim. I don't feel like it's who I am."

There's a fiery rage behind his eyes that he's trying so hard to contain. I can't blame him for that. If someone I loved told me something like that had happened to them, I'd be out for blood too, but he doesn't need to do anything – I'm okay.

"If I ever come across either of your parents, they better hope there are plenty of witnesses around."

I know he means exactly what he's insinuating.

He might be barely concealing the fact that he's threatening murder, but I only love him more for it.

"They don't even matter. They'll never mean anything, never *be* anything. I have all the love I need right here under this roof. I wouldn't waste even the littlest bit of energy on those low lives."

I can tell he's going to need some time to make peace with this the way I have, but I'm glad he knows. I know his secrets and he knows all mine now too.

"I will never, *ever* touch you in a way that makes you uneasy, Lily. I promise you that. If you ever feel uncomfortable with me, even if it's just over something little that you think is silly, you only have to say the word and I'll stop."

"I know, I trust you."

I wouldn't be here with him if I didn't trust him completely.

He brushes a strand of hair from my face and looks at

me with so much love and kindness. It's the sweetest thing.

"Sorry, way to kill the mood," I mumble.

He quickly shakes his head. "*No.* I'm glad you told me. I know how precious you are, I know how big of a step this is for us. It's not something I take lightly, especially now. We don't have to do anything tonight. I'll wait as long as you want."

"I don't want to wait," I tell him quickly. I'm not sure I can wait any longer.

He shifts to sit back on the bed, so his back is leaning against the wall, and lifts me like I'm light as a feather, so I'm sitting in his lap, straddling him.

I nibble on my bottom lip as he looks my body over, slowly, taking in every single inch of me.

Just having his eyes on my skin is enough to make me crazy.

So much for the mood being killed.

"My beautiful girl."

He skims his fingers lightly down my arms, barely making contact.

"Tell me what you want me to do," he murmurs.

"Don't treat me like I'm made of glass," I whisper.

He bucks his hips underneath me, and I moan as I feel the hardness between his legs.

I'm so screwed. He's barely even done anything yet and I'm a quivering mess.

"I think you should kiss me now."

He grins. "Yes, ma'am."

TWENTY-FOUR

Pax

I don't know if it's because I know it's her first time, or what it is, but I'm nervous as fucking hell. I'm a mile off being a virgin – shit, for a while there, I spent way too much time with my dick in places it probably shouldn't have been – but this is the first time I've been in love.

This is all new to me.

I *love* this girl, and I want to make this perfect for us.

This isn't just some quick fuck where all I care about is blowing my load.

This means something.

She's so fucking beautiful. Not only that, but she's sexy too. I've never had a girl in my lap who wound me up the way Lily does.

I kiss her hard, controlling her mouth and swiping my tongue against hers in a frenzy. I want to make sure she knows what she's just told me doesn't change anything. I still want her so badly – it's taking every bit of restraint in me not to flip her on her back and make her mine, hard and fast.

I buck my hips again, and the noise she makes drives me crazy.

My girl is so ready for this.

She grinds her hips back and forth, pressing herself against me. Fuck it feels good.

Her hands are wound into my hair, tugging at the roots, and those sexy-as-fuck tits are pressed against me.

I drop my head, burying my face in them. She's so soft and sexy, her curves make me weak.

"I want you to touch me," she breathes. "Touch me everywhere."

I've never been one to deny a woman what she wants, and I'm sure as fuck not going to start with this one.

She's on her back in a second, her head caged in with my arms and my weight hovering over her.

A moan slips out and I can't help but grin at how much she's clearly enjoying herself.

I get straight to work, kissing every bit of exposed skin available to me. I touch her everywhere, and she moans, shivers and squirms under me.

I get to her jeans, and I don't even need to stop to ask her for permission, she's already lifting her hips and trying to wiggle free of them.

I make quick work of those, leaving her only in her underwear. I sit back on my knees between her legs for a second, just soaking in the sight of her.

Fuck.

She's got on these little lacy knickers that cover fuck all and leave even less to the imagination.

The curve of her hips and the dip of her waist is so God damn hot. She's all woman and I'm so here for it.

"I want to fuck you so bad right now."

Her cheeks go red. I've never met someone who gets so easily embarrassed. It's cute as hell.

I look into her eyes as I pull down the waistband of my pants, taking my boxer briefs with them.

My dick's been painfully hard for a while now, and it springs free, standing at attention, ready to play its part.

I leave my pants around my knees and grip my dick in one hand.

She's staring, watching my hand move up and down my length ever so slowly, her cheeks a soft pink now.

Fuck, I'm so desperate to be buried deep inside her.

I lower myself down, my mouth going to her pussy. She gasps in surprise as I kiss the scrap of lace covering her.

I run my tongue from bottom to top and she moans loudly.

"You like that, don't you?"

She nods quickly, her whole body moving.

"I want to taste you."

She nods again and reaches for her underwear.

I do the job for her, slipping them off and tucking them under the pillow before diving back in and getting to work.

I'm not magic, but I like to think I can do a half decent job of this.

I run my tongue along all her most sensitive parts,

focusing on the bits that make her squirm and moan the most.

I suck, lick and tease until she's panting, her back arched off the bed.

She's got handfuls of blankets and her breathing is ragged.

"Come for me, Lily," I coax.

She lifts her hips, and I flick my tongue on her clit over and over until she cries out in pleasure.

I barely let her ride it out before I'm up on my knees. I find my pants and pull a condom out of my pocket.

She's breathing heavily as she just watches me, a sated expression on her face as I rip open the foil packet and roll the rubber down my length.

I lower myself down and rest my forearms on either side of her head.

"You have to tell me if this hurts, okay?"

She nods. "Just kiss me while you do it."

I move my hips around, lining myself up while kissing her softly.

"Are you sure you want this?"

"Literally never been more sure about anything in my life."

That's good enough for me. Lily is the smartest person I know, she must have been sure about a lot of shit, and if this is the thing she's most sure of, then the least I can do is meet her halfway.

I push, slowly at first, and then all the way in.

She gasps as I still inside her, balls deep.

"Oh my god." I groan. She feels so fucking good, exactly as I expected. "Are you okay?"

"I think so," she whispers. "Go slow."

I focus on her beautiful face as I carefully draw out and back in again, so cautiously. I'll feel like a total prick if I hurt her.

She winces as I push back in, and I freeze.

"Don't stop," she breathes. "I'm okay, just keep going."

I kiss her hard, teasing her lips with my tongue and swallowing her gasps as I keep moving in and out of her.

I still can't believe I'm the guy she chose to do this with for the first time.

I'm not sure I deserve the privilege, but I'll do whatever it takes to be worthy from this point on.

"Harder," she whispers against my lips.

I move a little faster, pressing a little harder.

She squeezes my shoulders, her nails digging in hard. I don't care if I come out of this looking like a pin cushion. It's probably nothing compared to how she feels.

She starts to relax after a few more thrusts, and I give it to her a bit harder again.

Fuck.

She feels incredible. So tight and wet.

"Oh my god, Pax." She moans loudly, her concerns of being quiet, long forgotten.

Hearing her say my name just about pushes me over the edge.

"Jesus, I'm going to come soon if I don't stop."

"Don't you dare stop," she pants.

She looks into my eyes as I keep moving in and out of her until I feel myself lose control.

I come so hard I can hear ringing in my ears and I feel dizzy.

I grunt as I finally finish, my breathing is so heavy you'd think I just ran five kilometres.

I slump onto her shoulder, absolutely fucked.

She runs her nails gently up and down my back while we lay there, our chests rising and falling heavily.

I carefully slide out of her, and she grimaces.

"Are you alright?"

She nods, her cheeks turning a soft pink.

I can't stop myself from laughing at her. She's so fucking cute. After what we just shared, she's still blushing about nothing.

"Are you sore?"

"A little, but I think I'm okay."

God, she looks so beautiful. Her hair is all crazy, her cheeks flushed and her eyes alive with excitement.

"I love you."

She smiles the most stunning smile. "I love you too."

***

"PAX. YOU'RE OFF THE BENCH."

I'm on my feet before coach even finishes his sentence. I've been waiting for this moment all game.

There's only eight minutes left in play, but eight minutes on the field is better than none.

He calls Kingston off the field – he's been limping a bit for the past ten minutes – and sends me on my way to take his place.

Fuck yes.

I can hear cheering and yelling as I run out to join my teammates.

Bryson gives me a low five as I pass him to head over to the right wing.

Cullen is down the back, barking orders. He grins at me and gives me a chin lift.

It feels so good to be back out here with my brother. I feel good. Fit. Fast. Strong. My ribs aren't giving me any more shit either.

Fuck, I've missed this. My spine is tingling and my legs are itching to run.

I can't wait to get hands on that ball.

There's something about knowing Lily is in the crowd watching that makes me want to play better than I ever have.

I want to show her that I'm good at something. That all that pent-up energy I'm always pinging around her lab with can be used for something productive.

I'm going to make these eight minutes something to remember.

The other team has got the ball, and I know exactly what the play is going to be when we get hold of it, we've practised it a hundred times over the past couple of weeks.

With a bit of luck, it'll end with one of us over the try line.

Richmond High kick the ball and it come's sailing down the field into Smithy's waiting hands. He runs it up hard, taking a few guys down with him. Bryson plucks the ball out the back of the maul and fires it out wide to Tonksy, who sends it on to a flying Cullen.

He gets taken down in a grunty tackle and the backs pile in over top of the ball.

Bryson has it again and this time he sends it to the left, away from me.

I can see it happening before it does; Richmond High's star player – Mikey – is too quick. The guy was a track star who's recently moved over to rugby and is taking the game by storm.

Nick fumbles the ball, and that's all the opportunity Richmond need. Mikey comes flying through, scoping the ball from the air mid-fumble.

I didn't even realise I was running, but I'm halfway across the field already and gaining ground quickly.

They're two points up with fuck all time left on the clock.

We can't let this ball go. It's now or not at all.

I've got this fire inside me, it's what's been missing from the game for me all this time, but it's here now, and with a vengeance.

I blindside him with a tackle, catching him completely off guard. He thought he was away and gone.

I can hear the crowd screaming as the ball is lost backwards.

I get to my feet and pick it up off the ground and I'm sprinting for the try line before I can even really register what's happening.

I'm flying down the centre of the field, the opposition scrambling to get their defence together. I throw off one guy, then another, but I'm not going to be able to shrug off the four coming for me. I can feel Jack sprinting alongside me on my right, but I wait, making their defenders fully commit, before offloading the ball with a flick of my wrist out the back.

I go down like a sack of shit, four guys piling on me, but the eruption of the crowd tells me that Jack got over the line.

Fuck yes.

Didn't exactly go to plan, but we got there.

I hear the whistle blow for the try, and then another long blast signalling that it's the final whistle – the game's over.

The conversion doesn't even matter. We won.

It's a nothing game – it's not going to change our standing on the table, but coming off the bench and getting the win means a hell of a lot to me.

The Richmond guys pile off me, bitching and moaning, but offering me a hand up.

I'm barely on my feet before all the guys are flying at me, jumping around and smacking me on the back, celebrating. Everyone is buzzing.

"Where the fuck did that come from?" Cullen pulls me in for a bro hug. "You were flying."

I chuckle. "Thought it was about time I pulled my weight around here."

Coach comes over and shakes my hand – he's beaming from ear to ear.

Jack catches my eye across the chaos and gives me a grin and a chin lift. I can only hope my fuck up with asking him to get my gear has long been forgotten.

I look over to the stands trying to see Lily, but there's people everywhere.

I'm dying to get my hands on her. I can't stop thinking about last night and how fucking incredible it was.

"I bet that felt good." I turn back around, and Cole is standing in front of me.

I grin wide. "Shit, yes it did."

His smile matches mine. I'm stoked he's here. I'm stoked *I'm* here. Maybe this whole having a dad thing is exactly what I needed.

"Not bad, Golden boy." I hear Berlin's voice and turn just in time to see her run into Cullen's arms, not even sparing me a look.

Hello to you too, sis.

I don't actually care, she's not who I'm dying to see, but the smiling, shy girl who's wandering over behind her is.

My beautiful girl.

I'm smiling so wide it's hurting my face.

"Lily-boo," I say as I bowl up to her.

"Living up to your reputation there, Ace," she teases, looking up at me with those stunning green eyes.

"What'd you think?"

"I think it was hot," she replies.

That's not at all what I was expecting her to say, but I'm not mad about it.

I hold her face in my hands and dip my head to kiss her lips.

She melts into me, her hands clinging to my forearms.

I keep it short and sweet, even though I feel like doing a hell of a lot more to her right here and now.

I drop my head further, so my mouth is at her ear. "Does that turn you on?" I whisper so only she can hear.

"*Yes*," she breathes.

"Meet me under the stands in five minutes," I growl.

She looks up at me, eyes wide in surprise, but she doesn't argue.

I kiss her forehead and slip away to do a quick round of the boys before sneaking off to meet up with Lily again.

I want her so fucking bad. I've had a taste and now I feel like an addict.

I manage to get away from everyone after about ten minutes – five was being ambitious, and duck under the stands when no one is paying attention.

She's already there waiting for me like the good girl that she is.

She's in jeans and boots and a big warm, winter coat. She's almost covered head to toe, but she somehow still manages to look sexy as hell.

"You're late."

She's fighting back a smile, so I know I'm not really in trouble.

I stroll over to where she's leaning against a large concrete pole. "I can think of a few ways to make it up to you."

"I guess you could try."

I smirk at her. I like this quiet arrogance thing she's got going on. It's hot as fuck. I take her by the hand and lead her in deeper, to a more secluded spot, tucking her in behind another pillar.

I kiss the corner of her mouth, then lower on her jaw, her neck, up to her ear until she lets out a breathy moan.

I'm not about to stop now though, there's no time to fuck around down here.

I undo the button on her jeans and slowly lower the zipper before roughly tugging them down her legs to her ankles. I drop to my knees and waste no time pulling her underwear to the side so I can taste her.

There's chatter and footsteps coming from the stands above us, but I don't care, I'm interested in one thing and one thing only.

She moans, loud as fuck, and her fingers weave into my hair, tugging at the strands.

I drag one leg of her jeans off over her boots to free it and throw it over my shoulder so she's open to me.

"Oh my god, Pax," she cries out as I slip a finger inside her while I suck and lick at her clit.

It's not going to take her long to come, I can feel her tightening around my finger and her legs shaking already.

I keep working her until she cries out that she's coming, and her body begins to slump.

I slip my finger out of her and use my hand to steady her while I keep teasing her with my tongue, taking every last bit of her pleasure from her.

"*Fuck.*" She whimpers.

She's pulling my hair so hard it's kind of painful, but I like it. I'm hard as rock.

"That's it, baby." I coax another couple of shudders out of her.

I want to fuck her so badly, but I don't have a condom, and this has probably got out of hand enough. The last thing I want is for one of the boys to come looking for me and see Lily like this.

She slowly releases my hair and I get to my feet, not

even bothering to brush the loose dirt off my already filthy knees.

I help her back into her jeans, resisting the urge to fuck her right here and now.

"I guess I forgive you for being late."

I chuckle. "Don't be too hasty. There's still more where that came from. It's just not happening here."

"There's more?"

"I'll be climbing in your window tonight to finish the job," I promise her.

She licks her lips before pulling me in for a kiss. "You better be."

TWENTY-FIVE

Lily

"So how was it?" Berlin asks me.

All eyes swing to me in anticipation of my answer.

I glance around nervously. The silence is *so* loud.

"How was *what*?"

All I can think about is how *it* was. How it felt when Pax slid inside me. How it felt when he licked and sucked until I came. How absolutely sated I felt lying in his arms afterwards. Between the first time and him having his way with me after the game, all I can think of is *it*. But I'm pretty sure that's not the question Berlin is asking. She couldn't possibly know.

She exchanges a look with Carissa.

"The *sex*, obviously."

I almost spit out the water I just drank from my drink bottle.

"*What?*"

She just gives me a look. Apparently, I'm not fooling anybody. That's so great.

"He told you?" I choke out in between coughing up water.

She grins triumphantly. "*No*, but you just did."

My eyes widen at my own stupidity.

It's not like it's a secret, but I hadn't planned to make a public announcement about the losing of my virginity. If I'd known that was how this worked, I'd have opted for a group text.

"Oh, come on, Lily, I'm not stupid. Your face says it all. You may as well have a 'I got fucked' sign stamped across you."

Keke gasps and points an accusing finger at me as though she's just noticed the non-existent sign across my forehead. "You had sex!"

A group of year nines look in our direction as they walk past.

"Shhhhh," I hiss. "Far out, Keeks, I think there might be some people down the back fields that didn't quite hear you if you want to go and get them up to speed."

"You had *sex*," she repeats in a whisper.

I don't know if she's disgusted or proud.

"Yes, okay, I did, alright. Now can we all just stop saying 'sex' please. Far out, you're making a scene."

Sophia laughs. "Absolutely not. Tell us everything."

I can feel my face getting redder and redder as all the girls just stare at me, waiting for the details.

"Please tell me that you used protection," Berlin begs.

"We love Pax, but I think he's been kind of a whore until now," Carissa adds.

I really try not to think too much about that, but it's not like its new information. There's been rumours about those boys for a year or two now, and I hang out in the science block, not on the moon. The gossip still reaches us nerds.

"All safe and well, thanks, Mum," I reassure them.

"God only knows this town doesn't need any more teen pregnancy." Berlin shudders.

"I can't believe you've had sex!" Keke says. Apparently, she's still in shock.

"You can't talk, you did it ages ago."

Keke hooked up with some guy at a summer camp when she was sixteen. They were both virgins and she said it was awkward as hell, but not entirely unpleasant.

She hasn't bothered doing it again yet.

That could be because she thinks she might be more into girls than guys. I guess she'll figure it out one day.

"Oh, I can still very much talk."

Lucky me.

"So can we," Sophia adds.

"Just so we're all on a level playing field, Carissa has had a couple of dicks, Mel is still clean as a whistle, Laura lost it to some gross bogan the other weekend." Laura shudders at the very mention of it. "And Sophia here is well on her way with Tonksy – as shocked as we all are about *that* turn of events," Berlin informs me.

I laugh at her delivery; it reminds me of the way Pax gave me the run down on all of them in the diner.

"Obviously her and Cullen go at it like rabbits at every possible opportunity," Sophia drawls.

Berlin shrugs, unfazed. "I make no apologies."

"Not to change the subject or anything, but can I please have the tea on this Tonksy situation?" I cut in.

"Can we stop calling him *Tonksy* please, it makes me feel icky." Sophia grimaces.

"His name being *Josh* is what *should* make you feel icky," Berlin tells her.

"What's wrong with being called Josh?" I ask.

"Oh my god, go outside every once in a while, watch a TikTok or something," Berlin teases me, although I'm sure she's only half joking. "Josh's are the *worst*. I swear to God, the female population, all over the world... we've come together to absolutely *crucify* anyone called Josh. J names in general are a concern, but *Joshua* is like the leader of the bad news pack."

"That's not only ridiculous, but it's also totally unreasonable," I reply.

"Thank you," Sophia agrees. "Josh has been nothing but sweet to me."

Berlin rolls her eyes when Sophia isn't looking.

"Pax told me he thought you had something to do with setting this whole thing up," I question Berlin.

"Correct," Carissa answers. "But it didn't exactly go to plan."

"*Didn't go to plan* is an understatement, she wasn't meant to actually fall for the local drug dealer," Berlin grumbles.

The what now.

I look back at Sophia in shock.

"Oh, don't look at me like that," Sophia tells me, outraged. "He was selling to your boyfriend, you know. Josh doesn't even take drugs himself. He just moves them for his cousin sometimes, and he's not even really doing that anymore."

Damn. I think I've misread Sophia. She comes across as super sweet and innocent, but now I hear that she's dating a drug dealer and it's got me questioning everything.

"Whatever helps you sleep at night," Berlin mutters.

Sophia looks like she's sick of this shit. "Look, I don't know what you expect from me. Bryson isn't interested, *okay?* He had his chance. All of this was meant to give him a push and it didn't work. I can't spend the rest of my life just waiting for a guy who may or may not make a move. He shat the bed, I got to know Josh and I'm happy. Just deal with it."

"*Fine,*" Berlin replies quickly. "Don't blow a gasket."

I'm almost sorry I asked. Almost, but not quite.

Mel and Laura are trying to cover their laughs, Carissa looks like she's bored of hearing this argument. I doubt this is even close to being the first time they've blown up at each other over it.

Keke looks surprisingly into this little gossip session.

"Can we just go back to talking about Pax giving Lily one," Sophia insists.

I definitely have more questions about this whole love triangle situation, but I can sense that it's not going to happen right now.

Berlin joins in. "Yeah, give us the details."

"You really want me to tell you about how your brother is in bed?"

"Yeah, fuck it, why not. Can't be any worse than thinking about the fact that I've kissed him."

"I'm sorry, you've what?" Keke demands.

It's lucky Pax told me this story already, or I probably would have just gone into cardiac arrest.

"Yeah." She shrugs. "We kissed once at a party, before we knew we were related, obviously. I'm not into weird incest kinks. Anyway, it was a bet for losing a game of beer pong. No biggie. Everyone got over it pretty quickly."

"You openly admit to necking on with your *brother* and then follow up with *no biggie* and people just go along with it? Man, your confidence is *wild*. I respect that." Keke shakes her head in disbelief.

"Thank you, Keke. Your hair is wild, and I respect that."

God, trying to keep up with this conversation is *tiring*. I'm barely used to talking to one person, let alone five at once.

"Okay can we just focus on one thing at a time," Carissa suggests.

Finally, some sense.

They all look at me pointedly.

Dammit.

"Okay fine, it was great. He was great. Everyone was very satisfied. That's all I'm saying."

"Was he romantic?

"Did you do it more than once?"

"Have you guys said the 'L' word?"

"Was it big?"

The questions all get fired at me at once.

Far out, I didn't know my lunch break was going to turn into a press conference. I'm not prepared for this.

"This is why I prefer to stay in the lab," I warn them. "If you guys can't chill, I'll stay in there for the rest of the year."

Not a single one of them look sorry.

I glance at my watch. "I don't mean to be *that* guy, but the bell's about to go, and I have to go to my locker before class."

I get to my feet and grab my bag while they all bitch and moan and protest.

The bell sounds as I swing my bag onto my shoulder, and I grin.

Can't argue with that.

I'M TYPING on my laptop, and Pax is doing... whatever it is Pax does when he's here, when I hear his phone make a noise, and I feel the vibration on my wrist from my watch, notifying me of a message on my own phone.

I ignore it, I'm eyeballs deep in chemical compounds and research theories and if I stop now, I'll probably lose my train of thought.

"What the fuck!" Pax yells.

I jump, nearly knocking over the coffee sitting next to my laptop.

I scramble to make sure it stays upright. Thank fuck for travel cups with lids.

I look over at him, and he's off the couch and on his feet. The look on his face scares me.

"What is it?"

My first thought is that someone is hurt. He looks like he's seen a ghost.

"Look at your phone," he demands.

I frantically feel around for my phone in a panic. I have no idea what to expect, but it's bad, I already know it's bad.

I swipe open the screen and see that I have a group message with Pax in it and some name I don't recognise. I tap on the message bubble and nearly drop my phone when it loads.

All there is, is a photo. It's me and Pax, under the stands on Saturday night. He's on his knees in front of me, and my jeans are down my legs. His face is between my thighs and my head is thrown back in pleasure. I'm not exposed, but it's pretty obvious he's eating me out. It's a little bit grainy, you can tell someone zoomed in a bit to get a closer shot, but there's no mistaking who it is.

"Holy shit," I whisper.

I didn't even hear him cross the room, but he's right next to me now.

"Who is that?" I ask, frantic. "Who sent that to us?"

"It's a fake account," he tells me. "No pictures, joined two days ago. It's someone hiding behind fake bullshit."

"Why would someone want to take a photo of us like that?"

"I don't know. It doesn't say anything. It's just a photo."

"I don't understand. Maybe it's just one of our friends being silly?"

He looks at me with an expression that makes it clear that we both know this isn't some harmless prank from a friend.

I stare at the picture. Holy shit. Someone took a photo of me having an orgasm.

"This can't be happening." I feel a tear slide down my cheek. I'm sure it won't be the last.

I think I'm in shock.

He wraps me in his arms and pulls me tight into his chest.

"I don't know what's going on, but we'll figure it out, okay?" He kisses the top of my head and lets me cry.

I can't believe this. I don't know who would do something this creepy and violating.

I can't afford to have pictures of me that resemble amateur porn doing the rounds. I'm working towards achieving an extremely exclusive scholarship to my dream school. I doubt they'd look too fondly at an applicant who's got a picture of her boyfriend going down on her, floating around the internet for everyone to see.

I don't know if professional rugby clubs would be too stoked about the scandal either.

We're both *screwed* if this goes public.

"That picture cannot get out." I sob.

"I'm going to do everything I can to make sure that doesn't happen, okay? I promise you I won't stop until I figure out who's behind it."

"What do they want from us?"

He holds me even tighter and sways me side to side. "I don't know, baby."

I'm getting hysterical, I can feel it.

I'm not the girl who finds herself in some high school sex scandal. I never even thought I'd lose my virginity in high school, let alone have something like this happen.

"This is all my fault. I never should have made you go down there."

He didn't *make* me do anything, I went down there willingly and was more than keen to be involved. And this isn't his fault. This is some weirdo invading our privacy.

"No. We're in this together."

"You and me, baby," he whispers.

I hold him tighter too.

Right now that's all we can do.

TWENTY-SIX

Pax

"Alright shut the fuck up, this emergency team meeting is in session."

Everyone falls silent.

Lily and I called in everyone we could trust.

Berlin, Cullen, Bryson, Sophia, Carissa, Mel, Laura and Keke are all sitting around the living room at mine and Cullen's house.

Lily hasn't stopped crying all day and it's *breaking* me.

Everyone is up to speed with the situation, but no one seems to know what the fuck to do about it.

"I'm telling you, it's got to be Liana. She's the only person crazy enough to do this kinda weird shit," Berlin says, crossing her ankles.

"Liana always has a motive," Cullen argues. "If it was

her, she wouldn't be able to resist adding in some bitchy fucking comment or blackmailing them for something."

"You said the account's not active anymore?" Bryson asks.

I shake my head. "Nah. I tried to check it out again about an hour after the message came through and it was deleted."

"I did a reverse image search and it didn't show up anything," Mel says.

I don't really know what the hell that means, but hopefully that's a good sign.

"You okay, Lily?" Berlin asks.

Lily is curled up in my lap. Same place she's been since we got back from the lab.

"Yeah." She sniffs. "Sorry I'm such a baby."

"No one thinks you're a baby," Cullen says gruffly. "This is some serious bullshit, and we won't let them get away with it."

"Thank you all for helping us," I say sincerely.

This might be a shitty situation, but the people in this room are pretty fucking incredible. Not everyone has friends like this, and I'm lucky they've stuck with me through all my bullshit. I sure as fuck haven't deserved their loyalty.

"I'm going to confront Liana," Berlin says, all that sass and attitude in full force.

Cullen physically places his hand on her to stop her, as though she were going to get up and go right now.

"But what if it *is* her, and then you get her all fired up and she puts that pic on her Insta story or something?" Keke says. "She seems to be a big fan of that shit."

She makes a good point. We're not in control here. We need to be smart, which unfortunately for me, isn't my forte.

Fuck, I wish I knew who was behind this, or what they want. I wish I knew just *something*.

I don't know how I'm meant to protect Lily from something like this.

"Oh my god, get Jaxon to get it out of her," Sophia half yells excitedly.

"Who the fuck is *Jaxon*?" Bryson grunts.

Shit must have gone further south between the two of them, because Sophia doesn't even acknowledge that Bryson has spoken. She just carries on talking.

"Do your catfish thing and find out if she's behind it," she tells Berlin.

"Can't." Berlin pouts. "She's pissed at him because he's still refusing to meet her."

"*Seriously?*"

"Wouldn't you be pissed if some guy had been leading you on for months, but wouldn't meet you in person?"

Sophia pouts. "Couldn't possibly imagine how disappointing it'd be to be let down by a male like that," she replies dryly.

I bite back a laugh at the obvious dig at Bryson. I don't know when she got so ballsy. She's been hanging around Ice too much. All that attitude is rubbing off.

"Who is Jaxon?" Bryson repeats.

Berlin smirks. "The catfish account I've been using to gather intel on Liana. She thinks it's this hot guy, but really it's just me using my mate's pictures, fucking with her."

Bryson pauses for a second. "Remind me to never get on your bad side."

"I hope not either. For your sake."

"Maybe she's finally onto you," I suggest.

Ice shakes her head. "*Nah*. She got a bit suss at one point and wanted a pic of him holding up a fork, it was weird, but I just asked my buddy to take the pic and she ate it up."

"She doesn't want to video call?" Bryson asks. "I'd want to video call."

"She mentioned it once, but I dunno, it's never really come up again."

"Well make up with her, and get the information, because we're going to need Lily to stop crying," Sophia states.

Fuck, it'd be great if she'd stop crying. I can understand why she's so upset. And this shit always looks worse for the girl than the guy, because society is fucked up like that, but I'm getting worried about her. She's borderline catatonic.

I'm also concerned about what else this asshole might have to share, but I don't even want to bring that up... her tears are cutting me deep.

"I'll try." Berlin shrugs. "Maybe I'll send her flowers. Kiss her ass for a bit."

"Keep your friends close but your enemies closer," Keke mutters.

"One day when this is all over and Liana has got her

karma, can we arrange for Jaxon to meet her and then when she shows up, we're all just sitting at a big table?"

Berlin grins wickedly. "Fuck yes."

"That sounds fun, but it doesn't really help with me not becoming an unwilling porn star." Lily sniffs.

"Unless you want to take it to the police, or the school, I think we just need to lay low, keep a real close eye on social media and try and figure this thing out quietly," Berlin tells her. "I know it's shit, and that you're scared, but whoever is behind this isn't being brave with it. They could have shown that picture to half the school by now if they wanted to, and they haven't. That's a good sign."

"And maybe no more fucking in public, you two," Cullen suggests.

"We weren't actually fucking." I flip him off and dip my head down to talk quietly to Lily. "We can go to Principal Evans, or the police if you want to. I'll do whatever you want."

"No," she replies quickly. "Not unless something else happens."

I'm pretty happy she feels the same way I do about that. The last thing I need right now is old man Evans putting another black mark next to my name.

"Right then, so for now, we stay vigilant."

"You make us sound like some kind of crime fighting gang."

"Stay Vigilante," I amend, smirking.

Lily actually laughs a little bit at that one.

It's a start.

I SNEAK around the side of the building, my hoodie pulled over on my head, covering as much of my face as it can.

I don't know what's made me think that *this* is the best idea in the world, but I'm here now and I'm not going to chicken out.

The store closed about thirty minutes ago, and from what I can tell, there's no one here. The owner has gone home for the night.

It's just me and my choices now.

I slink past the doors, looking inside. It's dark, the doors are locked.

I'm all alone.

It's now or never.

I shrug off my backpack and start grabbing out the supplies I'll need to get the job done.

I haven't been this close to the doors of this bottle store since the day I got myself on their most wanted list. I probably shouldn't be here now, but after I drove past here today and saw what I saw, I can't help myself.

Call it karma.

Call it destiny.

Maybe Scorpios moon is the microwave or whatever.

I don't care, I'm here and this is happening now.

I'm not going to get caught. I didn't tell anyone, not even Lily or Cull. As far as everyone is aware, I'm asleep for the night.

It's just me out here.

I grab the metal pole from next to my foot and get started.

"AREN'T you meant to walk the other way when you see me?"

That's pretty much exactly what I've been doing since *that* day.

He slams the door of his locker shut and crosses his arms across his chest. He's trying to look staunch, and he's actually nailing it. I'm impressed. I don't blame him for the tough guy act. I've probably messed his head up.

Getting punched on school grounds for no good reason would probably leave a lasting impression.

God, I'm an asshole.

"I just wanted to tell you in person that I'm really fucking sorry, bro. I had no right to lay hands on you and you didn't deserve it."

I already said sorry in the letter, and I've been warned to stay away from the kid, but I can't – I owe him more than some words on a sheet of paper.

"You should be sorry, bro, that shit was messed up."

He's eyeing me cautiously, like he's not sure what to make of me.

"I want to make it up to you."

"You want to swing at my nose from the other direction? Straighten it back up?"

"I was thinking more along the lines of doing a beer run for you and your mates or something. Me and the boys can carry a lot of piss."

He looks like he's about to tell me to go take a hike, when I see a light bulb go off over his head and his expression changes.

It's concerning to say the least. Hopefully he's not going to ask me to be a target for paintball shooting practice or something.

"Actually, I *can* think of something you can do for me."

"Yeah? What is it?"

"You're on the rugby team, right? You guys are all pretty close?"

I nod, unsure of where he's heading with this.

"You know Carley, your mate Bryson's sister?"

Ah shit.

"I don't like where this is going."

"You broke my nose," he says.

Touché.

"I really like her, man. I've had a crush on her since year ten."

He's only year eleven now, so it's not like he's been pining away after her for years on end. Still pretty weak that he's been crushing all this time and apparently hasn't done anything about it.

"Does she know you like her?"

He shakes his head quickly, like that's the stupidest question ever.

"Does she know you exist?"

He looks like he's not sure.

I groan. "Seriously, bro?"

"We sat next to each other in English last year and she's in my PE class this year. I don't know if she knows my name, but she's definitely seen me before."

"You have no idea how sad that sounds."

"Probably about as sad as a year thirteen with everything going for him, turning up to school drunk and getting suspended."

Well, fuck me. Another point to Brent.

"Bry is going to kill me if I try pimp out his sister."

He frowns at me. "You're not *pimping* her out, you weirdo. Just talk me up or something. I don't expect miracles, but at least get me on her radar."

I guess he's a good-looking dude. Blond, tall, fit, he seems like he's not a total dumbass, I don't really know why he wouldn't be able to get a girl that he liked.

"Alright, alright, I'll do it. Have you ever spoken to her?"

He shrugs. "A couple of times, but nothing more than basic, polite kinda chat. I get nervous when she's around."

Jesus Christ. I wonder where he keeps his vagina.

"I'm just going to push through and pretend that you're not a total pussy."

He looks like he wants to argue, but I keep talking. "You're going to have to tell me what kind of shit you're into... what you're good at... I can't talk you up if I don't know anything about you."

"You know I can brawl."

I smirk at him. Kid's got jokes.

"Yeah, one of you smoked my ribs," I admit.

"I'd say sorry, but I'm really not," he drawls.

I kind of like this kid. He seems like quite a good dude. Bit of backbone, at least when it doesn't involve girls.

"So I'll tell Carley that you can throw a punch then."

"Nah don't do that," he replies quickly. "She'll think I'm a dickhead."

"Come on, man, just forget being modest and tell me what you're good at."

He thinks about it for a second. I glance at my watch. I want to help the guy, make it up to him and all that, but this is taking longer than I planned.

"I'm on the basketball team, I'm not bad either. I'm really good at writing and... fuck I dunno... I'm not an asshole?"

"Good start," I tell him. "Leave it with me and I'll see what I can do."

He nods his head. He seems happy enough with that.

I just hope I can do something for the guy. All jokes aside, the way I behaved was lower than low, and I owe him.

He could have come after me for assault if he wanted to. I wouldn't have blamed him either. I'd have deserved whatever I got.

"I gotta go, but I'll do my best, and for what it's worth, I am really fucking sorry. I was going through a low point and I didn't deal with it well. I'm sorry you got caught in the crossfire."

"It's all good, man. You hit like a girl," he jokes.

We laugh together, and even though I still feel like a total asshole about it all, this seems like a step in the right direction.

I hold my hand out and he slaps his palm against mine.

"See ya round, bro."

"I'll keep my guard up."

TWENTY-SEVEN

Lily

It's been a couple of weeks since the photo landed in my inbox, and I've finally stopped flinching when I get an alert for a message. Those first few days, every time I saw people talking, whispering or laughing, my heart rate spiked, and I freaked out that they were looking at the picture and talking about me. Thankfully that didn't last long. Pax has done a good job of keeping me calm.

I probably shouldn't relax about things just yet, but there hasn't been anything more. No more pictures, no more messages, no nothing.

It's almost like whoever sent it had regrets and decided to bail. Dreams are free.

I mostly try not to think about it too much. I hate an unsolved mystery though, and this definitely qualifies, but as long as the photo stays off the internet and away from the public, then I can probably learn to live with it.

Pax groans and rubs his hand over his face.

I lower my book. "What are you doing?"

"Trying to play match maker." He frowns.

He looks not only totally bewildered, but also completely out of his depth.

"Match maker for who?"

He looks at me sheepishly. "Just this guy I know. He's into this girl but he's kind of a little bitch and doesn't know how to talk to her."

I narrow my eyes at him. He's up to something, I can tell.

"Who's the guy?"

My money is on it being someone from the team, but it doesn't really explain why he's acting so fishy about it.

"He's younger, you probably won't know him."

More suspicious behaviour.

I raise a brow at him and just sit there waiting for more information. I've spent enough time with him now to be able to read him pretty well.

"It's the guy I got into a fight with that time," he finally admits. "His name is Brent, he's a year eleven. I ran into him the other day and properly apologised. I told him I wanted to try and make it up to him somehow and he asked me to do him a favour."

This is not *at all* the direction I was expecting this story to take. It's not the time to tell him, but I'm a little proud that he went and apologised properly.

"Who's he crushing on?"

His expression tells me that *this* is the part he's feeling bad about.

"Bry's little sister, Carley."

I crack a smile. "*Awkward.*"

He runs his hand through his hair and finally spills his thoughts. "Tell me about it. He seems like a good dude, and Carley is old enough to take care of herself, but I don't know if I should be telling Bry that I'm trying to help this guy get into his sister's pants."

"Well, if you do, I'd avoid wording it like *that*," I tell him.

"You know what I mean." He groans. "I don't know where to start. I don't even know how the hell I got you, how am I meant to help someone else pull?"

I bite back a laugh. He's so cute when he's flipping out over silly things.

"Is he hot?"

He gives me a look. "He's not my type, if that's what you're asking."

I swat at his shoulder. "You know what I mean."

"Yeah, he's a good-looking guy. Tall, blond, athletic."

"Sounds like a good start."

If there's one thing I know about females, especially fifteen-year-old ones – it's that you'll never get them to do something they don't really want to do. Especially not girls with the privilege and looks that Carley Decker has.

Pax can have all the good intentions in the world, but if Carley doesn't think this Brent guy is cute, he doesn't have a hope in hell of changing her mind.

"Doesn't mean fuck all if Carley doesn't know who the kid is."

"Can't you just tell her that he's a good guy?"

"Last time I went around to Bry's I gave her some shit about her skirt being so short it was up around her neck, and I swear to God she nearly killed me with a look. She's so feral she may as well hiss when people come close. She's not going to listen to my opinions on potential boyfriends."

I bite back a laugh.

Sounds like she's full of teenage girl hormones and sick of her brother's friend's shit. She's probably a sweet girl outside of that, but that's not about to extend to Pax – or the kid he's trying to help out. In fact, it'll probably have the opposite effect.

"This sounds like it's going to be a complete clusterfuck."

"I appreciate your confidence in me."

"You're welcome. I do actually have one idea."

"I'm all ears."

"Tell her you overheard a couple of guys talking about her. Play it off like one of the guys didn't think she was a big deal."

"You want me to insult her?" He's looking at me like I've lost my god damn mind.

"*No.* Jesus. We don't want to set the poor boy up to have his eyes scratched out. Act like one guy was really into her – she won't be interested in hearing about that. But some attractive, tall basketball player who isn't tripping over himself... that'll get her attention."

"I don't understand."

I can't help but laugh at how lost he looks.

"Don't worry, Ace, we'll iron out the details."

"Are we like... treating 'em mean, to keep 'em keen?" he asks, excited that maybe he might be getting it.

"Something like that." I shake my head in amusement. "That won't work with me, just so you know."

"I wouldn't dream of being mean to you, nerd."

"Good. I wouldn't be mean to you either."

"That's a shame, I think your mean streak could be sexy."

"You're a pig." I laugh.

He's laughing – at his own joke.

"You want me to change... turn into a bitch?" I tease.

He shakes his head, his laughter dying off as he pins me with those dark eyes.

"I wouldn't change a single thing about you, Lily."

That's the sweetest thing I've ever heard. It's bound to be a total lie, but it's very sweet anyway.

"Actually, that's a lie. I'd change *one* thing."

I bet it's my ass. Maybe my stomach rolls. Love handles. Cellulite. I should probably wait for the answer, this guessing game isn't doing much for my self-esteem.

He's watching me. Almost plucking the thoughts straight out of my head.

"*That*. That right there is what I'd change, Lily. The self-doubt. The way you're so mean to yourself. You're funny, kind, beautiful and sexy. Everything about you is how it's meant to be."

I take it back. *That* is the sweetest thing I've ever heard.

I don't agree, and I'm rarely good at accepting a compliment, but he means it. I can see it in his eyes how serious he is about it. He means every word. He truly thinks I'm amazing the way I am.

He doesn't care what size my jeans are, or if I overindulged with that block of chocolate. He doesn't give two shits if my butt jiggles when I run, or if I have a roll over the top of my jeans when I sit down. He likes me for me, and I don't think I've ever felt so seen and appreciated in my whole life.

PAX CLAMBERS THROUGH MY WINDOW, not even attempting to keep the noise down. I don't know why he still comes in this way instead of using the door, but I think he just enjoys the excitement of it all. He's a bad boy at heart and old habits die hard.

"Lily-boo, I missed you."

"You only dropped me home a couple of hours ago." I laugh.

"A couple of hours is too long. Ma and Mum have not shut up about you since you left," he tells me, before closing and locking the window behind himself.

God, that makes me nervous. I hope they didn't hate me. That'd be so awkward.

It was my first time meeting them both and I was *so* nervous. Pax means so much to me, and meeting not only one woman who is responsible for raising him, but two, was daunting.

They're lovely women, and it was obvious how much they both love both of the boys. Pax's ma was ridiculously excited to meet me. It was quite sweet, but their relationship is still noticeably strained. I hope one day they'll be able to get back to the way they were before this whole saga.

"What'd they say about me?" I ask warily. "I hope they approve of me."

"What *didn't* they say?"

"That's not helpful, Pax. I'm freaking out here."

He chuckles and pulls me in for a hug. "They adore you already. Seriously, you're giving Berlin a run for her money in the favourite girlfriend-in-law stakes."

"They really liked me?"

"They *love* you. I swear to God, it was all... Lily is so sweet, Lily is so nice, Lily is so pretty. It was almost embarrassing, they're like a couple of fan girls. Big points for me though, apparently I have good taste."

I blush, because of course, it's me and someone just gave me a compliment that I don't know how to accept. "Well, that's very sweet of them to say."

"Bet they wouldn't think you were so sweet if they knew how you'd sucked my dick an hour before they met you. I still can't believe you went in there with penis breath." He laughs.

"Pax!" I smack his chest lightly, going a much deeper red.

"Don't be embarrassed, that was the best blow job I've ever had."

"Oh my god, stop!" I try to turn around to escape from him, but he grabs me around the waist and pulls my back against his front.

His mouth is at my ear, his breath warm on my skin. "I'm being serious, Lil, you keep doing such a good job and I might be out here knocking on your window every night."

"I wouldn't be complaining," I murmur.

He presses his crotch into my back, and I can feel how hard he is again. He's like an energiser battery; he never stops, he's already ready.

"Mmmm," I murmur.

I don't know if it'll always be like this, but right now, I can't get enough of him. The feeling seems mutual.

"Am I really doing an okay job?"

It's not like I have anything to compare to, but I did some serious research on how to do it right, so hopefully that paid off.

I really am such a nerd.

"Mind blowing, Lily, trust me."

I'm quite proud of myself for that. I'm not sure I entirely believe him, but since we got the... *result*... I figure I didn't do the worst job.

"You're welcome to conduct further hands-on research if you want to."

He knows me well. I do love research.

I'm definitely not opposed to getting more experience. Not if he's going to make noises like he did last time.

That was seriously hot.

"I think maybe it's my turn to get a little more hands on experience." He slips his hand from my stomach down between my legs.

I make a humming noise.

I love it when he touches me.

He sweeps the hair away from my neck and trails kisses from my ear down to my shoulder.

It feels so good, I shudder as tingles race up and down my spine.

"I'm going to strip you naked and bend you over that desk," he growls in my ear.

Yes. Please.

Even just the thought of that has me wet.

Now that I'm having sex, I can't believe it took me this long to get started. It's lucky that I'm nearly done with my scholarship work though, all this sexual tension is very distracting in the lab.

I turn around in his arms and kiss him, while I run my hands over his arms and shoulders – he's so firm and toned, I love feeling his muscles flex under my palms.

I gasp as he slides his hands under my ass and lifts me up, I clamp my legs around his waist and cling onto his neck.

I still can't believe he can hold me up like that, but it doesn't seem to bother him, it's like I weigh nothing.

It makes me feel feminine and sexy.

We're still kissing like crazy, neither of us can seem to get enough.

He backs up and lowers himself into my desk chair, so I'm sitting in his lap.

"*Lily*," he whispers against my lips.

"I love you," I whisper back.

"I love you more."

He grips my hips and rocks me back and forth over the bulge in his pants.

I'm about ready for that whole being stripped naked part.

He pauses for a second, listening, so I do the same.

His ears must be better than mine, because it takes a second longer for me to hear the unmistakable sound of Grammy's slow footsteps down the hallway.

They get closer and closer until they stop outside my door.

Impeccable timing.

There's a little knock on my door.

Grammy and I haven't exactly sat down and had a conversation about Pax staying over, but I'm sure she knows he does. She's pretty fond of him, and she's not shy about having him do a variety of 'man jobs' around the place.

"I'm just doing my homework," I yell out loudly. She normally takes her hearing aids out at this time of night, so she probably can't even hear me.

"I might be deaf, dear, but I'm not silly. You two use the front door, would you? Dorinne from next door is about to call the police. She phoned me up on the telephone and told me someone was trying to break in through the window."

I grimace. That is seriously embarrassing. Nothing like getting called out by the local old lady neighbourhood watch.

"Busy body Dorinne," I grumble. "Sorry, Grammy, we were just being silly," I call out to her.

"And bring that boy out here for some cake."

"We don't need any cake, Grammy."

"What was that?"

I was right. The hearing aids have been put to bed for the night.

"I said we don't need any cake!" I yell back a little louder.

"You both want cake?"

I cover my face with my hands.

Pax is pissing himself silently.

"I'll get it ready, dear," she replies, clearly not having heard a god damn word I've just said.

We both listen to her shuffles head off back down the hall.

"I think we're going to have to have some cake." I sigh.

He leans down, kisses my forehead and squeezes my butt. "I'd love some."

TWENTY-EIGHT

Pax

I nearly shit myself when I hear the footsteps behind me. Like no lie, it touches cotton.

I've clearly gotten complacent out here, because I had no idea I wasn't alone until someone was right behind me.

"You missed a spot."

I spin around, already planning to make a run for it, even though I know I'm cornered. I'm a moron.

"Don't run," he tells me.

It's pretty dark out, but I remember the voice. It's the guy who owns the bottle store.

Fuck.

I hope he's not going to chase me down the street again, or worse, call the cops on me. There's no way he's not going to recognise me once I take my hood off, and when he does, I'm bound to wind up in cuffs.

Shit. That'll learn me. It's what I deserve anyway. Karma is a bitch.

Goodbye rugby season.

"How long are you going to keep this up for, kid? I'm not complaining, but I think you've repaid your debt by now."

"*What?*" I ask. That's not at all what I was expecting.

"That box of beers was worth about twenty bucks. You've been here for *hours*, night after night."

Hold up...

"Wait. You already knew it was me?" I ask, turning to face him.

"Of course I knew it was you. I've been watching you on the security camera feed for weeks. I knew it was you the day you showed up here and cleaned all that graffiti off. I assumed that'd be it – you'd call it even, but you just keep on coming back."

"It doesn't feel like enough. I was a dick."

He nods his head and looks me in the eyes. "You were a dick."

I quickly tug my hood off. I'm making a total mess of this, but I want to be as respectful as I can be – the opposite of my past behaviour.

"I wanted to try and make it right."

"Do you think you have?"

I'm not sure. I owe him an apology. One that I've been too scared to give in case it landed me in a cell, but I'm here now, may as well put all the cards on the table.

"I'm really sorry for the way I acted. I wasn't in a good space, but I'm doing better now. Got my head on straight. I know cleaning up spray paint and broken glass doesn't make what I did any better, but I'll do whatever you want me to do to make up for it."

He doesn't say anything for ages. He's probably trying to decide if he can be bothered calling the police at this hour of the night, or if he'd rather make me his private clean-up crew for the next twenty years.

"You can call the cops if you want to. I won't run this time."

I don't know why the fuck I'm putting ideas in his head, but it's too late now.

He looks me dead in the eye, contemplating it.

"I don't think that'll be necessary."

"You don't?"

He shakes his head. "I was young and stupid once too." He shakes his head at himself. "God, that makes me sound so old."

I want to laugh, but I'm too on edge. I don't want to do anything that might spook him back to his senses and earn me a free ride in the back seat of a cop car.

"You can relax, kid. I've known who you are for a while now. This is a small town. If I wanted to press charges, I would have."

"I don't know what to say."

I don't think I've ever been this lost for words.

"Say 'thank you' and tell me you'll stop lurking around here at stupid hours of the night. You're giving my wife anxiety."

I give him a questioning look and he rolls his eyes. "Tell me about it. She's a softy. Doesn't like you being out here alone. I reminded her you're an adult, and I pointed out how much money we were saving on getting this mess cleaned up."

"How'd that help your case?" I ask him, relaxing a little bit.

"A small reprieve. Couple more nights of free labour. Here I am though, so obviously she got her way. As per usual."

I still don't really know what to say. I feel a lot like a little kid who's been caught doing something naughty. Only this time I'm trying to do something good. I'm stumped on where to go from here.

"It's Paxton, right?"

"Pax. Yeah." I step forward and hold out my hand. I wouldn't be surprised if he just lets it hang there, but he doesn't, he steps forwards and shakes my hand.

"Jeff."

I clear my throat. I don't know what else there is to say.

"Is everything alright with you? You know, at home or whatever."

I don't know what makes me do it, but I give him an honest answer.

"Yes and no. My mum lied to me about not knowing who my father was for my whole life, and now he's here and everything was kind of a mess for a bit, but I'm coming to terms with it all now. Building bridges and stuff."

"That's a tough break. I can see how that might result in some dodgy decision-making."

"I do a good downward spiral."

"I'm glad to hear things are getting better."

Him and me both.

"Your mum know you're out half the night?"

I shake my head. I feel bad about that. I know I'm eighteen – legally an adult, but I still live under her roof. She'd die if something happened to me out here.

"Go home. Don't tell my wife that she was right, but you really shouldn't be out here in the dark all alone."

"I'll just finish up and then hit the road. I'm parked around back."

"That's the other thing. If you're ever planning some kind of getaway in a vehicle, you might want to do a better job of checking for security cameras. You're on the other side of the block, but I clocked your number plate on the second night."

Fuck, I'm a rookie. Lucky I don't have any plans to hold up a bank any time soon. Sounds like they'd have me tracked down in about thirty seconds if I did.

"Maybe you should be a detective."

"Maybe." He chuckles. "Think I'll stick to selling beer for now."

I nod my head. It's probably not too bad of a job until assholes like me come along and fuck shit up.

"Maybe I'll even calm down on the school uniform thing."

"Yeah?"

"Nah." He laughs. "Probably not."

He turns, like he's about to leave.

"Thank you. Jeff." I clear my throat again. "And I really am sorry. I've learnt my lesson. And I hope you can forgive me."

"Consider it forgiven. I'll even take your picture off the wall of shame."

"Yeah?"

"Yeah. It takes a man to own up to his mistakes and try to make it right."

I kick a bit of timber with the toe of my shoe. "I'm trying."

"I know you are, kid. Now hurry up and get out of the cold. I'll never live it down if my wife finds out you got sick."

I nod my head quickly.

He waves as he disappears around the corner of the building.

I look around at the last of the graffiti I have to clean off, give myself a moment to appreciate the fact that I managed to do something right for once, and then I get back to work.

ME AND BRY are playing pool in their huge, second living area, when an opportunity not only finds me, but smacks me right in the face.

Carley and a couple of her little mates stroll in, mid gossip session.

Exactly what I need.

Carley doesn't even acknowledge us, but her friends sneak us glances and smiles. I'm not stupid. I know they hang out here in the hopes of seeing Bryson or his even hotter mates. Carley would be the same with any of her friends' older brothers. It makes me laugh at how much they try and play it cool.

They stroll past and sit themselves on the couches.

"Nice to see you too, ladies."

Carley glares at me.

"I'm good, thanks for asking," I carry on.

"What do you want, Pax? I have better things to do than talk to losers."

She might have to spend more time with Ice. Her insults need some work.

"You should be thanking me, Carley, I overheard something about you the other day – had to stand up for you and set the dude straight."

That gets her attention. "You did *what?*"

"You know. Defended your honour."

"That better not have involved you speaking my name, aloud, in public." She grimaces, as though I've told her something absolutely feral, like I skinned a cat during lunch and served it up on a lunch tray.

"It involved all three of those things, but don't worry, I had your back."

She actually looks like she could throw up.

The horror.

"Tell me everything. *Now,*" she insists.

"Was just a couple of dudes. No biggie."

"Details, *immediately.*"

I turn away to hide my smirk.

"I'm not sure but I think it was that kid Johnathan from the basketball team, he was with Brent – you know the kid I got into the fight with? Tall, blond, pretty good-looking guy actually."

"I know who Brent is."

Solid. That's a good start. Brent may have underestimated himself.

"And everyone knows about that fight. Embarrassing for you much." She smirks.

I push on. "Anyway, that John kid was going on and on about how hot you are and how he wants to ask you to the formal at the end of the year and all this shit."

"I told you he was into you," one of her friends says to her.

"Boring," she replies quickly.

I hope I'm not landing this kid Johnathon in hot water here. Word around the gym is that he *is* hot for Carley, so it should be no harm done, but I'm making the rest of it up as I go along. I don't even know if the two guys are mates. I'm flying by the seat of my pants.

I might have failed creative writing in English, but I'm thriving out here talking shit as a wannabe cupid.

"He wouldn't stop banging on and on about how you were the hottest girl in school. Brent didn't even know who he was talking about, but he still wouldn't sto–"

"*Excuse me?* Brent didn't know who he was talking about?" Carley interrupts me.

Bingo.

"Yeah, I dunno. I think he figured it out eventually," I say dismissively.

"I've been in *so many* of his classes," Carley says, her confidence clearly dented.

I have to hold back a laugh at this point.

"What exactly did Brent say?"

I shrug. "I dunno. Didn't seem that interested I

guess... I think he said something like... *oh yeah, her, she seems alright.*"

One of her friends gasps. Like actually gasps out loud at the apparent audacity of this boy and his ability to be unfazed by the greatness that is Carley Decker.

The other friend looks a little smug if I'm honest. She's probably tired of living in Carley's shadow.

Carley looks... *frustrated.*

This is fun.

"Anyway, I told Johnathon he better not fuck you around or he'll have me to deal with."

"Ew. *Don't* try and act like my protector. And Johnathon has *nothing* to worry about, because I'm *not* interested."

Well, well, well. Lily was right after all.

"And don't talk about me to people, it's gross. I don't want anyone thinking you know me."

I flip her off.

Carley gives me a look that dismisses me, and I turn back around, biting down a grin.

"I can't believe he didn't know who you were right away," I hear one of them whisper.

"Like, right? I sat next to him in English last year. He's in my P.E class."

"Did he ever try and talk to you?"

I glance over at the three of them out of the corner of my eye. They're in full girl mode – dissecting everything.

Carley shakes her head. "No... not really."

"Maybe he's shy."

"Maybe he's just not into her."

Carley gives the friend who said that a spicy-as-hell look.

Fuck, I envy her confidence. It's not like I'm a shy dude, but she lives her life like any and every person would be tripping over themselves for the privilege of being spoken to by her, and while it'll probably fuck her over at some point, it's getting her places right now. She's the top of the teenage girl food chain.

"He's obviously confused," the friend who has the least balls says, trying to calm Carley down.

"Well maybe I better make sure he knows *exactly* who I am. Clear up any of that confusion."

"I bet he won't think you're just 'alright' after that."

I smirk to myself. Girls are weird, but it's mission accomplished for me. Brent is on her radar. What he does from here on out is up to him.

Bryson is staring at me.

"It's your shot," I tell him.

He gives me a *what the fuck are you up to* look, but thankfully for me, playing dumb isn't just a skill, it's a life-style choice, so I just shrug and get back to my game like I didn't just cultivate potential young love.

TWENTY-NINE

Lily

I was expecting the final game to be one of those nail-biting close games where it all comes down to the last minute – a runaway try maybe where the star player saves the day and makes a legend of himself, but this game is nothing like that.

The Black Diamonds have left absolutely no room for their opposition to even get a point on the board, let alone make it a close score.

The boys are absolutely dominating out there. It's a total whitewash. Pax has played a full game so far and he's killing it. They all are. They look like the most well drilled high school team I've ever seen.

I don't know what these boys have been getting fed, but they look fitter, stronger and faster than ever. They're so in tune with one another, the other team never stood a chance.

There's just under five minutes left on the clock, and the whole crowd is going crazy, celebrating the win before the final whistle has been blown.

They can't lose it from here. Even if all fifteen of them forgot how to catch the ball, they'd still win. They're the champs. Again.

Pax scored the try of the game just before half-time and it doesn't matter what happens with us in the future, or where life takes me, I'll *never* forget the way he searched for me in the crowd, tapped his fist to his heart twice and pointed at me.

The blinding smile on his face.

The pure adoration in his eyes.

The privilege of being his is an all-consuming feeling that I *never* expected.

Two minutes to go.

"They've done it again," Berlin yells from next to me.

From what I can gather, she doesn't really give two shits about rugby, but she loves Cullen, so she's here, cheering and yelling and clapping in all the right places, for every single game of the season.

Sophia is just as excited, and Carissa is pretty into it too. Keke declined the offer to come with me, so it's nice I get to be here with friends instead of on my own like a loser.

I think I can safely call these girls friends now.

I never saw that coming, but they're nice girls, if not a little unhinged, and they help bring me out of my shell a bit. They're good for me.

One minute left...

"Woooooooooooo!" I cheer at the top of my lungs.

We're all clapping and yelling and going crazy as the seconds tick away.

"Ten! Nine! Eight! Seven! Six! Five! Four! Three! Two! One!"

Time's up.

We're already in possession of the ball, and Bryson kicks it, sending it out of field, effectively ending the game.

The whistle blows.

It's over. They won.

If I thought the cheers of the crowd were loud before, it's nothing compared to the deafening noise that fills the stadium now.

The Westlake High supporters are losing their shit, the four of us included.

I'm *so* proud of him.

And not just for winning this game, but for being the man I deserve, for cleaning up his act, for coming back to the game he loves with a whole new passion. I couldn't be prouder of the man he is today.

The boys all run around like crazy, hugging and jumping all over each other.

This is a huge moment for them. Those who are new to the team are tasting victory for the first time, where the guys who are in their final year are probably soaking in the feeling of their last ever time putting on this jersey and playing for an incredible team.

It'll be bittersweet for Cullen, Bry, and Pax. The

three of them have been in this team a long time, and it's all over now.

I don't know what their plans are for next year, but there's a chance they'll never all play for the same team again. It's kind of sad to think about everyone going their separate ways next year, but it's exciting too.

I feel tears welling in my eyes as I watch Pax and Cole embrace. Father and son. I know what this moment means to him. It's something he never thought he'd get.

He's really leaned into his relationship with his dad lately and I've seen such a change in him because of that.

He's so happy.

It's like he's carrying a little less weight on his shoulders. He's finally been able to unload it to someone strong enough to bear the load.

"Let's go!" Berlin yells to me over the screaming. "We're going down onto the field."

I shake my head quickly, my eyes wide. There's *no way* I'm going down there in front of so many people. This is the big league. I don't want to get in the way. This isn't *my* moment, and I'm sure Pax would prefer to celebrate with his teammates.

"I'm good here, I'll see him after," I yell back. "Later. Whenever."

She rolls her eyes and leans in closer. "Don't be a party pooper. He's going to want to see you down there."

I don't know about that.

I can feel myself blushing at the idea of going down there in front of everyone.

I don't want to embarrass myself – or him. What we have is so private – potential photo leak aside.

"I'll come down when the crowd thins out a bit. You should go though. I'm fine here."

She looks like she's about to get settled into an argument with me over it, but Carissa and Sophia drag her away down the stands, smiling and waving at me as they go.

"Lily will catch up when she's ready," Sophia says.

They probably think I'm being silly too but I'm glad they respect my shyness at least.

I watch them with a smile as they make it down onto the field. Soph and Carissa fall behind as Berlin runs off into Cullen's waiting arms. They look like they're in a movie as he swings her around, celebrating. Love oozes off them.

I see Sophia and Tonksy come together out the corner of my eye, their moment is nowhere near as passionate, but it's still kind of cute when he kisses her forehead as she hugs him.

I also can't help but see Bryson standing off to the side, watching their interaction with a blank expression on his face.

I kind of feel sorry for the guy, but I guess he had his chance. You can lead a horse to water, but you can't make it drink.

Right now he looks pretty damn thirsty too.

Silly boy.

The stands around me are still super crowded so it takes me a moment to figure out what the sudden increase in cheering is all about.

I push up on my tippy toes, trying to see what has got everyone below me so excited.

He's about halfway up the stands when I spot him, climbing over rows of seats, getting pats on the back and congratulations from everyone he passes.

I feel my cheeks go bright red as he makes a beeline for me, not stopping to talk to anyone. He's a man on a mission.

I can feel everyone staring as he parts his way through people to get to me, eventually stopping right in front of me, a row below, his head still higher than mine.

He's got grass-stained knees and a smear of dirt across one of his cheek bones.

God, he's so *hot*.

"What are you doing hiding up here, brains?" He grins.

I open my mouth to talk but my explanation gets caught up with my congratulations and nothing coherent comes out.

He just chuckles and wraps his hand around the back of my neck, pulling my mouth to his and kissing me in a way that is absolutely not appropriate for public viewing.

I don't even care – I just let him do it – he's the champ after all, he deserves it. At least I've got pants on this time.

"I love knowing that you're watching me out there," he breathes, his forehead resting against mine.

"I love it too, Ace."

"Why didn't you come down with the girls?"

I shrug. I feel kind of silly now. He clearly isn't worried about being seen with me. "I wasn't sure if I should."

He pulls back and looks me in the eyes with an expression so serious I almost don't recognise him. "You *always* should, Lily. With *me*, always. I'll want you there, trust me."

All I can do is nod my head. My mind is so caught up in him I couldn't string together a sentence if I tried.

It's going to take some getting used to – the pride in which this man claims me as his.

He taps my butt. "Let's go, my little nerd, we're celebrating and I'm not letting you out of my sight."

I take his hand in mine, and let him lead me along the row, and down the stairs of the stands, he stops and accepts the congratulations this time, making sure not to let go of my hand while he does, and introducing me to anyone important that we come across.

I never imagined that this would be my life – it's not the fact that I can see he's destined for greatness, or that I can see myself at his side while he achieves it, it's the fact that he's so proud to have me next to him while he does it.

***

"I CAN'T BELIEVE your dad is letting you have a party like this," I say as I look around at the people crowded in Berlin's living room.

Berlin waves her hand. "Pfft. *Please.* It was his idea. He's reliving his glory days; I swear to God."

"He doesn't need to relive them, he's still in his peak, look at the guy. Prime meat," Pax boasts.

Berlin gives him a grossed-out look. "I'd have thought your weird little man crush would have dissolved when you found out he was *your* dad too, but I see it's still alive and well. Feels kind of *incesty.*"

"It's not like I'm tickling his balls, Ice, I'm just saying he's a good-looking dude. Like father, like son."

"You're so weird sometimes."

"Weird, but right."

He's certainly not wrong. Cole Davids is an attractive man.

I smile as I watch the two of them banter back and forth. They're more similar than they probably realise. Those Davids genes are strong.

They even have some of the same mannerisms. DNA is crazy.

Tonight has been so fun.

It's not like I have anything to compare it to, since I'm not exactly a seasoned party goer, but I think this is probably the party of the year. It's not too crowded, but the whole team is here, and a few of the guys' girlfriends aside, there's no blonde cheer bitch brigade.

Everyone is on such a good buzz, the team is still on a huge high and there's no real drama. There's definitely no Liana bullshit.

The drinks are flowing, even for me, which is probably quite a risky game since I've barely touched a drop of alcohol in my life.

"I think I should have a water."

Sophia nods at me, knowingly. "Good idea. I got so smashed at one of these parties – Cullen had to carry me inside Berlin's house to sleep it off so my parents didn't find out."

"Seriously?"

She sighs. "Seriously. Turns out Liana slipped something in Berlin's drink, and then I drank it, but *still*, I definitely had my body weight in drinks prior to that happening."

I never did get all the details on that wild drugging story, maybe tonight will be the night.

"You really don't want to be the girl who throws up at parties – some people will remind you of it *forever*," she carries on, glaring at Pax as she does.

He chuckles. He's behind me now, his arms wrapped around my middle, his chin resting on my shoulder. "*Hey*, you can't blame me for that. It was a lot of puke for such a little girl. It would have been impressive if it wasn't so gross."

Sophia flips him off before looking around the room again. Her man is here somewhere, but I haven't seen them together. She's doing the casual sweep of the room every few minutes though, clearly looking for him.

I'm pretty sure I saw him head outside with a group of people as soon as we arrived. He hasn't seemed overly concerned about spending any time with his girlfriend, but it's not my place to point out how weird that seems. I can't help but wonder if it was him I overheard behind the art block that day, but I've never said anything to anyone.

Cole swaggers over to us, his whole vibe a little more drunk than it was when we arrived. I haven't actually been properly introduced to Cole yet, but I have a feeling that's about to change.

"Is this my future daughter in law?" He smirks, looking to get a rise out of Pax.

"Maybe, if she plays her cards right," Pax retorts.

Cole looks amused.

"Lily," he says warmly, reaching out to pull me into a hug.

"Hey, Mr. Davids."

"Gross. Call me Cole."

"*Cole*," I repeat as he releases me. I can feel my cheeks going red – yet again. This whole blushing at the drop of a hat is getting really old. "It's good to finally meet you."

"You too, I was worried this knuckle head was going to mess it up before I got the chance."

He reaches over and playfully punches Pax's shoulder.

Pax flips him off. "Lucky I have an old man with a hundred years of experience to turn to for advice, huh?"

"Smart prick." Cole chuckles.

"Just wait until he starts one of his stories with *back in my day*, right, old man?" Berlin chimes in.

It cracks me up the way they give him shit like this when he's the youngest – and hottest – dad around. I guess that's the gag. Got to keep him humble.

"Where's your date tonight, Cole?" I ask him.

He grins and shakes his head, but there's a sparkle in his eye that makes me think he's not short of options.

"She's probably hiding in the bushes outside his window," Berlin drawls.

"Oh be nice," Cole tells her, biting back a laugh.

"I feel like there's a story here," Pax prompts.

Berlin rolls her eyes dramatically. "Oh, there's a story alright. Genius over here got himself caught up with a stage five clinger. *And* she knows where we live."

Cole just laughs, thoroughly amused. "She's not a stage five clinger."

"She's at least a four and a half," Berlin barters.

"But she looks like a ten," Cole mutters, smirking.

"I don't care if she's so smoking hot that she's literally on fire. She's as crazy as a bag of cats."

Pax howls with laughter. My face hurts from smiling so much.

Berlin turns to us. "She showed up here, the day after their *first* date with a basket of muffins. Like, what the fuck? This isn't a suburban sitcom, and it's not the nineteen fifties. The woman needs to pull herself together. It's embarrassing."

We're all cracking up laughing.

Cole just shrugs. He seems pretty proud of himself. "What can I say? I've got the special recipe to keep them coming back."

"I swear to God, I cannot hear the joke about your secret sauce again. I'll need therapy." Berlin shudders.

Carissa's drink comes out her nose, she's so caught off guard by the comment.

"I think it's time to wrap this conversation up." Cole claps his hands together. "Lovely to meet you, Lily, you're welcome for the free trauma. Let's do this again some time without the inappropriate comments. Pax can bring you over for dinner one night. I'll order in and pretend I cooked it myself."

"Sounds like a great idea."

"It's a better idea than him actually cooking, I can tell you that for free," Berlin teases.

Cole saunters away, still laughing. I really like Cole.

He seems like a good dad. He's fun, but I don't doubt he'd do anything to make Berlin and Pax happy and keep them safe. He's what a father should be. Plus he's *very* nice to look at, so that's never a bad thing. Pax is going to look just like him in twenty years.

The boys all fall into an easy banter, and I slip out of Pax's arm to join the girls on the couch.

He pulls me back to him, kisses me hard and then lets me go again.

He's still totally engrossed in their conversation, but somehow, he makes me feel like I'm the centre of his universe.

"Where's your *man?*" Berlin asks Sophia, barely concealing the fact that she clearly thinks 'man' isn't an accurate description.

She shrugs, trying to play it cool. "He's here somewhere."

"He's probably outside dealing drugs," Berlin whispers to me and Carissa when Sophia turns to look around the room, yet again.

She might be trying to play it cool, but she's failing miserably. I feel bad for her. It must feel like shit to put in more than you get back out.

Berlin starts to whisper something else, but Sophia turns back around, and Berlin pretends she was about to sip her drink.

"Did you find out anything more about your creepy stalker picture?" Sophia asks me.

I shake my head. "Haven't heard or seen a thing."

"Liana still hasn't said a word to Jaxon about it. As much as I hate to say it, I don't think it was her."

Oh well. It was worth a shot.

It's not keeping me awake at night anymore, but it's always there in the back of my mind. I just want to know who it was, and why. It'd be great if I could get an iron-clad agreement to make sure it never got sent to someone else ever again, but at this point I'd probably be happy to just know who was behind it.

I'll be forever grateful for the support I've gotten from these girls. Without them, Keke, and Pax, I don't know how I would have kept myself afloat.

I don't even want to think about it tonight. That can be tomorrow's worry. Tonight, I just want to enjoy this party with my boyfriend and my friends.

Fourteen words I never thought I'd hear myself say.

"Hopefully it'll never resurface," I say.

"I'll drink to that," Berlin replies, raising her bottle.

We all nod in agreement and clink our bottles together.

THIRTY

Pax

I'd be lying if I said I didn't like the attention at least a little bit.

I love the game for what it is, but winning, and even more than that, being the champion team in our final year of high school, is pretty fucking epic.

Doesn't hurt to have hundreds of people cheering for you.

The Black Diamonds are the best of the best – *again*. And I never expected to say this, but having my dad there alongside me for the ride has made it even sweeter.

The awards ceremony today is where we're all officially awarded our championship medals, in front of the whole school.

It's hard to believe it's the last term of the year. I don't feel old enough or wise enough to be ready to go out into the world and make something of myself in only a few months, but that's what's going to happen, whether I'm ready or not.

I glance over my shoulder. Trying to find Lily in the crowd. The team is seated up the front, with the rest of the year thirteens all behind us, and the rest of the school filling the hall behind.

My old mate Mr. Evans has been droning on for about ten minutes now, talking about the team and the history of our successes. It was interesting the first time I heard it all, but this is far from my first rodeo. The West-lake High Black Diamonds have been winning for years now, long before my time, even before Cole's time.

Being part of this team and its legacy is something I'll never forget.

Principal Evans comes to the end of his speech – thank fuck – and calls Coach and Cole forward to help him do the honours of presenting our medals.

One by one we're called up to the stage to receive our medal, a certificate and a handshake from two of the most influential men in my life.

I grin widely as my name is called and I hear cheering coming from the sea of students. I can hear Berlin's voice over everyone else's – no surprises there.

Cullen is called up after me, and then Bryson – alphabetical order and everything – and standing up here with my two best mates, knowing that I pulled my head out of my ass and actually got my shit together... I'm pretty proud of myself.

The whole team is up on stage, we pose together for a photo, and just like that, the season is officially closed.

My high school rugby career is no more.

We all exit the hall, and everyone starts to disperse, but I linger around a while, hoping to find Lily. There's students going everywhere, so I'm probably going to have to wait until lunch to get my pat on the back.

I feel a hand slide around my waist and I grin.

I guess I was wrong.

I turn around and nearly fucking jump when I see Eve touching me.

"What the fuck are you doing?" I demand, shoving her hand away.

"Don't be like that."

"What do you want?"

"Your dick inside me, preferably."

Jesus Christ.

I grab her arm and drag her behind one of the pillars. The last thing I need is someone overhearing her acting like a hoe, talking about my dick.

I narrow my eyes at her. "Don't ever touch me again."

"*Come on*, Pax, we had fun... didn't we?" She pouts.

Fuck's sake. I need *that* kind of fun about as much as I need a hole in the head.

She starts going on and on about the 'good times' and talking about herself like she belongs in a porno. It's pathetic.

I run my hand through my hair in frustration. This chick just will not quit it. I don't know if her pride is hurt or what, but she's been standing here trying to convince me to hook up with her for a solid two minutes now.

Two minutes too long, but every time I try to leave, she grabs my arm and gets this deranged look in her eye that makes me think she's going to make a scene if I tell her to get fucked.

"I don't give a fuck, Eve. We're not hooking up again. Ever. Get that through your head."

She pouts and sticks out her tits. It doesn't do anything for me. Not a single dick twitch. "But I miss your cock in my mouth."

That makes *one* of us.

I have absolutely zero desire to put my dick anywhere near anyone other than Lily.

Eve's trying to be all sultry and alluring, but it's coming off desperate and skanky. She's nothing but a cheer hoe. We won the comp and she wants a piece of the glory.

"You know I'm with Lily now. Stop fucking around," I warn her.

She glares at me. That's clearly not the answer she was hoping to hear.

"You'd *seriously* rather her than me?"

The question sounds like a fucking joke, but this clown is being serious.

"In every fucking possible universe," I drawl.

She makes a disgusted face. She's turned into such a snobby bitch.

I'm bored of this now. I don't care if she does make a scene, I'd rather walk away now than have to listen to another second of this bullshit.

There's hardly anyone around outside the hall now anyway, she can have at it.

"Leave me the hell alone, Eve. I won't tell you again."

I turn to walk away, but I only get a couple of steps away before she's yelling after me.

"At least *I'd* be the one to get down in the dirt and suck you off after you win a game, not like that bitch."

What the fuck?

It all clicks into place as her words sink in. She's said too much.

It was her.

She took that photo. She's been creeping around, watching me and Lily like some kind of pervert. Not only that, but she sent it to us to try and scare us.

The sick bitch.

I turn around so fast my head spins.

"It was fucking *you*, wasn't it? You took that picture." I'm all up in her face in a couple of strides.

Here we were, thinking that Liana was the most mental blonde bitch in town, but maybe Eve is just as fucking insane.

This stunt just might take the cake.

All the colour drains from her face. "I don't know what you're talking about."

Like fuck she doesn't. She's overplayed her hand.

"Delete the photo," I sneer.

"Pax, I –"

"Delete the photo!" I roar, making her jump.

She fumbles her phone in her hand and unlocks it in a rush. It takes her three attempts to get the right pin number in. She's given up trying to deny what she did – that's something.

"*Every* fucking trace of it. Empty the recycling bin."

Her hands are shaking as she hurriedly does what she's told.

"That photo so much as sees the light of day ever again, and you'll regret the fact that you were stupid enough to take it in the first place."

"Are you threatening me?" She tries to make her voice sound strong, but it comes out sounding as weak as she looks.

"You can fucking bet I am."

"You can't lay a finger on me."

I laugh a humourless laugh. "I don't have to touch you to hurt you. You fuck with me again, with *her*, actually, you so much as look in her direction again and I'll make it my life's mission to destroy everything you care about."

It's pretty clear that I'm not playing. I've never been so serious in my entire life. She'd have to have no brain at all for her not to understand that I'll end her over this if I have to. She's clearly fucking stupid, but she's not *that* stupid.

"I'm sorry, Pax."

"Save your bullshit apology. It's too late."

"I was jealous, and I followed you and then I saw you together down there," she rambles, trying to explain herself.

"And then what? You thought you'd just take a photo and then send it to us, as what? Some kind of threat?"

"I felt bad as soon as I sent it. That's why I deleted the fake profile. I didn't show anyone else, I swear. I was just angry that you ghosted me."

"Get a fucking grip, you psychotic bitch. You could have ruined lives because you were *jealous*? I was never going to choose you. You were nothing but a bit of fun to pass the time. Lily is *everything*."

She looks like she's about to burst into tears. I couldn't give a single fuck. She's lucky I'm not going to the police with it. That's what she deserves.

"Is it gone?" I demand.

She nods her head, the bobs quick and jerky. She even holds her phone out for me to look at myself, but there's no point in even checking. If it's not gone, and she digs it up again one day, then it'll be war. She's been warned.

"Get the fuck out of my sight."

Her eyes look like they're going to bug out of her head, but she does what she's told and turns and flees.

I'm shaking, I'm so fucking wild about this. I can't believe Eve would stoop that low. I don't even know why the hell I'm surprised she's turned into a slightly less insane version of Liana after all.

Crazy bitch.

At least Lily will be able to sleep at night again, knowing who was behind it, and that it won't happen again.

Lily.

I need to go and find her. I need to tell her everything that just went on. I need her to calm me down.

I need my happy place.

I BUST INTO THE LAB, half expecting to find it empty, but instead I see Lily and Keke sitting at one of the benches. If I was thinking straight, I'd have known she would be here for her study period – but I'm not thinking straight at all.

I'm panting heavily. I ran over here, but that's not the reason. My heart is racing so fast after my confrontation with Eve that I almost can't get enough oxygen.

"Pax!" Lily says excitedly when she sees me.

Her expression quickly changes when she catches sight of my face.

"What happened?" she demands, going white as a ghost. She's out of her seat and meeting me halfway before I even get the chance to speak.

I can't blame her for jumping straight to panic. I really should have known this would happen and thought it through, but it's too late for that now.

"It's fine, everything is good," I tell her quickly, pulling her in close and breathing in the scent of her hair.

"Don't you dare lie to me," she says as she wraps her arms around my middle.

"I found out who took the photo."

Lily stiffens.

Keke gasps.

"Hey, Keke."

"Paxton," she replies with a nod. "Please spill the tea."

I look down at Lily. She looks terrified.

"It was Eve," I tell her.

She frowns. "Who?"

"Oh, I'm *so* sticking extra pins in her voodoo doll tonight." Keke is on her feet now, pacing.

I don't know what the hell she's talking about, but

she's kind of a strange chick, so I'm not really surprised. Lily seems to understand what that means.

"She's one of Liana's sidekicks?" Lily asks.

I nod. "She's a cheerleader."

"Of course she is," she mutters. "And let me guess, you two used to be a thing."

I hope I don't look as sheepish as I feel. "We ah, hooked up a few times."

Lily rolls her eyes. "You're really quite predictable."

I sweep the hair off her face and cup her jaw in my palm, grinning. "I *was* predictable."

She can't help but smile back at me.

"Can we please circle back and find out why Barbie was trying to shoot amateur porn?" Keke asks me. "No offence intended with the *amateur* comment."

I laugh, but Lily doesn't look as amused. It's easier for me laugh about this now that I know who was responsible and I've handled it. Eve won't fuck with us again, I'm as sure about that as I've ever been about something.

"She was pissed at me because I turned her down, so she was trying to follow me to change my mind, I guess, and saw me and Lily together. Apparently, she was jealous and angry."

"And psycho," Lily says.

"And that."

"What a crazy bitch."

My thoughts exactly.

"Why did she send us the picture?"

"I don't really know what her plan was, but she said she felt bad after she sent it and that's why she deleted the fake account. I made her delete the photos. We can relax. It's over."

"She could have it backed up somewhere."

I nod. "I know she could, but I also threatened to ruin her life if she went anywhere near you again, and she looked like she was about to cry at the thought of it. She's not going to cross me. She knows I could have her arrested if I wanted to. She's eighteen. She's an adult."

"Old enough to know better, is what she is," Keke mutters.

"You think it's really over?" Lily asks me, those stunning green eyes wide.

"I do. She's too embarrassed to try anything else. She's not as ballsy as Liana. She'll give up."

She wraps her arms around me and squeezes tight. I can basically feel the relief pouring off her. My poor girl has been holding onto so much stress, so much tension.

She smiles up at me with tears in her eyes. "Thank you," she whispers.

This is nothing. She hasn't even seen the half of it yet... the lengths I'd go to, to protect her. I'd do *anything* to keep her safe.

"I got the scholarship," she blurts out.

Wait. What?

"You *what*? The scholarship? You got it?"

She nods her head, a look of total disbelief on her face.

She leads me over to the table where her and Keke were when I walked in. I follow her in a daze.

She picks up a thick envelope and slides out a folder with a letter on the top, and hands it to me.

I skim read the first part until I get to the bit that says *we would be honoured to offer you the Cheryl Wilkinson scholarship for your work in the field of chemistry.*

She fucking did it. I don't know why I'm so shocked... I knew she would, but I didn't expect it to all happen so quickly. I didn't even know she'd submitted it yet.

"I didn't even know you were finished it."

"I didn't want to tell you until I heard back. I was too nervous."

Fuck, now I can feel tears pooling in my eyes. I'm so fucking proud.

"You did it, baby."

"I did it."

She's absolutely beaming with pride, and as she should be, she just made her dreams a reality.

This scholarship not only proves that her level of work is out-of-this-world crazy, but it means she can get a full ride to the university she's always wanted to go to, studying in an exclusive-as-hell programme.

It also means that in a few short months, she's going to be in the South Island, hours, and an entirely different island away from here.

I've given my future some thought, more so now than ever, but knowing that she's going down there for certain, makes me want to finalise plans of my own.

"I'm *so* proud of you." I hug her so tight I have to remind myself that she's a hell of a lot smaller than I am.

I don't want to let her go. I just want to stay here, with her in my arms forever.

"Look at the cover of my thesis," she tells me, her voice muffled against my chest.

I reluctantly let her go, just enough to look back at the papers in my hands. I slide the acceptance letter to the back and look at her cover.

It's a whole lot of big-ass words thrown into sentences that I don't understand, but down the bottom it has her name and a small list of contributors. There's two teachers, another student she did part of her research with, and one more name.

Mine.

Paxton Benson.

She actually did it.

I look back at her in disbelief, and she laughs at my expression.

"Congratulations, you're officially a nerd now."

"Never thought I'd say this, but fuck it feels good to be a geek. My brain feels too big for my head all of a sudden. It's huge."

"Pretty sure a big head isn't a new thing for you, pal," Keke pipes ups.

Point to Keke.

Truthfully, I'd forgotten she was even there.

"Touché." I chuckle.

"Couldn't have done it without you." Lily beams.

"Yeah... I think you probably could have got it done *sooner* without my input, but I'll take it."

"You *are* kind of a pain in the ass."

"I'm so happy I was such a dumb loser. It got me here. To you."

Keke makes a gagging sound. "Someone get Hallmark on the phone, Jesus Christ. We're all proud of her, and you two are very cute together, but if this little chat is going to continue then I'm leaving. I liked my lunch, but I doubt it'll taste as good coming back up."

The girl has a real way with words.

"Don't toss your cookies just yet, Keeks, we'll behave," Lily reassures her.

"I make no promises," I add in.

This girl. She makes me want to give her the world, while simultaneously not needing a single thing from me. She's more than capable of achieving everything she wants, all on her own. That's the beauty of it – she doesn't *need* me – if she gives me the privilege of allowing me into her life, it's because she *wants* me there.

THIRTY-ONE

Lily

Pax: I got offered a spot in Christchurch. I talked to the coach today. It's mine if I want it.

Lily: But I thought you wanted to go to Auckland?

Pax: I did, before…

Lily: And now?

Pax: Now I'm thinking that wherever you're going is where I'm going too.

Lily: Really?

Pax: Really Lily-boo

I'm smiling so wide my cheeks hurt.

"What are you grinning about? The fun hasn't even started yet."

God, I don't know *what* she's got planned for this assembly, but I have a feeling it's not going to spell good news for Liana. Berlin has picked the prime time for it. It's the end-of-year assembly. Not only is the entire school here, but every teacher, and a hell of a lot of parents are here too. It's a full house.

Today has been referred to as 'revenge day', and 'the day karma came to town', and as much as I want to see Liana get what's coming to her, I feel super nervous about *how* exactly that's going to happen.

Berlin won't tell me what they have planned – she didn't want me implicated if things go wrong. Apparently, it's for my own good.

Which is honestly only more concerning, but I can't say I'm upset about the fact that there's no way to put any of it back on me – my scholarship is worth too much to risk it over a prank or teaching a bitch a lesson once and for all. It gives me the warm fuzzies to know that my friends agree.

I guess I'll just wait and see the show along with everyone else.

"Pax might be coming to the South Island with me," I tell her. Saying it out loud makes my smile even wider.

Her eyes light up. "*Really?!*"

I nod excitedly. "He just text me. He got offered a spot in Christchurch."

"That's amazing!"

She looks so genuinely happy for her brother. They've all become really close in this final term. We all have. I'm going to miss everyone so much.

"You know, me and Cullen have been talking about

heading down south ourselves. We're still in talks with a few places, but it's a possibility."

I know Berlin got accepted to a few different universities across the country, and Cullen is no dumb jock either, so not only is he being offered rugby contracts to play professionally, but he's going to study photography too.

"That would be so cool."

"Right?"

We push open the door to the bathroom, and the first thing I see is Sophia hurriedly wiping her tears in the mirror.

"Soph, what's wrong?" Berlin asks.

Cue the water works.

Berlin rushes over to her as a fresh wave of tears roll down her face.

"Oh my god," Sophia sobs.

Berlin wraps her arms around her and holds her while she bawls. I just stand there like an idiot. I don't know what to do. I feel like I should leave but that also feels kind of heartless.

Berlin gives me a baffled look over Sophia's shoulder and I shrug. I've got less than no idea about what's going on.

"Did that sack of shit boyfriend do something to you?" Berlin asks.

Sophia shakes her head, sniffing.

She finally pulls free of Berlin's embrace and uses her sleeves to wipe her eyes.

"I'm getting worried, Soph. what's going on?"

"I should leave you two to talk," I suggest.

"No, it's okay. Stay. You're in this now too, Lily." Sophia snivels.

Given the look on her face, and the fact that she's as white as a ghost, I'm not totally convinced I actually want to be part of whatever this is, but since I have little to no backbone, I guess I'm sticking around.

"What the hell is going on, Soph?" Berlin demands again, losing her patience. "You look like shit. You're bawling your eyes out."

Sophia reaches into her pocket and holds up a white stick towards Berlin.

Berlin gasps, and when I move closer, I see why.

Oh my god.

No, no, no, no, no.

I can't see the result, but I doubt she'd be bothering showing us if it were negative.

It's a pregnancy test.

"I'm pregnant," Sophia whispers, the quiet words holding so much weight that she may as well be screaming them. "What the hell am I going to do?"

Mr. May

Mr. June

Mr. July

Mr. August

Mr. September

Mr. October

Mr. November

Mr. December

Calendar Boys Box Set – Books 1-4

Calendar Boys Box Set – Books 5-8

Calendar Boys Box Set – Books 9-12

Master Manipulator

The First Rule

<u>Royals of Westlake</u>

The King of Black Diamonds

The Ace of Westlake High

ACKNOWLEDGMENTS

Thank you so much to all my readers, new and old, who took a chance on *The King of Black Diamonds* and have followed the crew through into *The Ace of Westlake High*. I really love this group of mouthy, sassy characters, and I hope you do too.

Sophia's book is up next, and I can't wait to answer a lot of the questions that have been left hanging in Pax's story.

As always, thanks to my editors, beta readers, ARC readers and everyone who helped me get this book done.

Thanks again for all the support.

Nicole x

ABOUT THE AUTHOR

NICOLE S. GOODIN is a romance author and mother of two from Taranaki in the North Island of New Zealand.

In mid-2015, she started to write about a group of characters who wouldn't get out of her head. Her first book, Rushed, was published in mid-2016.

Nicole enjoys long walks on the beach, pillow fights and braiding her friends' hair. She dislikes clichés, talking about herself in the third person, and people who don't understand her sense of humour.

Please feel free to contact her either via her website, email, Instagram, Twitter or on her Facebook page, she would love to hear your feedback. If you're feeling really game, you can even sign up for her newsletter.